Other books by Karen McQuestion

A Scattered Life

Easily Amused

For Teens:

Favorite

Life on Hold

For Kids:

Celia and the Fairies

Secrets of the Magic Ring

The Long Way Home

Published by Amazon Publishing
P.O. Box 400818
Las Vegas, NV 89140

ISBN-13: 9781612183565
ISBN-10: 1612183565

The Long Way Home

Karen McQuestion

amazonpublishing

For Alice L. Kent

Chapter One

She arrived late.

They were nearly finished when the young woman rushed into the classroom, flustered and apologetic. When the door flew open and Marnie first spotted her, she assumed the girl had entered the wrong room. For one, she was so much younger than the rest of the group—in her early twenties, judging by her looks. And secondly, she was strikingly beautiful with straight blonde hair and pale blue eyes. The way she moved, too, was a sharp contrast to the rest of the women, all of whom had trudged in earlier like prisoners to the gallows. This girl was all energy. She bounded in, bracelets jangling, a large bag swinging off her shoulder. "I'm really sorry," she said. "The traffic was terrible, and then I couldn't find the room—"

The instructor, Debbie, a round-faced woman, pointed to the empty chair next to Marnie and went to get a name tag for the newcomer. Before the interruption, they'd been sharing things that cheered them up when they felt down. Debbie had given them five minutes to come up with their "day brighteners," but

Marnie hadn't been able to think of anything. While all the other women frantically filled out index cards, there she sat, empty.

The young woman accepted the name tag and pulled a purple marker out of her bag. When she leaned over to fill in her name, her hair fell forward, obscuring Marnie's view.

This was their first class, but already they knew the routine. They went around the circle in clockwise order, the instructor cueing them one at a time. Marnie hoped the hour would be over before they got to her, but it was dicey. Just two more to go and it would be her turn. Debbie pointed to a woman, who cleared her throat before reading off her card. "One thing that really brightens my day is when my husband warms up the car for me on cold days." She'd stumbled over the word *husband,* and a stricken look crossed her face, as if she were remembering something. Marnie knew what she was thinking. So many in the group were widows that the mention of a live husband seemed insensitive.

But she shouldn't have worried. This group knew pain, and they weren't wishing their particular brand on anyone else. "Nice," somebody murmured, and the rest nodded in agreement.

A woman named Leticia went next. "When I'm really down I like to stop at Starbucks and treat myself to a Skinny Vanilla Latte."

"And how does that brighten your day?" Debbie asked.

"Oh, I don't know." Leticia flexed her card. "I guess I love the way the coffee smells. And I like to people-watch too. It takes me out of my everyday worries."

"Excellent, excellent!" Debbie gave her the thumbs-up. "Class, this is a perfect example of being proactive. Leticia makes a point of stopping at Starbucks knowing it will give her a much-needed lift."

"Plus, I'm trying to use up my gift cards," Leticia added.

"Moving on," Debbie said, finger aimed at Marnie. "Your turn."

Marnie glanced down at her blank card, slightly panicked. Weren't classes offered through the Park and Rec supposed to be stress-free? She'd only signed up on the advice of the funeral director, of all things. People found the class comforting, he said. It helped them to cope with their loss. Looking at the grim faces of the other women in the room, Marnie somehow doubted it. She sat up and said, "I would like to take a pass."

"A pass?" Debbie looked confused. "Would you like someone else to read for you?"

"No." Marnie held up the index card to show it was blank. "I don't actually have anything to read. You can just skip me."

Debbie pressed on. "But surely you can think of *one* thing that brightens your day?" The awkward silence was punctuated by the droning of the fluorescent light fixture overhead.

The blonde newcomer gave Marnie a sympathetic look and then waved her arm from side to side, making her bracelets clink. "Oooh, ooh." At this angle, Marnie could see the name tag now positioned on the left side of her shirt. Jazzy, it said. The two *z*'s were slanted so they looked like lightning bolts.

"Yes?" Debbie squinted to see her name tag. "Jazzy?"

"I'd love to share some things that brighten my day." She looked at Marnie. "If you don't mind me taking your turn?"

Marnie exhaled in relief. "Please, go ahead."

Jazzy flipped her hair back. "One thing I love, love, love is when I walk past a guy and then when I glance back I can totally tell he's checking me out. Who doesn't love that?" She looked around the room grinning, and continued. "Or how about a bubble bath at the end of a really sucky day? If you add some really great music and a glass of wine, that's even better. That way you get like three sensory experiences at once." Debbie cleared her throat, but Jazzy didn't stop. She was just getting warmed up. "You know what else is fun? Going to the dollar store and buying all kinds of goofy crap just for the hell of it. One time I bought something totally random, this miniature flashlight keychain thingy, and then I wrapped it and gave it to this old guy at work. I hardly knew the guy, but I told him I was out shopping and just saw this one thing and had to get it for him. Oh my God, he was so puzzled, but really pleased too. It totally made his day, and that cheered me up." She beamed at everyone in the circle, and Marnie felt a shift in the room. Positivity, that's what this girl was putting out.

Jazzy was hurrying now, sensing Debbie was going to shut her down. "Another super great thing I do when I'm kind of depressed is find a song on the car radio I just *love* and I force myself to sing along. Loud, really loud, like at the top of my lungs. It always cracks me up, especially if I get caught at a stoplight. Sometimes I get the funniest looks from people. Then I wave at them."

The ladies leaned forward in their chairs. "Fantastic!" said the woman whose husband warmed up her car. A smattering of applause started up.

Debbie didn't look pleased at the way Jazzy had taken over the evening's discussion. Order, that's what she was all about. Marnie could sense it: her class, her rules.

Jazzy held up a hand. "Just one more thing, if I can—"

"You weren't here earlier, Jazzy," Debbie said, interrupting, "but the rule was that we were limiting our day brighteners to one thing per person. Just one. The very *best* one."

"Oh," Jazzy said, clapping a hand over her mouth. "Sorry." Her face reddened.

Debbie glanced at her watch. "That's all the time we have for tonight. Next week we'll be discussing exercise and its role in elevating mood. Please come on time."

As the women gathered up their handbags and went to lean their folding chairs against the wall, Jazzy snapped open her phone and began texting. Marnie didn't quite understand the allure of texting. What exactly were people sharing that required the constant back-and-forth? She couldn't imagine.

A woman with bobbed hair approached Jazzy and laid a hand on her shoulder. Her hair was that beautiful shade of silver that looked almost blonde. Marnie guessed her to be in her late fifties. She was slim and elegant with expensive-looking clothing, a silk scarf draped around her neck. What was her name again? Oh yes, Rita. "Your ideas were just wonderful," the woman said, leaning toward Jazzy, her eyes brimming with tears. "It was so much fun to listen to you. I can tell you're a sparkler, just like my daughter."

"Thanks." Jazzy closed the phone and smiled up at her. "How old is your daughter?"

"Twenty-three." Rita looked away for a second, swallowed, and then looked back at Jazzy. "I mean, she *was* twenty-three," she said, and now tears were streaking down her cheeks. "She died. Ten years ago. Murdered. We're sure it was her old boyfriend, but the police can't prove it."

Jazzy stood up so rapidly the phone fell off her lap and clattered to the floor. "I'm sorry," she said, holding her arms open. Rita walked into her embrace and clung to her. "There, there," Jazzy said, as if she were reassuring a child. Marnie, car keys in hand, froze at the sight of this woman finding comfort in the hug of a complete stranger.

"The thing is," Rita sobbed, "I still miss her so much."

"Of course you do," Jazzy said. She stroked the back of the woman's head. "Of course you do." For Marnie the rest of the room softened to a blur, and the only real thing in all the world was the sight of these two women clinging to each other.

Chapter Two

Jazzy hadn't planned to go to the grief group that Tuesday evening. Hell, she didn't even know there was such a thing. What she'd planned for was a quiet night at home alone. She'd just settled down on the couch with a can of honey roasted peanuts and a glass of wine, when a voice popped into her head. *You really need to go out tonight.* It came through real soft and low, like it was only a suggestion. Ha! As if.

Ignoring it wasn't an option, she knew that much. When she'd heard voices like this in the past, she'd tried to ignore them, but that never worked. They didn't let up, for the most part, and eventually she'd get an uncomfortable nagging feeling, as if she'd forgotten to do something important. And then it just got worse, and the rest of the night she would pace around the apartment suffering from a bad case of free-floating anxiety. Total madness, that way. Easier just to give in.

She called her brother, Dylan, at work to let him know she was going out and would probably need a ride home later. Where she was going, she couldn't really say. He understood, though.

This had been going on since they were little kids. Their grandmother went through the same thing—voices would come into her head like she was getting a phone call from the universe, and she'd drop everything to do whatever was needed. "They're guiding you, Jazzy," Grandma had said over and over again. "These voices, you get them for a reason." She also said every person on the planet had the potential to get them, but few did. And if Jazzy did as the voices asked, wondrous things would happen. If she ignored them, she'd never know what might have happened.

What Grandma hadn't told her, at the time, was that both of them heard dead people. That would have freaked out any ten-year-old. By the time she understood, she was used to having ghosts invade her thoughts. It was weird, but it was her very own version of weird. Everybody had something.

And now, ironically and comfortingly enough, Grandma was her most frequent spirit visitor. Just like when she was alive, her energy was pure joy and her advice was designed to make Jazzy think.

Tonight though, she had a different visitor. After Jazzy finished telling Dylan she was going out, she downed the wine and set the glass in the sink when the unfamiliar voice came back again. *You really need to go out tonight.* Talk about nagging. Hello! She'd barely had time to get out the door. Such impatience. "Maybe I *should* go out," she said, trying out the words. She had a sudden feeling of confirmation, like, *Yes, now you've got it.* She could tell it was a female spirit. Young, maybe about her age—twenty-two. How sad to die before you'd really lived. But maybe she, Jazzy, could do something that would make a difference.

Jazzy filled her big bag with everything she thought she'd need, and left the apartment, locking the door behind her. Dylan had the car, so her traveling options were limited, but she wasn't worried. It would all work out somehow.

She walked down the street, purposely pausing by the bus stop in case that was the plan, but something inside of her said to keep going. Fifteen minutes later, her neighbor Greta pulled up alongside her and called out, "Hey, Jazzy, you need a ride?" Greta lived in the apartment next to them and was, Jazzy had decided, one of the best people on the planet. A person really couldn't *not* like her, unless they were like really evil or something. It turned out Greta was headed to the rec center to take a knitting class. Something about the words *rec center* clicked with her, or rather, clicked with the voice in her head. She told Greta that, oddly enough, she herself was headed to the rec center and would love a ride.

"Such a coincidence," Greta said, smiling.

Jazzy climbed into the car feeling certain now she was on the right path.

"What wonderful weather we're having," Greta said, pulling away from the curb. "We're finally getting that rain we need. I love the way the air feels after a good rain."

Jazzy listened politely, looking out the window as buildings and street signs whizzed by. How lucky for her Greta had come by. Of course, she knew it wasn't luck: it was meant to be.

If things worked out the way they usually did, Jazzy knew that once she arrived at the rec center she'd be led to the one person who needed something only she could give, and they'd connect somehow. That was always how it went; there was no point in overthinking it. For now, she was content to look out the window and listen to Greta excitedly talk about the yarn and knitting needles she'd recently bought. Alpaca wool was really soft, Greta said, and she'd bought a boatload of it because she was going to make all her Christmas gifts this year.

Jazzy had a feeling there was a new scarf in her future. The thought made her smile.

Inside the building, Greta asked if Jazzy would need a ride home. "No, I'm good, thanks," Jazzy said, and they parted ways. She meandered through the hallways, divining for people the same way someone would dowse for water, all instinct and pull. If she'd just still her thoughts and wait, an unexplained twitch would steer her in the right direction.

She walked around some more, stopping to look at a bulletin board. The rec center had an impressive selection of classes. Cooking, crafts, yoga, writing—the list went on and on. And so cheap too. Twenty or thirty dollars for most of them. She wondered if she should sign up for one of them sometime. Cooking lessons might be fun. And useful.

At half past the hour, a classroom door opened and a surge of middle-aged women spilled out. She heard several of them gleefully call out, "Adios!" and guessed it was a remedial Spanish class. Jazzy flattened her back against the wall to get out of the way, and one of them, a grandma-type with curly white hair, smiled as she went past.

She waited a few minutes, then went over to the open door and peered in to see the Spanish teacher, a pretty young woman with dark hair, packing up to go. Upon seeing Jazzy she called out, "Hola!"

"Hola," Jazzy said. A second earlier she'd wondered if this woman was going to be her contact, but no, this wasn't it. Definitely not. She walked away before more Spanish would be required. At the end of the hallway, she found an elevator next to a staircase. Her radar was really kicking in now, and she followed her instincts and bounded up the stairs. When she got to the second story she headed purposefully down the hall until she came to a closed door. Through the narrow glass side panel she saw a group of women sitting on metal folding chairs and grouped in a circle. The sound of one woman's voice hummed, but she couldn't make out the words.

Taking a deep breath, she opened the door and rushed in. "I'm really sorry," she said. "The traffic was terrible, and then I couldn't find the room—"

Chapter Three

Marnie adjusted her rearview mirror, but didn't start the engine. Now that the class was over, she wasn't in any hurry. There was nowhere to be and nothing waiting at home. One place was as good as another.

Lately she'd felt mired. Not as depressed as before, but not too motivated either. Like she was waiting for some vague, unknown thing to happen. So far, whatever it was hadn't shown up.

The best of life was behind her now. She was thirty-five years old and it was clear she'd never be an Olympic athlete, or mountain climber, or rock star. It was too late for any of that. So many doors had closed. When she was young, there was only possibility ahead of her, but she hadn't felt that way in a long time. Two months ago, she had a house, a family, and a career. Now all of it was gone. Or most of it anyway. The career was still somewhere in the background. She had taken a leave of absence from her teaching job when Brian died. She'd go back to work at Lincoln Elementary in September, but it seemed a small consolation.

Marnie glanced into the rearview mirror and frowned. Middle-aged frump. Shoulder-length brown hair and glasses. The same weight as she'd been in college, but she lacked the muscle tone she had then. Probably she should start exercising. Yes, she should really look into a gym membership or a yoga class or something. Maybe tomorrow.

She drummed her fingertips on the steering wheel and watched the other women from the class walk to their cars. They waved to one another and called out, "See you next week!" She had thought them a likeable group, but hadn't connected with them or their stories. Even in loss and death, her situation was unique.

The woman with the lustrous silver hair walked past, giving Marnie a clear view of her face. Only a few minutes before she'd been sobbing, but now her steps were lively, and her face, though blotchy, showed serenity. No sign of that Jazzy girl. Marnie had hoped to get another glimpse of her, but she hadn't come out with the others.

The embrace between the two women had given her the oddest feeling. She could still picture Jazzy, her arms outstretched. And the older woman, Rita, a complete stranger, sinking into her like it was the most natural thing in the world. What should have been awkward was anything but. How could that be?

Jazzy didn't fit in with the group. She didn't even seem to understand what they were all about, and yet she had helped, Marnie could tell. Just her presence had livened things up. She wished the instructor, Debbie, hadn't interrupted her at the end. Marnie would have liked to hear more. She suspected Jazzy was selling something, or else working as a life coach and seeking clients. A grief group would be the perfect place to recruit lost souls willing to shell out money for the promise of a better life. Lately she'd been seeing people with a critical eye.

The parking lot was emptying out now. The sky was gray and the wind was picking up. After a long, difficult winter, spring had been overcast and rainy, and even now, at the beginning of summer, it didn't look much better. So typical for Wisconsin. You never got what you wanted. On hot days Marnie yearned for cool breezes; when it was cold she longed for the sun. She'd driven past her old house the day before and the garden was a muddy mess. Only a few flowers were in view, perennials that had struggled to come back, and even they'd looked beaten down. The For Sale sign was still in the front yard, now leaning a bit. She had taken a bit of perverse joy at the sight of the neglected house. It had looked better when she was in charge.

The instructor, Debbie, emerged from the building, carrying a large bag and talking on her cell phone. She didn't look happy. Marnie had a theory about people who worked in the mental health field. Therapists, psychiatrists, analysts, psychologists—all of them were screwed up in some way. Drawn to the profession by their own mental-health shortcomings. Her college roommate, now a psychologist, had told her horrible stories of childhood abuse. The year they lived together in the dorms, she'd gone through one nightmare of a boyfriend after another. Later Marnie heard she'd been married and divorced twice. That same woman now had her own local radio talk show—giving relationship advice, ironically enough.

Marnie watched as Debbie got into her car and drove out of the lot. Now the entire class was gone. Time to go home. She pulled her seat belt across her lap and clicked it in place. When she looked up she noticed a fine mist covering her windshield. Great, more rain.

Finally, she turned the key, expecting the usual sound of the engine starting. Instead she got nothing. Nothing at all.

Disbelieving, she tried again. Click. She took the key out and looked at it, then stuck it back in and tried one more time, getting the same results. Damn. It had to be the battery. She thought hard. The car was six years old. How long did batteries last? She didn't think they'd ever replaced it. The cars were Brian's department. She knew it was illogical to blame someone who was dead, but dammit, why hadn't he taken care of this? Once more he'd let her down. First by dying, and then with every bad thing that had happened since.

She unzipped her purse and fumbled around for her cell. She peered into the dark recesses, but couldn't see past the wad of receipts and jumble of cosmetics. Who could find anything in all this crap? Just as true panic set in (and she was just about to dump the contents onto the seat next to her), her fingers recognized the smooth plastic edge of the phone. With a sigh of relief she held the phone in her hand. Oh, yes. Help was just a phone call away.

But it wasn't that easy, and a few minutes later the panicky feeling had returned. The cell phone turned out to be dead, and the car charger, which she could have sworn was in the glove compartment, was gone. Not that it would have helped, since the battery was dead, she realized as she slammed the glove box shut. To make matters worse, when she went back to the building she found it was locked, and even though there were a few cars left parked on the outer edges of the lot, pounding on the door hadn't produced anyone. Defeated, she ran back to the dead car. And now it was raining, really raining, a true downpour. She calculated the distance home—at least five miles. And the rec center was surrounded by office complexes, none of which would be open this late in the evening. She thought she'd passed a gas station on the drive in, maybe a mile back, but she wasn't really sure. Oh why had she let that stupid funeral director talk her into signing up for this class? Stupid class. Stupid her for listening to him. And stupid Brian for leaving her behind.

Marnie rested her forehead against the steering wheel. She would sit here forever, if that's how long it took for the rain to stop. She would *not* get drenched in the cold rain, her hair dripping and her clothing clinging to her body. If it rained forever she would stay in the car for exactly that long, ignoring hunger, thirst, and the need for the bathroom, like any good martyr. The authorities would find her skeleton in this car and everyone would say, *You know, I'd wondered where Marnie was, but I was so busy being self-involved that I couldn't be bothered checking in on her. Now I feel just terrible.* And they should feel terrible, all of them. It would serve them right.

Her pity party felt good. The steering wheel dug into her forehead, but that was a necessary part of her suffering, so she endured the discomfort.

Marnie was working her way up to a good cry, when a knock on the window startled her into sitting upright. The view through the glass was blurred by rain, but Marnie instantly recognized the girl who'd barreled late into class.

Jazzy rapped again and then called out, "Hello there?" She moved closer. "Are you okay?"

In all of her life, Marnie had never been so happy to see anyone. She opened the door an inch. "Thank God you're here," she said, talking through the narrow opening. She saw then that Jazzy clutched some kind of metal rod. At second glance she realized it was the shaft of a large red umbrella.

"Are you okay? I saw you slumped over like that—"

"No, no, I'm fine," Marnie said hurriedly, "but my car battery is dead and my cell phone isn't working and the building is locked. I was getting desperate." Jazzy nodded kindly, and Marnie felt her despair melt away. "Can I use your phone or could you give me a ride? I can pay you for your trouble."

"Why don't you let me in"—Jazzy pointed to the passenger side—"and we can get this sorted out."

Marnie nodded and closed the door. She watched as Jazzy crossed in front of the car, making a detour to gleefully kick her way through a puddle with multicolored rubber boots.

When Jazzy got into the car she set her bag and the collapsed umbrella at her feet and turned to Marnie. "Can you believe this rain? Crazy, crazy weather we've been having lately."

"I like your boots," Marnie said. "I don't remember seeing them in class."

"Thanks, they're new. I had them in my bag and just put them on a few minutes ago. Funny thing, I'd just been wishing for a chance to wear them and then the clouds opened up and bam, a deluge!" Her eyes shone. "Like magic."

"I'm so glad you came along. I was having a breakdown wondering what I was going to do."

"Oh, you poor thing. Aren't car problems the worst? That, and computers. I always feel so helpless when something gets screwed up." Jazzy raked her fingers through her hair. "It's so frustrating when you can't fix things."

The rain pounded against the windshield, making the outside world a blur. Now that help had arrived, Marnie felt herself relaxing into the seat. She waited a moment, hoping for an offer of a ride, but when one didn't come, she said, "Is it okay if I use your phone? I'm sure you want to get home, and I don't want to use up any more of your time."

"Oh, don't worry about that. There's no hurry." Jazzy leaned over and reached into her bag. "You're welcome to use my phone." She flipped it open and handed it to Marnie.

The phone's screen displayed the words, "I'm awesome," surrounded by twinkling stars. The image made Marnie smile, but her smile quickly faded as she realized the phone wouldn't do her any good. She didn't know any phone numbers. She hadn't memorized a number in years, always relying on her list of contacts.

"It's on," Jazzy said, leaning over to point. "All you have to do is—"

"I know how to use it. I just can't think of any numbers. Isn't that crazy? I'm a complete blank." Marnie swallowed and thought hard. She knew Brian's number at work, for all the good that would do. She also knew her mother's number; it had been the same since she was a girl. That was no good though. Her mother didn't drive and would only fret. Although, on second thought, her mother could give her *other* numbers: her brother? her sister? They both lived nearly an hour away though. They'd come and get her, certainly, but she knew that they'd also be irritated by the inconvenience and she'd never hear the end of it. As the baby of the family, she'd been typecast as spoiled and helpless. Nothing could be further from the truth, but they stuck with that story, even looked for evidence to back it up, in fact. No, she didn't want to call them. Friends? She had a few, but they were lunch friends and volunteering friends, not car-problem friends. Besides, she didn't know their numbers. She suddenly felt more alone than she had since the funeral.

Jazzy interrupted her thoughts by patting her arm. "Don't feel bad, I only know one or two numbers by heart myself. I think that's pretty normal."

"Maybe I could call a mechanic to tow the car," Marnie said, but made no move to do it. Another number she didn't know. She could call directory assistance, if she knew how to do that, but she didn't. She had to be the biggest idiot in the world. The tears that filled her eyes matched the rain outside. "But at this time of night I bet it would be hard to get a tow truck to come out."

She sighed heavily. "I hate to impose on you, but would you mind giving me a ride home? I can give you gas money for your trouble."

"I don't actually have a car here," Jazzy said. "My brother is picking me up. Why don't we just drop you off at home and you can deal with this tomorrow?"

"Are you sure? I live over on the west side, about five miles from here."

"I'm sure." Jazzy took the phone back. "Dylan won't mind. I'll call and let him know."

Chapter Four

Dylan was more put out about it than Jazzy let on. Marnie could hear his side of the conversation perfectly, and he sounded exasperated. Still, when they were done speaking, Jazzy snapped the phone shut, turned to Marnie, and said, "It's no problem at all. He said he'd be glad to give you a ride home."

When he arrived, fifteen minutes later, it was in a black Toyota Camry. The two women made a mad dash from Marnie's car but still got drenched. Dylan opened the door from inside, and Jazzy motioned for Marnie to sit up front, while she got in the back. The windshield wipers whipped back and forth furiously, and the car smelled like pine air freshener. Jazzy leaned forward and made the introductions. "Marnie, this is my big brother, Dylan, the hero of the hour. Well, actually, the hero of my life."

"Glad to meet you, Marnie," he said, offering his hand. His tone was friendly. If he'd been annoyed before, he'd gotten past it. "Did you want me to try jump-starting your battery?"

She looked at the rain pelting the car and shook her head. "Thanks, but not in this weather. Besides, the battery is six years old. I think it needs replacing."

"Fair enough," he said, sounding relieved.

Marnie directed Dylan down the highway and then through side streets until they reached her duplex. It was an old building, red brick with white shutters, with colonial-style pillars flanking the front stoop. The pillars distinguished it from the other houses on the street, most of which were plain brick boxes. Marnie lived in the upper half and had use of the basement where she had her own washer and dryer. Tonight her half of the house was dark, but the lower, where her landlady, Mrs. Benner, lived, was lit up. Marnie made a mental note to keep a light on in the evenings when she was gone. This living alone took some getting used to.

"This is your house?" Jazzy said. "It's really nice."

"I just moved here and I'm renting," Marnie said. "I'm not sure how long I'll stay. I've been looking at condos." The last part wasn't technically true. Actually she'd been *thinking* about looking at condos, but then again she'd been thinking about a lot of things. Doing things was another matter altogether. The car came to a stop, and Marnie dug in her purse until she found a pen and paper. "I want to give you my number," she said, jotting it down and handing it over to Jazzy. "I'm so grateful for your help, and I'd love to repay you somehow. Maybe I could have you over for dinner some Sunday? I love to cook and don't get much chance lately."

"That would be nice," Jazzy said. "Sure. Thanks."

After saying good-bye, Marnie dashed to the protection of the overhang, where she discovered Mrs. Benner had already locked the front door for the night. Getting her keys straightened out took a moment, and she was glad when she finally found the right one and heard the click of the lock's release.

Although Mrs. Benner lived right below her, Marnie had never met the woman and wasn't likely to. She'd worked out the rental agreement with Dave Benner, who cautioned her against bothering his mother. "My mother likes to keep to herself. Please respect her privacy," he said, after showing her how the thermostat worked and explaining how to use the intercom that linked the front porch to her unit. "I can tell you now you probably won't see her at all. I'd appreciate it if you wouldn't try to contact her in any way. Don't knock on her door. Don't call. If you have any problems, you need to talk to me." He'd made it plain that Marnie's cooperation in this matter would make or break the rental agreement. Because she didn't have a lease, he could give her notice at any time, and the thought of moving again didn't sit well with her.

After their conversation, Marnie reflected on what he'd said. She wondered what Mrs. Benner's problem was but hadn't asked. That would have been rude. Don't try to contact her, was what he'd said. What an odd way to put it. Marnie wasn't planning on socializing with Mrs. Benner anyway, so it was a nonissue. She liked her privacy as well, so having a recluse live below suited her. The lower level was always quiet. Once in a while, she got a whiff of food cooking or heard the faint sounds of a cat meowing, but for the most part, it was like having the house to herself.

Tonight she remembered Dave's instructions and carefully locked the door behind her, then checked to make sure it was secure. She paused at Mrs. Benner's door and listened. Nothing. She knew the old lady was there, though, and to test her theory she paused partway up the stairs. Click—there it was, the sound of Mrs. Benner's door opening a crack—checking on her, no

Karen McQuestion

doubt. It happened nearly every time she came or went. If she backtracked, the door quickly shut. For a woman who liked her privacy, Mrs. Benner sure was nosy.

She wondered if acknowledging the landlady's presence violated the no-contact rule. "Good night, Mrs. Benner," she called out softly before heading up to her place. "Sweet dreams and sleep well."

Chapter Five

Marnie hadn't even had her second cup of coffee when the doorbell rang. In the two months she'd lived there no one had ever rung it, so for a minute she couldn't place the noise. By the time she figured it out and made her way to the intercom, the visitor had rung again and again.

She pressed the button to speak. "Yes?"

"Hey, Marnie, it's me, Jazzy. From the class last night?" As if she needed reminding. Jazzy continued, speaking in a rush as if they might get cut off. "I have my brother's car today, so if you need help, I'm here for you."

Marnie, who'd spent half the night lying in bed worrying about her dead car, felt relief wash over her. "Really?"

"Unless you made other plans?"

"Oh, no, no, no." Marnie pressed her mouth close to the intercom and spoke loudly. "I don't have it worked out at all. I'm so glad you came." She told Jazzy to hang on and went downstairs to let her in. When she opened the front door she saw that Jazzy had a different look than the night before. Today her hair was pulled back into a high ponytail, and she wore a dark blue vest with a laminated name tag clipped to the front. The name was in large bold letters: JESSICA.

"Hey," Jazzy said. "Good morning." Her smile was infectious, and Marnie found herself smiling back.

"Good morning." Marnie gestured to her smock. "Who's 'Jessica'?"

Jazzy looked down. "Oh that." She covered it with her hand. "That's me, sort of. My boss insists on using our given names. I like Jazzy much better, though. Please don't call me Jessica."

"I won't. I like Jazzy. It suits you," Marnie said.

Jazzy leaned against the doorframe and got down to business. "I bought a car battery and thought we could see if that was the problem. I can put it in for you, and if it works, your troubles are over. If not, we can call for a tow truck and I can just return it. If that's okay?"

"That sounds wonderful." What a comfort to have someone else handle things. Marnie went back upstairs to get her purse. A few minutes later, she was comfortably seated in the front seat of Jazzy's brother's car. Marnie had some trouble with the seat belt and Jazzy rushed in to help. "Let me get that," she said, after Marnie had fumbled with it for a minute or so. "These darn things are so tricky."

Sitting in this car reminded Marnie of the family cars her parents had driven when she was a kid. As the youngest of three, she'd always had to sit on the ridge in the middle of the backseat. "I call, Marnie has to sit on the hump," her brother would crow as the three of them ran out to the car. She was the smallest, so she had no say in the matter. She didn't remember her parents interceding to make things fair. Her brother and sister had seniority, and that's the way it was. She got whatever they didn't want. The leftovers.

Jazzy was a good driver, and talkative too. She said she lived with her brother, Dylan, for the time being. He'd gotten divorced the year before. It worked out well; she kicked in for the rent and used his car when he didn't need it. They got along fine. Lately though, both she and Dylan had been thinking about moving elsewhere, going their separate ways. "I've reached a crossroads in life. I can't live with my brother forever," Jazzy said. "I know that, and yet I still find it hard to get myself to make the change."

When they turned into the parking lot of the rec center, Marnie was relieved to see that her car was still there. She'd been afraid that it would be towed or ticketed, but there it was, just the way she left it. Jazzy pulled up so the cars were nose to nose. "I have the new battery in the trunk. If you want to pop the hood, we can get right to it."

"You don't think we should try jump-starting it first?" Marnie asked.

"No, you definitely need a new battery," Jazzy said firmly.

"Okay then," Marnie said, happy to let her take charge.

Jazzy proved to be an expert at replacing a battery. "I'm handy," she said, when Marnie commented on her skills. She'd pulled the old battery out and set it in a cardboard box she'd brought along. "Don't touch that," she said, when Marnie tried to help. "That battery acid is nasty stuff. I once ruined a pair of jeans carrying a used battery on my lap. It ate right through the fabric." After Jazzy set the new battery in place, she swiftly pulled the cables to the correct knobs. "The red cable goes to the positive terminal and the black one is negative. I always remember because it's Red Cross and black is negative energy." She looked up and Marnie nodded, even though she knew in ten minutes the information would fly right out of her brain. Jazzy tightened the nuts with a wrench and took a step back. "That should do it," she said. "Start it up and see if it works."

Marnie got into the car and held her breath as she turned the key. Not expecting it, she let out a gasp of joy when the engine came to life. Yesterday the car's death had been a calamity, but now it seemed to be only a minor interruption in the flow of life. It struck her that the fix had been remarkably easy. Five minutes ago the car had been an immovable behemoth, and now, just by replacing a small box, it could be driven anywhere. All because one person stepped in to help. Amazing.

Jazzy pulled the hood shut and came around to Marnie's window. "Yay for you," she said and applauded with hands extended, as if Marnie had been the one to fix it instead of the other way around.

Marnie opened the door. "No, yay for *you*," she said. "Between the ride home last night and the new battery today, I'm so grateful for your help."

"Oh, it was nothing."

"It wasn't nothing to me. It was…" Marnie stopped and searched for the right word. "…like you were sent from heaven. I don't know what I would have done."

Jazzy shrugged. "If I hadn't come around you would have figured something out," she said. "I have a knack for reading people, and I can tell that you're one of those smart, capable types."

"You think so?" Marnie asked dubiously. She didn't feel smart or capable. In high school she'd been the nerd girl, the one with drab brown hair and awkward bangs and glasses that were too large for her face. She'd daydreamed and been socially inept. The glasses she wore now were chic, and she didn't have bangs anymore, but most days she still felt like that girl. Lately she felt clumsy and out of sync. Like she'd been dropped into someone else's body and couldn't quite control the limbs.

"Absolutely." Jazzy's tone was assured. "When we were in the class last night and you told that bossy woman that you wanted to take a pass, I thought that was awesome. All of the rest of those ladies were like little sheep, but you weren't playing her game."

Marnie reflected on what Jazzy was saying. It was true that she had stood up to the very forceful Debbie, but she hadn't thought her refusal to be a strength. More like a failure for not coming up with something to say.

"And then, when Rita came over to us and was telling me about her daughter's death, I saw your face and you looked devastated for her. You have a lot of heart, I can tell."

"Thank you." A real compliment. When was the last time one had come her way? Certainly not from Brian, unless it was about her cooking. "Great meal, Marn," he'd say nearly every night. But that was a compliment to the food, not her as a person. And looking back, she realized it was almost reflexive on his part. The equivalent of "God bless you" after a sneeze. Troy was the only one who ever really complimented her; in fact, as a little guy he'd showered her with praise almost constantly. He said she was pretty and laughed at all her jokes. He preferred her to Brian for most everything from reading books to pouring juice to being tucked in at bedtime. So flattering for a stepmother. Or pseudo-stepmother, as her sister put it, since Brian had never married her. She was good enough to be a mother to his son for nearly ten years, but it was never quite the right time to legalize their relationship. Marnie had thought she'd had some fatal flaw that kept her from becoming a wife, but now a complete stranger had recognized her positive traits. She gripped the steering wheel and swallowed to keep the lump in her throat at bay. "Thank you for saying that."

"All true."

"So how much do I owe you? For the battery, I mean."

"It was just under sixty dollars. I can check the receipt to give you an exact amount."

"No, we can make it an even sixty." Even as Marnie reached for her purse she knew she didn't have that much money with her. And she could visualize her checkbook on the counter, right where she'd left it. "I'm sorry, but I don't have any cash with me. If you follow me to an ATM I can pay you right away."

Jazzy said, "I have to get to work, but don't worry about it. It can wait until the next time I see you."

The next time? Oh, their class! Marnie, who hadn't really planned on going back to the Good Grief class, suddenly found she was open to the idea. She could picture herself getting ready for class next Tuesday, making sure to tuck sixty dollars in her purse for Jazzy. Maybe she'd stop at Starbucks on the way and pick up one of those drinks Leticia mentioned. What was it? A Skinny Vanilla Latte? Yes, that's what she'd get. The thought of it made her feel good, gave her a sense of purpose. She was someone who had plans for next week. Maybe she'd even call out to Mrs. Benner as she left the house—"I'm off to my class at the rec center, Mrs. Benner. I'll be back at nine." As sad as she was, it had to be worse for Mrs. Benner. Poor lady, whatever she'd been through to make her a hermit had to be horrendous. Maybe if Marnie shared little bits of her life with her, it would make her feel less alone.

"Great," Jazzy said. "Well, take care then and I'll see you on Sunday."

"Sunday?"

"For dinner. Remember? You invited me for a home-cooked meal."

All the cylinders in her brain clicked into place. Yes, now she knew. The thank-you dinner. But had she said Sunday? Jazzy seemed so certain. Marnie said, "Oh, of course. My mind just drew a blank for a second."

"We're still on, then?"

"You bet." Marnie chuckled self-consciously. "I've been looking forward to it. Come around six. I'll leave the front door unlocked. Just come on up. It'll be great to have company."

Before Jazzy got into her car, a question came to Marnie. She leaned out the window and called out, "Jazzy!"

Jazzy turned questioningly. "Yes?"

"What kind of work do you do?"

"I'm a cashier." She twirled her keys around one finger. "At the Supercenter on Highway 63."

It sounded dreadful. Marnie's job, teaching four-year-old kindergarteners—now that was a wonderful job! The younger the kids were, the better she liked them. Little children were so energetic and curious. Even the ones who wore her out with their shenanigans had redeeming qualities. And they were a joy to look at, so fresh-faced and perfect with their flawless skin and pearly white teeth. In her opinion, everybody was beautiful when they were young. Dealing with children was a joy because there was so much potential there. Everything lay before them. But working with the general public? Standing at a cash register for hours on end? Oh my, that had to be depressing. She asked, "Do you like your job?"

Jazzy looked thoughtful. "I wouldn't say I like it, but it's what I need to be doing right now. You know how that goes."

Marnie nodded, even though she didn't completely understand.

"I know that my time there is limited," Jazzy said. "Actually, I feel that I'll be making a change soon. I have faith that when the time is right I'll find what I'm really meant to do with my life, and it will all come together for me. For now, this is good."

Chapter Six

Sunday evening, Laverne Benner peered through the blinds at the young blonde woman parked across the street and continued watching as she got out of the car and made her way up the walkway to the house. Laverne's cat, Oscar, made figure eights between her legs until she nudged him away. Silly cat.

She waited to see what the young woman would do when she reached the front door. Long ago, she'd had her son, Dave, disconnect the doorbell to her unit. The upstairs one still worked, and when it buzzed she could hear it through the ceiling. She ignored all visitors. Most of the time it was salespeople or church folk, no one she'd have wanted to talk to anyway.

As the girl got closer, she could see her more clearly. She was a pretty thing with blonde shiny hair that swung as she moved, all bounce and animation, a big smile on her face, although there was no perceptible reason to smile.

At the front door she didn't pause but came right in. Laverne tensed for a second, afraid, but she could tell by the movement in the front hall the girl was headed for the stairs. *Oh, okay, a guest of the new tenant.* What a relief. At the top of the stairs she heard a knock and then the tenant's voice greeting her guest. The girl said something and then let out a peal of laughter. Laverne found herself smiling. It was a lovely, infectious sound. Musical.

She went to the door and opened it, hoping to hear more. At her feet, Oscar joined her in peering out, and then, before Laverne could block him with her foot, squeezed through the opening and was out.

"Oscar," Laverne said, in a hiss. "Come back here."

Chapter Seven

Marnie had everything prepared. The money she owed for the car battery was in an envelope, ready to hand over as soon as Jazzy walked through the door. She'd cooked all day, a veritable Thanksgiving dinner of turkey, gravy, potatoes, rolls, and sweet potatoes. Too late she realized that everything on the menu was heavy. A green vegetable would have balanced things out nicely, but as it turned out, Jazzy didn't seem to notice the lack.

"This is delicious," Jazzy said, more than once. She loved to talk and was good at it, telling stories about the people she knew from her job. Her gestures, punching the air in enthusiasm, were the equivalent of exclamation points. Her joy was so evident; it was hard to believe she needed to be in a grief group.

It was nice to have company for dinner, Marnie decided. Before, when she lived with Brian and Troy, the mood was always serious. Brian had been so quiet, and not because he was paying attention. More often than not, he had mentally checked out. And it had nothing to do with her; she was sure of that because he was the same with his own son. Troy would talk about his school day—something funny about one of his teachers, or a food fight in the cafeteria—and later Brian would claim not to know anything about it. Living with Brian had been lonely, she could see that now. He was as much company to her dead as he was alive.

When there was a pause in the conversation, Marnie asked, "If it's not too personal, do you mind if I ask who died?"

Jazzy looked puzzled. "What do you mean?" she asked, helping herself to another serving of sweet potatoes. "No one died."

"I mean for the grief group at the rec center. Why did you sign up?"

Jazzy cleared her throat and said, "It's not really for me. It's just that I seem to come into contact with a lot of people who have lost loved ones. I wanted to learn how to be sensitive to what they're going through."

"Oh." That made sense. So why did Jazzy look like Marnie had caught her in a lie? Odd.

"I'm not technically signed up for the class," Jazzy said, tucking her hair behind her ear. "I thought I'd try it out first."

"I didn't know you could do that," Marnie said.

Jazzy shrugged. "I'm not sure it's allowed. I just sort of barged in on my own." She changed the subject. "Why did you sign up? Who died?"

"I was living with someone," Marnie said, sighing. "A man. He was my fiancé, but we never got close to getting married. We probably never would have married, actually," she said, being truthful. Brian had talked of marriage but never gave her a ring, never even discussed setting a date. Over the years, she found herself falling out of love with him, but she never considered breaking up and moving out, not even once. Even as her feelings for Brian faded, her love for his son, Troy, grew until it became bigger than anything she'd ever experienced. Sometimes when he had a bad dream, he'd call for her from his room, and his cry of "Marnie" was so frantic and blurred that it sounded just like he was saying "Mommy." The first time it happened, a swell of love for the boy imprinted on her heart. To leave Brian would have meant leaving Troy, and that was unfathomable. She'd been his substitute mom since he was four, and he depended on her. "He was only forty-five and he died unexpectedly. We were together almost ten years. I was very attached to his son. I felt like he was mine."

"I'm sure it was a great loss for you." Jazzy gave her a small smile, and something about her expression, the sympathetic look in her clear blue eyes, made Marnie want to cry. Brian's death had happened so quickly: she'd been in the basement doing laundry when it happened. First she heard a loud thump that turned out to be Brian falling to the floor, dead from a heart attack. Then Troy frantically yelled for her. "Marnie, Marnie, come quick!" She'd run up the stairs to see him kneeling over his dad, shaking and crying. The rest of what happened—the call to 911, the ambulance arriving—was all a blur. What was clear in her memory was how Troy had hugged her harder and longer than he had in years. After they carried Brian away, it was just the two of them left behind.

And then Kimberly, Troy's mother, came back and took over everything. Kimberly was still listed as a co-owner on the deed to the house, a shock to Marnie. Brian had named her as the beneficiary on his life insurance too. Kimberly took care of all the paperwork, arranged the funeral, and greeted the mourners at the funeral home. It was her show.

Kimberly. Even thinking the name made Marnie shudder. To make things worse, Kimberly was gorgeous—slim and blonde. One of those women who looked effortlessly glamorous. Everyone liked Kimberly too. She was even nice to Marnie, which under different circumstances would have made it hard to hate her, but in this case, Marnie made an exception.

When Kimberly left town, she took Troy with her and there wasn't a damn thing Marnie could do about it. It was like the last ten years of her life were letters on a dry-erase board and Kimberly had wiped it clean.

She looked at Jazzy through the lens of tears. "It's been difficult," she said, dabbing at her eyes with a napkin. "I really miss my stepson. I feel like someone ripped my heart out."

"Where is he now?" Jazzy asked.

Marnie swallowed. "In Las Vegas with his mother." She was going to lose her composure if they kept talking about Troy, and she didn't want to start blubbering in front of company. "Would you like coffee?" she asked brightly. "I'd be glad to brew a pot."

Over coffee and dessert, the conversation became more cheerful. Jazzy liked to read, something she had in common with Marnie. They talked about books, which led to a conversation about movies. "The next time I want to see a movie I'll give you a call," Jazzy said.

Marnie nodded, pleased. Jazzy was probably being kind, but who knew? Maybe this was the beginning of a friendship. At eight o'clock, Jazzy announced that she had to get up early to work the next day and had to go.

"I'll see you at the grief group, right?" Marnie said.

"Oh sure," Jazzy said. "I'll see you then."

They exchanged good-byes, with Jazzy pulling Marnie into an enthusiastic hug, which took her off guard. When Marnie opened the door to see her out, a gray tabby cat leisurely walked in and rubbed up against Jazzy's ankle. "Well, hello there, you cute little thing." Jazzy reached down to pet the cat. She looked at Marnie. "I didn't know you had a cat."

Marnie's mouth hung open for a second. Recovering, she said, "It's not mine. I've never seen it before. It must belong to the lady downstairs. I hear a cat sometimes."

Jazzy scooped up the cat and held it like a baby. "What a cutie you are. Yes you are." She rubbed its head then looked up at Marnie. "I'll drop him off on my way out." She stepped out into the hall and headed toward the stairs.

Marnie got a panicked flush and started speaking rapidly. "Mrs. Benner doesn't like to be bothered. Why don't you just leave the cat in the hall? I'm sure it will find its way home." But Jazzy was already at the bottom of the stairs.

Jazzy called out, "Really, it's no trouble. I'm going that way anyhow." The clattering of her shoes on the wooden stairwell suddenly sounded thunderous. Marnie debated going after her and taking matters in hand, but it was too late. She could already hear Jazzy knocking on Mrs. Benner's door.

Chapter Eight

When Laverne heard a knock, she stiffened with dread. Lately that was her reaction to everything, and she was getting tired of it. Tired of being a hermit, tired of being homebound, but not quite sure how to end her reign of solitude. Interacting with others felt like an ordeal. Recently she'd managed small outings—the post office, the library, the grocery store. Luckily all of them were within walking distance because she'd let her driver's license lapse.

She was, she sensed, starting to overcome this nonsense, this feeling that the world was too big and frightening to navigate on her own. But it wasn't that easy. Nothing ever was. She had times, like now, when she couldn't even force herself past her threshold. The cat had run out and she couldn't make herself go up the stairs after it. She knew it was ridiculous. The whole thing irritated her. What she really needed was a kick in the butt.

Another knock at the door. This person wasn't going to go away. "Yes," she said, her voice quavering.

"Hello!" a female voice called out. "I'm here to return your cat."

Laverne fumbled with the deadbolt and unhooked the chain. "Just a minute," she said, her voice catching in her throat. It was the young woman who'd arrived earlier. She was even prettier up close, with friendly blue eyes and a ready smile. Laverne meant to just take the cat and slam the door shut, but when the girl waved Oscar's paw and said, "Hi, Mom, I got lost, but this nice lady helped me," in the silliest voice, something inside of her melted a little. Laverne smiled, something she hadn't done in a while, and she let the door swing open a little wider.

They stared at each other for a minute, until the girl said, "Hi, I'm Jazzy. I was visiting Marnie upstairs and your cat wandered up." She held the cat out and Laverne took Oscar into her arms.

"Thank you," she said, the words a struggle. "It's very kind of you."

"Your cat is sweet," Jazzy said. "She purrs like an engine."

"It's a boy cat," Laverne said. "Oscar."

"Oh, cute," Jazzy said. She leaned against the doorframe and ran a hand through her hair. It was the kind of hair, Laverne thought, that would fall into place no matter what. Let the wind come—this girl's hair would always look good.

Jazzy waved, fingers fluttering. "Well, it was nice meeting you—Oscar's mom. Have a good evening."

Laverne watched her go and, after closing the door, set Oscar down. The cat yawned and slinked away. She locked and chained the door, then went to the window to see Jazzy getting into the car.

Funny how even this short conversation felt unusual. She'd been avoiding strangers for at least three years. Since her husband died, she found everyday interactions to be an effort. Even normal pleasantries exhausted her. If she accidentally made eye contact with someone at the grocery store, she'd be pulled into a conversation about the possibility of rain later. The UPS man couldn't hand her a package without cheerful commentary. Going to the bank was the worst. The tellers felt compelled to ask after her health and offer her candy or free pens. Couldn't anyone perform a basic task without the extra chitchat? Was that too much to ask? Her son thought she suffered from depression and begged her to go for therapy. But she knew she wasn't depressed, just tired, tired of everyone and everything. She wasn't suicidal exactly, but she didn't leap out of bed every morning waiting to greet the day. Well, maybe she *was* a little depressed. Everything took so much effort.

Her son interpreted her reticence as fear, which wasn't really the case, but she didn't correct the notion. He was going to believe whatever he wanted, no matter what she said. The truth was that she wasn't afraid to be alone. Her neighborhood was safe enough. Even when Laverne went on early morning walks (the best time to avoid people), she was never fearful. It helped that she carried a handgun that had belonged to her husband and had been used by both of them for target practice. When he'd first bought it, he'd claimed it was the same gun James Bond used, but somehow she doubted it. It looked too small. When she'd found the handgun in his sock drawer a few weeks after the funeral, she put the safety on and tucked it into the secret compartment in her purse. She didn't think she'd ever use it, but she believed in being prepared. Life was uncertain.

Chapter Nine

When Jazzy arrived early for the grief group she found the door locked and a note attached that read: *Tuesday night's grief group cancelled due to emergency in instructor's family.* She tapped her chin, wondering at the irony of Debbie encountering some kind of grief of her own. Jazzy took down the note and tucked it into her purse. She pulled out a credit card and slid it up and down between the door and the frame until she heard a click. Aha! Sweet victory. She'd seen the credit card maneuver on a show about criminal tricks on a cable channel and had tried it a few times in other places without success. You had to have just the right kind of locking mechanism, apparently. As luck would have it, the rec center did.

She got the room ready for the group, turning on the lights, opening the blinds, and arranging the folding chairs in a circle. She found some colored markers in the tray of the dry-erase board and drew a forest complete with a unicorn and assorted squirrels. Since grade school she'd been told she was good at squirrels, and so she drew them with enthusiasm, shading their tails with a flourish. Above the drawing she wrote, "Do the thing you long to do and become the person you're destined to be." When she was finished she surveyed the room but wasn't quite satisfied. Something was missing.

Suddenly remembering, she rifled through her bag until she found her iPod and the portable speaker system Dylan gave her for Christmas. Once it was plugged in, she picked some upbeat music, keeping in mind the group's collective age, which was mostly ancient with some middle-aged thrown in. She started with Frank Sinatra's "The Sunny Side of the Street" and "The Best Is Yet to Come," George Harrison's "Here Comes the Sun," and Katrina and the Waves' "Walking on Sunshine." There was nothing like music to lift a person's mood.

The group filtered in one at a time, each person noticeably brightening as they saw the changes in the room. "Nice drawing!" one of the women said, and Jazzy smiled in response.

When Rita arrived, she made a beeline to Jazzy and sat right next to her. "I brought photos of my daughter," she said, pulling out a small photo album. Jazzy shifted in her seat to look. In every picture, Rita's daughter had a wide smile with straight white teeth. In a few of the shots she had her arms draped around her mother's shoulders. They looked comfortable together, Jazzy thought. Such a beautiful girl. Her death was such a loss for the world.

"She was a sparkler," Rita said, smiling wistfully.

"I can tell. I'm sorry."

"I think about her every day."

Jazzy said, "How could you not?"

Rita gave Jazzy's forearm a squeeze. "And it's not just me. Everyone loved her. Her friends filled the church at the funeral, and all of them had a story of how she touched their lives. Her death was such a loss." She shook her head. "And the one who did it still walks free. I worry about him out in the world doing this to someone else's daughter."

"You think it was her boyfriend?" Jazzy asked.

Rita nodded vigorously. "Oh yes. He was very charming and good at covering his dark side. Melinda alluded to some problems they were having, but I thought they were the usual problems all couples go through." She sighed. "I didn't know the half of it. Things felt off, but I just didn't see the signs. After she died, one of her friends told us some things that convinced us he had murdered her. He had a bad temper, they'd been fighting, his alibi was questionable." She sighed. "But it's one thing to know something, another to prove it."

"The police couldn't pin anything on him?"

Rita sighed. "No."

Jazzy nodded and waited, sensing there was more.

"We were supposed to go out to lunch that day," Rita said. "When she didn't show up, I got worried. And when she didn't answer her phone, I knew something was terribly wrong." She looked down at her hands, and her voice dropped. "The police found her in her parked car, strangled with her own scarf, one I had crocheted and given to her as a Christmas gift. Glenn and I had to go and identify her."

"I'm sorry." Jazzy could feel Rita's emotion as if it were her own. Even ten years after her daughter's death, Rita suffered agonizing pain and loss, and now it poured out of her in an unstoppable surge, straight to Jazzy's heart. This was the part of being intuitive she could have skipped.

"Davis, that was his name, didn't come to the funeral, and about a month after she died, he up and moved to God only knows where."

"I'm sorry," Jazzy said, again. Sometimes words were so inadequate.

"Thank you. I do appreciate it."

The room was filling up. When the last of the group trickled in, Marnie was among them, talking to another woman as she came through the door. She waved to Jazzy and took a seat, easing her purse off her shoulder and onto the floor. The chatter in the room became questioning: Where was Debbie? What's the story with the music?

Jazzy stood up. "Hey, everyone. My name is Jazzy. I was told that Debbie won't be coming because of a family emergency. It was suggested that as long as we all made the effort to be here, we could use the time to talk amongst ourselves." Jazzy herself was the one who was suggesting it, so it wasn't technically a lie. "If it's okay with everyone, I'd be glad to moderate a discussion."

"Debbie's not coming?" one of the women said, irate. "You'd think the rec center would have called to let us know."

"They should give us a partial refund," another one said, frowning.

Marnie spoke up. "I, for one, am happy to get a break from Debbie. I vote we let Jazzy lead the discussion."

"I second the motion," Rita said, thrusting her arm up in the air.

"Debbie was sort of bossy," said the woman who only a moment before wanted a partial refund. The women looked around at each other, and one by one announced that they were fine with having Jazzy take charge. This didn't surprise Jazzy, who'd been told by an unseen voice it would go this way.

Within the first half hour, every woman in the room had cried or laughed, and some had done both. Jazzy went with the theme she'd written on the board: do the thing you long to do and become the person you're destined to be. One by one, each woman confessed her most secret desire, her long-buried goal, her childhood dream. No matter how outlandish the idea, the women were encouraging and brainstormed ways the dream could become a reality.

Leticia, the lady who last week had mentioned brightening her days with the occasional Vanilla Skinny Latte, admitted that as a child she'd envisioned herself as a Broadway actress. Another woman in the group said she belonged to a local theater group, and mentioned upcoming auditions. Leticia took paper and pen out of her purse to jot down the information. She chuckled. "It's not exactly Broadway, but it's a start."

One of the other group members had just started talking about her dream of being a professional chef, when the woman next to her (who, as it turned out, hated to cook) said, "You're hired!" The one who despised cooking was scheduled to host a dinner party for twenty guests in three weeks and dreaded preparing the meal. The first woman offered to cater it, and they exchanged contact information on the spot. Jazzy loved it when the universe aligned like this.

— — —

Finally, Marnie's turn arrived. Uneasy, she shrugged and said she had nothing to say.

"No unrealized dreams?" Jazzy asked.

"No, not really. I mean I always wanted to be a teacher and I am. I love to cook and garden and read and I do those things all the time," Marnie said. "I've got it pretty good compared to a lot of people."

Jazzy looked around the circle and saw that the other women weren't convinced either. Leticia leaned forward in her chair. "So, is the life you're living the one you pictured when you were a kid?"

Marnie squirmed in her seat. "Not exactly, but I was a pretty unrealistic child." She smiled, recalling. "I wanted to be a princess and wear diamonds every day. I wanted to own a thoroughbred horse that came when I called his name. His name was going to be Lancelot. When I was grown up I was sure I'd have five children: three girls and two boys."

"And did you?" Leticia asked. "Have five kids, I mean."

"I didn't have any," Marnie said sadly. "But I raised one, and he was mine in every way. I taught him how to tie his shoes, and I took care of him when he was sick. I went to his parent-teacher conferences." She had the job, but not the title. Every day after school she'd spent time working on homework with Troy, something Brian had no patience for. She'd packed hundreds of school lunches, provided snacks for Troy's visiting friends, called other parents to coordinate driving to school events. And she always referred to herself as Troy's stepmom, and he did too, but she realized too late that it had all been a façade, a beautiful dream taken away by Brian's death and Kimberly's reappearance.

When she started to cry, one of the women handed her a yellow Kleenex. Marnie suppressed a sob and forced herself to speak through tears. She told them about the funeral and how Kimberly waltzed into town, smelling like expensive perfume and toting patterned luggage, the kind with designer tags. Upon arriving at the house, Kimberly immediately gave Troy and Marnie hugs and listened while they talked about how Brian had collapsed and died right in front of them. "Oh, you poor, poor things," she said, tapping her long, glittery nails on the kitchen counter.

She didn't hate Kimberly then: in fact, she felt a kinship with her. The hatred came later, when she realized the woman was stealing Troy. Kimberly was matter-of-fact about it too, asking Troy what he wanted to take with them on the plane. "Anything that doesn't fit in two suitcases will have to be shipped," she said. "Or else I can get it when I come back to sell the house." Troy looked shocked, the blood draining from his face. Marnie felt like she'd been struck from behind. She should have seen it coming, but she didn't. "Can't he just stay here with me?" she asked Kimberly. "He's fourteen. He starts high school next year. His friends—"

Kimberly laughed, the kind of low, throaty laugh men found sexy. Marnie wanted to choke it out of her. "They have high schools in Las Vegas," she said. "And Troy already knows a few kids in my neighborhood, right, Troy?" Troy had nodded mutely, which astounded Marnie. What happened to the mouthy, opinionated, moody boy she loved so much? Like all males, he was mush in Kimberly's presence.

Marnie spilled out the tale to the group of women and found herself staring at eight sympathetic faces. The woman next to her reached over to give her a hug. Marnie had never been so grateful for the kindness of others.

Rita raised her hand slightly. "How is it that Troy knew kids in her neighborhood?"

"Oh, that." Marnie wiped at her eyes and blew her nose. "Troy always went to visit her for three weeks in the summer. And then sometimes for long weekends during the school year. He hated going, but it was part of the agreement." She didn't mention that Brian often joined Troy midway through the summer visit and that both Troy and Brian returned in bad moods. Sometimes it would take weeks for them to get back to being themselves. She was never invited to Kimberly's house. Even if she was, she couldn't have gone because Brian and Troy always flew to Las Vegas. She'd had a traumatic incident on a plane trip during her high school years and hadn't flown since.

"Do you keep in touch with Troy?" Jazzy asked, leaning forward, a hand on each knee. She had the expression of someone determined to solve a problem.

"I try," Marnie said. "When I text he answers with one or two words. And when I call, it's never a good time. He always seems like he's in a big hurry and he wants to get off the phone. The last time he sounded like he was mad almost. I finally told him he should call me when he's ready." She paused. "I don't know what's going on with him. All I know is that I miss him."

"That's terrible," a woman said. "You poor thing." All the women agreed that Marnie had been wronged, which validated her pain. The only other time she'd mentioned the situation with Troy, it was at a family gathering, and her sister had said, "Well, what do you expect? She's his mother. You're really nothing to him." The words were a dagger thrust through Marnie's heart.

"So what are you going to do about it?" Leticia asked.

Marnie shrugged. "What can I do?"

"I know what I'd do," Jazzy said, looking around the circle. "I'd go to Las Vegas and see Troy. I'd get to the bottom of things." One of the women clapped while a few others murmured in agreement.

"Oh, I couldn't do that," Marnie said.

"Why not?"

Jazzy's tone was encouraging. How simple she made it sound. Marnie exhaled. "Legally I don't have a leg to stand on. And if I just showed up like that she'd probably tell me to leave." Nothing good could come of it. Troy had probably already adjusted to his new house and new neighborhood and she would be an unwelcome intrusion.

"You could get on a plane tomorrow and be there in four hours," Jazzy said, not giving up. Her brow furrowed. "Or maybe three. I'm not sure how long the flights are, but it has to be somewhere in there."

Now Marnie felt pushed. "I don't fly," she said firmly. "Never, ever. I have a huge problem with planes."

"You could drive," Jazzy said. "I would go with you." She turned to the group. "Is anyone else game? Who wants to go?" The room was suddenly quiet. "Rita, how about you? Do you like road trips?"

"I used to go on road trips all the time," Rita said wistfully. "But I haven't for years."

Jazzy gestured enthusiastically. "It sounds like you're due for one then. Have you ever been to Las Vegas?"

Rita shook her head. "My daughter and I talked about going, but we never got around to it."

"Well, see," Jazzy said to Marnie. "Now there are two of us who could go with you."

"That's really nice of you," Marnie said. "But I couldn't ask you to do that."

"You weren't asking. We offered." Jazzy ran her fingers through her hair. "It's really no big deal. What is it—a twelve-hour drive or so?"

"Double or triple that if you want a more accurate number," Rita said. "But still, it's manageable. You could do it in two or three days, if you were motivated."

Jazzy said. "I love car trips. Some good snack food, good tunes, you're there in no time."

Marnie shook her head. "No, I'm not going to drive to Las Vegas. I appreciate the offer, though."

The room grew silent. By looking at their faces, Marnie thought she could almost read their minds. Some of the women thought she should go to Las Vegas, make a ruckus, and try to convince Troy to come back with her. Others thought she should let go and move on with her life. But all of them were sympathetic because they were women and they understood. It seemed to her that men coped better with loss, or maybe they just didn't show it in the same way. This group understood what she was going through.

Marnie cleared her throat. "I've taken up enough time." She looked around the room. "Who's next?"

"Rita," Jazzy said. "I don't think you've shared your heart's desire yet."

"Oh, Jazzy," Rita said, sadly. "I showed you photos of my heart's desire. My daughter was the world to me. There's no getting her back."

"Still," Jazzy said. "You must have hopes and dreams that haven't been realized yet?"

"Not really."

"Not even one hope or dream?" Jazzy's voice was wheedling now. "Even one?"

Rita looked at the floor. "Lately I *hope* for justice and I *dream* of vengeance. Is that what you had in mind?"

"No." Jazzy's face clouded. "I'm sorry."

"It's okay," Rita said. "It's fine that you're upbeat and full of great ideas. I like your energy. But you're young. You'll find out someday that some things can't be resolved that easily." She shifted in her seat. "Or at all." For a moment it looked like she might bolt out of the room.

Leticia, who was sitting on the opposite side of the circle, said, "Maybe it would help if we said a prayer for Rita to find peace? Would you mind?" Marnie could feel the change in Rita: it was just the right thing to say. Rita nodded gratefully. Without being cued, the women linked hands and bowed their heads. "Dear God or the Goddess or whatever entity we each believe in," said Leticia. "Please help our friend Rita find peace and joy in her life. Some justice would be good too. And let Marnie make peace with losing her stepson." And one by one, she included everyone in the group, ending with, "And thank you for connecting us and for bringing Jazzy to our circle."

When the prayer was done, Marnie found herself joining the others in saying a heartfelt "Amen," which was odd because lately she'd lost faith in almost everything.

Chapter Ten

The next morning in the grocery store Marnie had just put bananas in her cart when she spotted Matt Haverman, Troy's best friend since third grade. "Hey, Marnie," he said. He leaned against a display, his butt resting up against a row of pomegranates. "How's it going?" The confidence of this younger generation amazed her. What a difference from her own teenage years when she barely made eye contact with grown-ups. Matt could converse with any adult with ease. In fact, sometimes when he'd been at their house, he'd wander out of Troy's room just to talk with Marnie. She'd had better conversations with him than she had with most adults.

"Hello there," she said, her smile genuine. Matt was one of those long-limbed kids, the kind who stretched as they grew. Today, wearing loose khaki shorts, she could see that he had hairy man legs. She thought of the old saying, *So long the days, so short the years.* So true. At least that's how it seemed when children were growing up. Her thoughts were interrupted when an automatic sprinkler off to one side kicked in, misting a section of vegetables.

Startled, she and Matt both turned to look. Matt laughed. "Whoa, dude. That scared me. I didn't know the vegetables took showers here."

Matt was in a chatty mood. He pointed to where his mother stood talking to another woman and explained that he had come along to help. "Mom needs me to carry the dog food and water softener salt. She says the bags are too heavy." He rolled his eyes.

"That's good of you," Marnie said. "I'm sure she appreciates it." She rifled through her purse looking for her list.

"Hey, what's the story with Troy?" Matt asked.

"What do you mean?"

"How come he's going to that camp?"

Marnie's heart sank. How was it that Matt knew all about Troy's life, but she didn't? "I don't really know anything about what's going on with Troy," she said slowly. "Kimberly has custody of him now. I don't have any say in things." She looked back into her purse, a distraction to keep her eyes from filling with tears. Aha, there it was—a folded piece of notebook paper with her handwritten grocery list. Bananas were at the top. "So he's going to camp?"

Matt nodded. "The middle of the month. It's some survival camp thing not too far from his mom's house. It lasts like six weeks. Troy said his mom had to find some place to put him because she's going to be in Europe. He's really pissed off about it. I told him not to kill himself."

"Why would you say that?" Marnie asked, alarmed. "Did he *say* he wanted to kill himself?"

"No."

"Why would you say such a thing, then?"

Matt shrugged. "I don't know. His dad just died and he had to move. The dude's depressed, that's clear. He's never on Facebook, and when I text him he's in a mood."

"I would have taken him for six weeks if he needed a place to go. They didn't even ask," Marnie said.

"Yeah, he wondered about that, but his mom was pretty set on this camp."

"I miss him so much," Marnie said. "I can't even tell you how much. My heart hurts."

"Yeah," Matt said. "He misses you too."

"How do you know?"

"He said he did," Matt said, shrugging. Then seeming to lose interest in the conversation, he picked up a pomegranate, tossed it up in the air, and effortlessly caught it.

Marnie reached out and plucked the fruit out of his hand. "He *said* he missed me?"

"Well, yeah."

"Those exact words. He said, 'I miss Marnie.'" She moved closer and clutched his arm. "That's what he said?" From the look on Matt's face it was clear her death grip alarmed him, but she didn't care. This was important.

"No, not exactly those words. He said—" Here Matt looked up as if the ceiling tiles might give him a clue. "He said he wished he was still here living with you. His mom is gone a lot, I guess. Even nights and weekends."

Marnie let go. "Where does she go?"

Matt looked uncomfortable. "I don't know."

"She shouldn't be leaving him there by himself."

"Troy's old enough to be home alone. He just doesn't like it." He shifted and looked away. "I have to get going. I think my mom needs me." And without saying good-bye, he turned and ambled away.

Behind him, Marnie called out, "Matt, wait!"

He paused. "Yeah?"

"You said Troy is going to camp the middle of this month. Did he tell you the exact date?"

"Not really. Just that it was coming up."

"Okay. Thanks."

Marnie stayed by the bananas, processing what he'd said. Troy missed her. He really missed her. And he hated Las Vegas. Okay, Matt hadn't used the word *hate,* but it wasn't much of a stretch. And Kimberly was never, ever home. Typical. According to Brian, Kimberly liked to go to upscale boutiques, classy restaurants, and new art gallery exhibits. Hardly the type of places that would interest a teenage boy. And now she was discarding him by sending him off to camp for six weeks when Marnie would have been overjoyed to take him. How unfair.

Marnie had been hearing about Kimberly for years, but she realized now she didn't know the woman at all. God only knew what went on there, what Troy was being subjected to.

A portly red-haired lady stopped her cart and leaned around Marnie to pick up a bunch of bananas. Marnie stepped out of the way and resumed her shopping. As she pushed the cart toward the pasta aisle, she made a firm decision.

She was going to Las Vegas.

Chapter Eleven

Jazzy had to finish up the work week, and Rita needed time to cook and stock the freezer with meals for her husband, so the trip was scheduled for Saturday. Marnie hated to wait, but she didn't want to go alone.

When the day came to leave, Marnie was ready. The post office had been notified and would hold her mail; she'd finished the milk and tossed other perishables, and she put the living room lights on a timer. She considered telling her mother and siblings that she'd be out of town, but decided against it. It would only be a week. It's not like they talked more often than that anyway. And she'd have her cell phone with her. If someone really wanted to reach her, they could.

She'd had difficulty sleeping since encountering Matt in the grocery store. His words kept running through her mind. Troy was alone. He was unhappy. He missed her. In her memory he was the little boy who'd cried during thunderstorms because he was worried about the animals outside. He'd been a sweet, sensitive child. She knew that underneath the surly teen exterior that sweet child was there still.

After hours of not being able to sleep, she got up and brushed her teeth. When she caught sight of herself in the mirror, it was like looking at a stranger. Alone in the world, she didn't know who she was anymore. She put on her glasses and smoothed her shoulder-length hair, studying her face for clues to her identity. During the school year she was Ms. Mayhew, to her siblings she would always be little Marnie, and to Brian and Troy she had been Marn. Troy. The thought of him made her smile. Oh, she loved that boy beyond measure, but she wasn't his mother, and never would be.

Marnie had picked up the phone a dozen times that week, and each time, she had decided against calling and set it down again. She wanted to catch Kimberly off guard. Part of her too worried that Troy would put on a brave face and tell her not to come. That wasn't an option anymore. Marnie had made up her mind. She had to see him in person because she needed something. What that something was, she couldn't quite say. Closure? Reassurance? Knowing that she had mattered.

And part of her wanted to steal Troy away. To tell Kimberly that he wasn't going to camp, that he was coming home with her. To reclaim her child. Marnie shook her head at the thought. She'd never have the nerve.

When Rita and Jazzy arrived, they pulled up next to the curb in front and gave a little honk. Marnie went to the window to see them climbing out of Rita's car. With Rita's silvery gray hair cropped into a bob and Jazzy's flowing blonde hair, the age difference was obvious; they could be mother and daughter. Jazzy wore a loose-fitting sundress that tied in the back while Rita was her usual classy self in capri pants, a white blouse, and strappy silver sandals. When Jazzy glanced up, Marnie held up a finger to indicate she'd be down in a minute.

She'd already dragged the cooler onto the upstairs landing and was back inside double-checking the thermostat and lights when Rita came through her open door. "If you need some help, we're here," Rita said, then turned around to see Jazzy hadn't followed her. She shrugged. "She was right behind me a second ago. Anyway, I'm here. Can I help you with something?"

Shimmying the cooler back and forth, they managed to get it down the stairs. Rita took the lower part and stepped backward, one stair tread at a time. "What do you have in this thing?" Rita asked, straining from the weight.

"I know it seems like I went overboard," Marnie said, "but I believe in being prepared. My philosophy is that it's better to have it and not need it, than need it and not have it."

"My philosophy is that it's better to travel light. If you forget something you can always pick it up on the way," Rita said, pausing to rest for a moment. She turned and bellowed, "Jazzy!"

When there was no response she said, "I do believe we've lost our young friend." She wiped her forehead with her palm. "Which is unfortunate, because she's the navigator."

They continued down the steps, making the turn at the half-way point. "If you don't know the way, I have maps," Marnie said.

"Maps, schmaps," Rita said. "Who can read those things anyway? Jazzy brought a GPS."

When they got outside, Marnie was relieved to see that the car had a sizeable trunk. "Nice car," she said, as they wrestled the cooler into the opening.

"It's not just a car. It's a Crown Victoria," Rita said, her tone mocking. "My husband is in love with it. He was a little nervous about letting me have it."

"I appreciate you driving," Marnie said. "My car is on the small side."

"No problem. I like to drive, and I haven't been on a road trip for years." She held her keys and looked at the house. "Do you need more help?"

"No, all I have is the suitcase. I can do that by myself."

"I was hoping you'd say that."

When Marnie came back down, luggage in hand, Rita again brought up the fact that Jazzy was nowhere in sight. "Is this something she does?" she asked, looking around.

"Not that I know of," Marnie said. The sun was high in the sky. It was comfortably warm, in the midseventies, and not too humid. At last they'd gotten ideal weather—and she was leaving it behind.

"So she doesn't generally wander off?" Rita brushed her hands against the front of her pants.

"Well, I don't know," Marnie said. "I haven't known her for very long."

"You haven't known her for very long? Aren't you two related?"

"No. I just met her at the grief group, same as you."

"Hmmm. For some reason I thought the two of you had a connection. Relatives or neighbors or something."

Marnie shook her head. "She gave me a ride home one night when my car wouldn't start. After that I had her over for dinner as a thank-you. I like her and she seems very nice, but I can't say I know her well."

Rita frowned. "So we're traveling with a complete stranger? Seems a little dicey to me, not to know someone and be sharing car space for a week."

Complete strangers. It occurred to Marnie that the same could be said of Rita. In fact, she barely knew either of these women.

For all she knew, they had homicidal tendencies. Or were just really annoying. Before she could say anything in response, Rita pointed to the house. "Oh there she is now. Odd that we didn't see her when we were inside." Marnie looked up to see Jazzy coming down the walk, a skip in her step.

"Good news!" Jazzy said, breaking into a wide grin. "Laverne wants to come with us."

Chapter Twelve

Rita leaned against the car, a puzzled look on her face.

"Who's Laverne?" Marnie asked.

"Laverne," Jazzy said, pointing back at the house. "You know—Laverne."

This was going nowhere. Marnie tried again. "How do you know her?"

"Your neighbor, silly."

"My neighbor?"

"The lady who lives downstairs from you." Jazzy stopped just an arm's length from where the two women stood. At this distance, Marnie could really see Jazzy's clear blue eyes and a scattering of very light freckles across her nose. "When I told her we were going to Las Vegas, she said she wanted to come along."

"The lady downstairs. You mean Mrs. Benner?" Marnie asked, astonished.

"I don't know her last name. She just said Laverne."

Rita spoke up. "I wish you had talked to us first, Jazzy. There's simply not enough room for another person. You're going to have to tell her she can't go." Her voice was firm. A mom voice.

"Oh, sorry." Jazzy looked crestfallen. "I wasn't thinking I guess. It's just that she was so excited, and I figured since she was Marnie's neighbor, it would be okay. The more the merrier is my philosophy."

"But I've never met Mrs. Benner," Marnie said, protesting. "I don't even know what she looks like."

"You've never met her?" Now it was Rita's turn to be astonished. "How can you live above someone and not know what they look like?"

"Her son told me she wants to be left alone. That under no circumstances should I bother her. He was very clear on that."

"You need to march back inside and tell her that you made a mistake," Rita said to Jazzy. "Blame me if you need to. Tell her I said there's not enough room in the car, and that she can go with us the next time." She ran her fingers through her hair.

Jazzy took a deep breath. "But see, I have this gut feeling that she needs to be on the trip with us."

Rita sighed. "Jazzy, I hate to be a party pooper, but we've reached our limit already. It's going to be hard enough with the three of us."

"I don't think she'll take up much space," Jazzy said, reminding Marnie of a kid pleading for a new puppy. "Two in front and two in back would work out fine."

The front door flew open then and a small elderly woman with white poodle hair and wire-rim glasses stepped out onto the stoop, dragging a suitcase behind her. "I'm ready, I'm ready," she called to them. When she stepped down onto the walkway, the door clattered shut behind her. "I can't thank you gals enough for including me on your trip."

Chapter Thirteen

Watching Laverne pulling her luggage down the walk, Jazzy thought about how much her appearance had changed in the last ten minutes. Funny that people used the word *aged* to describe when a person looked older, but there was no word for the reverse process. No one ever said someone had "youngered." But Laverne definitely looked like she'd shed some years. The lines in her face were still there, but her smile made them less noticeable. Her posture was different too. Instead of walking hunched over, she stood upright and moved with lively steps. The woman had to be at least seventy-five, but you couldn't tell it by the way she moved.

"Hey, Laverne," Jazzy said.

Laverne stopped on the sidewalk and patted her suitcase like it was an obedient dog. "Thanks for waiting. I could've been quicker, but I had to call my son and tell him to take care of Oscar."

"Oscar?" Marnie asked.

"My cat," Laverne said.

Jazzy said, "Laverne, I'd like you to meet Rita. This is her car. And of course this is Marnie, your upstairs neighbor."

"Hey," Laverne said gruffly, waving a hand in their direction. "I hope you don't need me to share in the driving. I didn't keep up with my license and it expired a while back."

"About that," Jazzy said. "I'm sorry to have to tell you I have some bad news."

"Oh?" Laverne's brow furrowed.

Jazzy twisted her hands together sympathetically. "Yes—"

Rita interrupted. "Let me tell her, Jazzy, since it's my car." She gave Laverne a big smile. "You'll probably have to ride in the backseat for most of the trip. We already had the seat arrangements worked out before we knew you were coming along."

Jazzy had an inkling Rita was going to change her mind, but it clearly took Marnie unawares and she raised her eyebrows in surprise.

"Okeydokey," Laverne said. "I don't care where I go as long as you don't put me in the trunk."

"Don't be silly," Jazzy said. "The trunk is full."

Indeed, it was nearly full. There was only enough room for Laverne's suitcase and that was all. Jazzy slammed the lid down and joined Rita in the front. In the back, Marnie and Laverne fumbled with seat belts. Two clicks later, Marnie gave the okay to go.

"Now," Jazzy said, looking at her GPS, "if we drive for four hours straight, we can stop to eat in—"

"Oh, honey," Rita said, overriding her. "I can tell you right now that we won't be driving for four hours straight at any time during this trip."

"Why not?"

Rita laughed and pulled away from the curb. "You're just a baby, so you probably don't know this, but when you're traveling with old broads you have to factor in a lot of bathroom stops."

Chapter Fourteen

Following Jazzy's directions, Rita headed west, then eased her car onto the expressway. GPS, she decided, had to be the best gift to car trips since air-conditioning. Jazzy had named hers "Garmina" and had set it to speak in a British accent, an option Rita didn't know was possible. "Garmina just sounds more polite when she has an English accent," Jazzy said. "The American version sometimes sounds irritated, especially when she says, 'recalculating,' over and over again. Like she thinks I'm some kind of idiot."

Rita's husband, Glenn, had found it hard to believe she was going on a car trip with two women she'd just met, but he was pleased for her too, she could tell. She hadn't been herself since Melinda died. Time and again she'd tried to get back to being the person she was before the murder, but even her best moments were a charade. Like she was going through the expected motions of life. With each passing month she thought it would get easier, but that didn't happen. Every day was one more day without Melinda.

She once heard a radio show psychologist say that death was painful, not because people couldn't see their loved ones anymore, but because they couldn't *communicate* with them anymore. That made perfect sense to her. Rita could stand not seeing Melinda and not having her as part of her everyday life, if only she could have some contact, some assurance that things were the way they should be and that her daughter was fine. The violence that had taken her life marred the memories of her vibrant self.

This trip was the first time she'd felt even a smidgen of joy. She wanted to help Marnie reconnect with her stepson. Someone should be able to hug her child even if she couldn't. When it was time to go, Glenn had helped her carry her things out to the car, and asked if she had her phone and enough money. "Make sure you call me," he said. As if she wouldn't.

"I'll be back in a week or so," she said, giving him a kiss. "And I'll call you every night." Wait until she told him they'd picked up a fourth passenger at the last minute. She still couldn't believe she'd allowed Laverne to go with them. The old lady just looked so overjoyed to be going that Rita didn't want to be the one to cast a storm cloud over things.

"Everyone comfortable?" Rita asked. Jazzy nodded vigorously and a double chorus of "Yes!" came from Laverne and Marnie in the backseat.

"I'm so glad we don't have to go through Chicago," Jazzy said. "With the construction this time of year it's a nightmare. I hate those orange cones."

"Worse are the concrete barricades," Marnie said. "I'm always worried the car will scrape against them."

"It's probably a good thing neither of you are driving," Rita said. She prided herself on her good driving record. She'd never had an accident, never even had a speeding ticket for that matter. Nerves of steel behind the wheel, that was Rita.

When Rita's daughter, Melinda, turned sixteen and got her learner's permit, Glenn took her out driving once and it had been a horrible experience for both of them. They came into the house afterward with Melinda crying. "Daddy yelled at me," she sobbed.

Rita gave Glenn an accusing look. He threw up his arms and said, "See if you can do it any better." From then on, she was the one who took Mel driving and that was fine. Every summer after that, mother and daughter went on a road trip and shared the driving. Glenn opted to stay home the first year and after that he wasn't invited. There was something sacred about traveling together, just the two of them. They talked and laughed and talked some more, stopping when they had to and taking detours when something interested them. Rita realized with a pang that she missed Melinda not just as a daughter, but as a friend too. And she also missed future Melinda, the daughter who someday would have been a mother, making her a grandmother. Melinda would have been a good mom.

Laverne opened the window a bit and tentatively stuck out a hand. "Ahh," she said, closing her eyes. She looked euphoric.

Rita glanced at the rearview mirror and smiled. "If you want the air on, just let me know."

Laverne, eyes still closed, said, "For now, this is perfect. Just give a holler when we hit the state line. I've never been out of Wisconsin. I want the full experience."

"You've never been out of Wisconsin? You're kidding!" Jazzy's eyes widened. She turned around. "Why not?"

"We never had the cash to be gallivanting around. I had a bunch of kids and they needed shoes and food and whatnot. And then when they grew up, we were saving up for retiring. It went on and on."

"Still," Jazzy said, "to not go out of Wisconsin your whole life!"

"My life isn't over yet." Laverne closed the window. "And I'm getting out of Wisconsin now, aren't I?"

"You're not only leaving Wisconsin. You're heading to Las Vegas," Rita said.

"Sin city!" Jazzy said.

Rita said, "Home of the Hoover Dam."

"An oasis in the desert," Jazzy added.

"Gambling," Laverne said, her eyes shining.

And Marnie softly added, "The place where I can finally see Troy."

Chapter Fifteen

Jazzy hummed along to the music. At the start of the trip, she'd asked if she could hook up her iPod to the car stereo and the ladies were fine with it. Since then, she'd spent a lot of time scrolling through songs to make sure the music matched the view.

They'd established a routine. Every hour or so they made a bathroom stop. Marnie said she didn't really find it necessary, but joined the other two anyhow, just in case. Jazzy declined. She couldn't even imagine having to pee that often. "Have you guys thought of seeing a doctor about this condition?" she asked, which made them laugh. When Rita had first mentioned frequent bathroom breaks, Jazzy hadn't dreamt it would be this often. Good Lord, how could a person function in life with having to stop and hunt for a toilet all the time?

Most of the time the group kept a lookout for their restrooms of choice—the parklike rest areas found along Wisconsin highways. When they stopped, the other women visited the bathrooms, while Jazzy checked out the display case and studied the large state map, complete with red arrow labeled, "You are here."

Her third-grade teacher had said Wisconsin was shaped like a mitten, and that was sort of true, although she noted now that Michigan was clearly even more mitten-shaped.

Marnie spent a lot of her time in the car looking at a road atlas, tracing their path with her finger. Jazzy knew Marnie was wishing they could get there faster. Jazzy had involuntarily tapped into Marnie's stream of consciousness, and was picking up her thoughts and emotions. It wasn't a fun place to be. The woman was down on herself a lot. Her latest mental self-flagellation involved her fear of flying. Marnie had been thinking the same thought, over and over again, ever since the trip began. *If I wasn't so afraid to fly, I could be in Las Vegas already. If I wasn't so afraid to fly, I could be in Las Vegas already.* It was driving Jazzy crazy. She wanted to tell Marnie to ease up on herself. Everyone had something—some fear, some shortcoming, some problem. And some people had multiples in each area. The problems were what made people human beings—they fostered compassion and encouraged growth. What would be the point if everyone was perfect? She wanted to tell Marnie this, but Jazzy knew from previous experience that the words wouldn't reach her. This was something Marnie would have to learn for herself.

Out of all of them, Laverne was the most interested in the view. She looked out in rapt attention, clutching her large purse. She gawked as they passed farm fields dotted by Black Angus cattle. When they passed a sign for the city of Fitchburg she said, "Sounds like a Civil War name." She nudged Marnie when she spotted a hawk flying overhead. Marnie feigned polite interest and then went back to reading the atlas. As they got closer to the Mississippi River, the route became hillier, and the road often dipped between walls of rock three stories high. Laverne gaped unabashedly.

At the end of the afternoon, when they were within reach of the Iowa border, they saw a sign for the last of the Wisconsin rest stops until the return trip. "Does anyone want to stop?" Rita asked, once again.

"You betcha," Laverne said. Rita veered off the freeway and headed down the long exit toward the rest stop. In the distance they saw a parking lot and building fronted by a flagpole. A US flag topped the pole, with the Wisconsin state flag below, both waving in the breeze.

"I was here with my daughter once," Rita said. "The building was inspired by Frank Lloyd Wright—prairie style. There's a really nice deck in back that faces the Mississippi. You can't see the river, but you get the sense it's out there." She sounded sad, but when she caught Jazzy's eye she managed a small smile.

When they exited the car, Rita turned back to lock the doors with her remote. *Beep, beep.* Laverne lagged behind the others as if she were moving through water. "Just go ahead of me," she said to the others. "I know I'm slow."

Jazzy stayed by her side. "Don't worry about it. There's no hurry." She accompanied Laverne inside and watched as she entered the ladies' room on the left. Then Jazzy stopped to take a drink at the bubbler, sipping slowly before pausing to let the arc of water wet her lips. Cold and pure and refreshing, like spring water. She went back outside and lifted her face to the sun. Such a beautiful, sunny day. Just the sort of day one dreamt of when winter was at its worst.

She meandered down to one of the covered picnic tables scattered behind the building and stopped to lean on one but didn't sit down. It was nice in the shade. A thought suddenly came, telling her to walk down near the edge of the clearing, closer to the trees and the tall grass. Was it her own thought or something from outside her? It wasn't always easy to tell. Either way, it seemed like a reasonable thing to do. Jazzy made her way down the incline. Now she was near a cluster of trees, a thicket of trees so deep that the area was nearly a woods, and the voice said, *Close your eyes.* She felt compelled to stretch her arms out wide and became fully aware of the rustling of the wind in the trees, the smell of exhaust wafting from the parking lot. She imagined herself linked to all that was around her. The air in her lungs, the energy in her limbs, the electricity in her brain, all connected to everything and everyone else in the universe. She took a deep breath, keeping her arms extended. She wanted to embrace the world.

Stay still, the voice said. *Be open to the possibilities.*

Chapter Sixteen

Rita was the first one out of the bathroom. She lingered at the display, glanced at the brochures in the rack, and took a sip of water at the bubbler before going outside to wait for the others. They'd only been on the road for a few hours, and she was already starting to doubt the wisdom of this trip. It had seemed like a good idea when Jazzy had broached the subject at the grief group. God knew Rita needed something to pull her out of her rut. Glenn had tried for years, bless him, with no success. They'd gone on trips, gotten a kitten, volunteered at a homeless shelter. Every step of the way she thought how much more fun it would be if Melinda were there.

This trip was different, mostly because Glenn wasn't with her and also because she'd met these women after Melinda died. She'd thought that maybe, just maybe, this would keep her mind off herself. And it was working, at least somewhat. Driving required concentration, and the other women were nice, so far. So why did she feel so alone?

A woman pushing a baby in a stroller approached the glass door, and Rita opened it from the inside. The woman, who wore training sneakers, spandex shorts, and a tank top, had a decidedly athletic look. "Thanks so much," she said brightly, guiding the stroller with one hand and taking a sip from a water bottle with the other. Rita nodded, and after the stroller cleared the door, she headed outside to wait for the others.

To stretch her legs Rita strolled down the slight incline, away from the building, alongside the V-shaped deck in back. The sun warmed her face and she lifted her chin to get the full benefit of the rays before stopping by a covered picnic table.

After a few moments, she spotted Jazzy standing in front of the tree line, sixty feet away. She had her arms extended and eyes closed, and she was turning slowly, so slowly. Rita was about to call out to her when she was stopped short by the sight of an animal coming boldly out from between two bushes. The words froze in her mouth. The animal, a good-sized doe, stepped deliberately toward Jazzy. Rita sucked in a breath and held it. What a remarkable sight.

Laverne appeared at Rita's side and watched the animal approach Jazzy. The deer came right up to Jazzy and nuzzled her hand.

The two women leaned forward. Laverne leaned over and whispered loudly, "Holy guacamole! A tame deer, what do you think of that?"

Rita shook her head. "I don't think it's tame." She fixed her eyes on Jazzy, willing her not to move, afraid that even the slightest twitch might scare the deer away.

"Oh," Laverne said, the word so soft it was more of an exhale than a verbalization. She lifted her arm and silently pointed to the thicket of trees behind Jazzy where one by one, a group of deer loped out from behind the trees.

Rita counted. Five, now six, now seven of them. Eight total, all does. They came out in a cluster and stopped just outside the woods, their gaze fixed on Jazzy and the first deer. The sound of a semi pulling out from the other side of the building didn't spook the animals, although it did startle Rita, who registered the sound right before she got a whiff of exhaust fumes.

A breeze kicked up and lifted Jazzy's hair up off her shoulders. It rose and fell with the motion of a tablecloth being shaken out. Jazzy opened her eyes but didn't seem shocked to see one deer nosing her palm and eight others watching intently. The young woman and doe locked eyes, and then the deer stepped closer. Jazzy stroked its head and murmured something undecipherable. The doe raised its head and nuzzled her shoulder.

In the parking lot beyond, Rita became aware of the sound of a vehicle pulling into a space and car doors opening and shutting. A small boy yelled, "Mommy! Look at all the deer." Out of the corner of her eye, Rita saw the boy running toward them. "Just a minute, Tyler," his mother called, but he wasn't listening. As the boy got closer, the deer changed from tame creatures to wild animals. Their reaction was physical—heads raised as if sensing danger, bodies turning, legs pumping—their white tails the last thing seen before they disappeared into the woods.

The little boy turned back in disappointment. "They didn't wait for me," he said, wailing.

"It's okay, baby," his mother said. "You can pick out a candy bar in the vending machine." The family went into the building, passing Marnie as she came out. She walked down the incline and joined Laverne and Rita at the picnic table. "Did I miss anything?" she asked.

Chapter Seventeen

As they approached the Mississippi River on Highway 151, Rita called out, "Once we get to the other side of the river we'll be out of Wisconsin and into Iowa."

Rita looked in the rearview mirror to see Laverne's face light up like a kid at a county fair. Hard to believe that crossing an invisible line held such significance for a woman that age. Laverne put her palm on the glass as the car made the seamless transition from solid road to bridge. "Oh, it's so big," she said, her eyes wide at the sight of the river. "I didn't know it would be so big."

"The mighty Mississippi," Jazzy said, suction-cupping Garmina to the windshield. "The same one that Huck and Big Jim traveled by raft."

Jazzy had made light of her meeting with the deer in the picnic area at the wayside. She admitted it was odd but shrugged it off. Who knew why animals did what they did? Maybe they thought she had food. Rita wasn't about to let the subject go that easily. She waited until they were firmly in Iowa and the others were occupied: Laverne with her nose pressed to the window and

Marnie reading a magazine. While Jazzy adjusted the angle of the GPS screen, Rita said, "I'm still wondering about those deer. Why do you suppose they came right up to you?"

"Pretty crazy, huh?" Jazzy said. "They must be used to people."

"That's really what you think?" Rita asked. "The deer are just used to people?"

Jazzy pushed her hair behind her ear. "What else could it be?"

Was Rita imagining things, or did Jazzy stiffen up? She lowered her voice so the others in the backseat wouldn't hear. "You can tell me what you think," Rita said. "Please. Whatever it is, I need to know."

There was a palpable tension now, the silence punctuated by the vibration of the tires on the road. Jazzy turned and gave her a cautious look. "How much do you want to know?"

"All of it," Rita said. "Everything."

Jazzy tapped her fingers on the dashboard, considering. She sighed.

Rita said, "Whatever it is, just tell me."

"I have a lot of weird stuff happen to me. I don't usually tell people. It changes things."

"Please."

"You'll think I'm a nut job."

"I promise I won't think you're a nut job."

"You say that now." Jazzy looked straight ahead for a minute or so and then gave Rita a long, questioning look.

"Try me." Rita said.

"Okay, if you have to know, I have this talent," Jazzy said finally. "Or maybe it's a curse. I'm still not sure. The truth is, and I know it sounds unbelievable, but I'm psychic. I pick up on people's thoughts. And I get messages from the dead."

Rita's grip on the steering wheel tightened. She'd suspected as much, but it was another thing to know for sure. "I had a feeling," she said, struggling to keep her eyes on the road.

Jazzy said, "It's not as dramatic as in the movies. I don't see apparitions, at least not in the way most people think of apparitions. I don't know the future, although sometimes I get inklings. Most of the time it's not clear-cut. I just get…"

"What?"

"Thoughts," Jazzy said. "Messages. I have no control. They just come. Little flashes of ideas or words. I get these thoughts and they're like voices in my head making suggestions or passing on information."

Rita listened in fascination. "How do you know the voices are from dead people?"

"My grandmother used to have the same thing. She was the one who told me it was spirits. It's like having a radio receiver in my head."

"And the deer?" Rita asked.

"Animals pick up on things," Jazzy said slowly. "They have to rely on their instincts more than people do. I think the deer were directed to me. To get my attention and serve as a conduit. As weird as that sounds." She ran her fingers through her hair. "When the one touched my hand, I got a message. A female voice. She said we needed to stop in someplace in Colorado. I couldn't quite catch the name. It sounded kind of like Preston Place. Anyway, we're supposed to stop there."

"Why?"

"Why do we have to stop, or why did I get the message?"

"Both, I guess."

Jazzy sighed again. "I don't know. Lots of times it's confusing. Usually though, it all works out for the best."

"The female voice—" Rita tried to keep the words steady, but it was hard going. "Was it a young woman? In her early twenties, maybe?"

"I don't know. Maybe," Jazzy said. "Not old, anyway." She continued, apologetically. "It happened so quickly. All I got was a sort of impression. It's like overhearing part of a conversation in another room."

"But it could have been a young woman?"

"Maybe. Female definitely. I'm not sure about the age. Young-ish, I guess. Why do you ask?"

"I think it was my daughter," Rita said and then, reconsidering, spoke with more assurance. "No, I don't think. I *know*. I know it was Melinda."

"I can't tell you that for sure. I didn't get that she was connected to you," Jazzy said.

"But it was a young woman." Rita didn't even try to keep the excitement out of her voice. "And it came through the deer."

"I don't want you to get your hopes up," Jazzy said, carefully. "Sometimes it's totally random, not connected to anything around me."

"No, it was Melinda."

"Why do you think so?"

"I've been at that wayside with Melinda many times. We always stopped there on our road trips. And using deer?" Rita felt something light up inside of her. "That's so Melinda, you don't even know. She collected deer figurines and stuffed animals. Her friends nicknamed her Bambi because she cried when she saw the movie for the first time when she was in high school. She told me once that she hoped she could be reincarnated as a deer."

"Wow," Jazzy said, but somehow Rita didn't think she was all that shocked. A person who got messages from dead people couldn't be surprised by too many things.

"It was Melinda," Rita said, almost to herself. "It's exactly what she would do." A wave of raw emotion came over her and she had to swallow hard to keep from crying. The feeling was similar to when she first held Melinda as a newborn. Awe and wonder and hope. Now, like then, a miracle had happened. Heaven had split open and allowed her daughter to send down a message.

From the backseat, Marnie said, "What are you two talking about up there?"

"We were talking about the deer," Jazzy said, with a nonchalant wave of her hand.

"What about the deer?" Marnie asked.

"I was just telling Jazzy that they reminded me of my daughter," Rita said, willing her voice to stay level. "Melinda collected them."

Laverne perked up. "She collected *deer*?"

"Stuffed animals. Plastic figures. It was sort of her thing."

"Oh," Laverne leaned back. "That's real nice, I suppose."

When Rita glanced over, Jazzy gave her a knowing smile, a signal between them. There was no need for the other two women to know their secret.

Chapter Eighteen

Riding in the backseat for hours gave Marnie too much time to ruminate. It was only the first day on the road, but she was already questioning the wisdom of driving to Las Vegas. If it were just her, she might have turned around and gone back by now, but it wasn't just her. The other women had already eased into the kind of camaraderie you usually only saw among longtime roommates or agreeable coworkers. Jazzy was the impetus, teasing a smile out of Laverne, threatening to make everyone play car games if they didn't talk. Laverne opened up pretty readily, telling how she met her husband at a high school dance. Rita had a better story. Her husband, Glenn, literally bumped into her at a diner, spilling the contents of his coffee cup down the front of her best blue blazer. The only reason she'd stopped at the diner was to kill time before a job interview. "Glenn was so embarrassed," she said, laughing. "And he turned beet red. He was so cute it was hard to get mad at him, although I was a little, at first." She didn't get the job, but she said that by then she didn't care.

"How did you meet your guy?" Jazzy asked, turning the conversation to Marnie.

Marnie had hoped the fact that Brian died recently would make them believe it was a raw subject, but no such luck. She cleared her throat. "I don't have a great story," she said. "We met at work."

"So you worked together?" Laverne said.

"No," Marnie said. "I met Brian because I had his son Troy in my kindergarten class. His wife left him and moved to Las Vegas, so he needed someone to watch Troy after school. He asked if I knew of a babysitter, and I volunteered to do it."

"Wow, that was nice of you," Rita said, her eyes still on the road.

Marnie shrugged. "I wasn't doing much else anyway, and he seemed to be in a real bind."

Jazzy said, "I think that's an awesome story. What did you think when you first saw him?"

"Oh, he was the cutest little thing," Marnie said. "He used to come to school with this little scrap of blanket. He called it his Biffy."

Laverne chortled, and Marnie realized her mistake. Jazzy had been asking about Brian, not Troy.

"Brian was a very handsome, charming man," she said, clearing her throat. "I just always thought of them as a package." Odd, but she couldn't get a clear picture of Brian from that time. Troy she remembered well. He was a shy boy, small for his age, always on the edge of the group. Cute, with brown hair that went every which way. His big, dark eyes framed long lashes.

In the classroom, he sometimes called her Mommy by mistake, which was as heartbreaking as it was endearing. "My wife abandoned us," Brian had said when she asked about Troy's mom, or lack thereof. Kimberly. Even then she'd had harsh feelings about the woman. What kind of woman could leave a precious boy like Troy for even a day, much less forever?

When Brian said he needed someone to watch Troy after school, she didn't think twice about it. They agreed she'd babysit at Brian's house. That made the most sense. Bit by bit, she made herself familiar and then indispensible, cooking dinner so that a hot meal was on the table by the time Brian came home from work. He was grateful and complimentary too. Her meat was perfectly seasoned; vegetables had never tasted so good; her desserts were decadent. The way he ate her meals had a sensual quality to it. He ate each bite slowly, groaning with pleasure.

It hadn't taken long before they became a couple. Marnie moved in when the school year ended. She was twenty-five. For a year or so she was happier than she'd ever been, happier than a human being deserved to be. Brian stopped and picked up flowers for her on the way home, complimented her endlessly, swept her into the bedroom every night as soon as they were sure Troy was sound asleep.

After about a year, it all fell apart. He pulled away when she went to hug him, stopped complimenting her or even noticing her. When she asked if she'd done something wrong, he denied it and said she was being paranoid. The sex stopped completely. She was puzzled, he was defensive. All relationships cooled off, Brian said. Meanwhile, her family asked when there would be a wedding. As the years went by, they stopped asking.

The permanent divide came when Brian was diagnosed with sleep apnea and had to sleep with a CPAP machine. He said it made him nervous to have her next to him when he had the mask up to his nose and the straps over the top of his head. She never understood that. What difference did it make if she was there? To make it sound like he was being selfless, he said he didn't want the noise of the machine to bother her. Odd, because the CPAP noise was a gentle hiss of air, almost like a vaporizer, but somewhat more soothing. Certainly a better sound than the snoring he did when not using the machine. But really, what could she say? If he didn't want to sleep with her, it would be pathetic to argue the point. Eventually she moved all her clothes and personal items to the guest bedroom. One advantage was that she finally had her own bathroom and didn't have to look at the remnants of shaving cream and whiskers in the sink each morning.

She should have moved out at the first sign of trouble, and she almost did, but every time she threatened it, Brian begged her to stay and reverted back to his old self. He'd rub her shoulders and whisper in her ear. "I love you, Marnie. You know that. I'm just not good at relationships. I'm working on it. Please give us another chance. Please. We need you."

Oh, he was charming, all smiles and flowers and nice messages on her voice mail. She usually got a few good weeks out of it, anyway. What Brian didn't know was that his tactics weren't what kept them together. It was Troy. That little boy adored her, and the feeling was mutual. They had private jokes that didn't involve Brian, or anyone else for that matter. He was a perceptive child, able to tell from the look on her face when she was troubled or had a headache. As he got older, their house became the place where all of Troy's buddies hung out. She provided the best snacks and joked with them in a comfortable but not overbearing way. Brian, for the most part, was just a guy who was there. The two of them got along and he was glad she took care of all the household details, but he didn't go out of his way for her. She continued teaching and because she had few living expenses was able to bank nearly her entire paycheck year after year. Now she was financially stable, but thirty-five and alone.

Jazzy interrupted her thoughts. "So you always thought of them as a package?" she prompted.

"Always," Marnie said firmly. "In fact, I wouldn't have stayed with Brian if not for Troy." It was, she realized, the first time she'd said that to anyone. It wasn't a flattering thing to admit.

"How come?" Jazzy asked.

"He was..." Marnie searched for a diplomatic way to put it. "Not a very warm man. I was lonely."

The car was silent for a moment. Laverne said, "Men. For Pete's sake. It's always something with them," and they all agreed. To change the subject, Laverne pulled a large Ziploc bag out of her purse and held it up. "If anyone is feeling under the weather, I brought my whole stash. Anything that's wrong, I got something that will fix you right up." The bag was filled with vials of prescription drugs and over-the-counter pain medication.

"Good Lord," Jazzy said, reaching for the bag. "You have a whole pharmacy in here. Where'd you get all this stuff?" Her brow furrowed as she looked at the labels through the plastic. "Yowza."

"Don't worry, it's nothing illegal," Laverne said. "They were all prescribed, at one time or another. And some are just regular medicine. Aspirin and such."

"Who's David Benner?" Jazzy asked, reading off a prescription label.

"My son. He had a hernia operation a while back and didn't use all his pills."

"And Christopher Benner?"

"My youngest grandson. They tried him out on that ADD medication, but he didn't take to it too well. It's good if you want a little pep in your step." Noticing the look on Jazzy's face she added, "Only for emergencies. I'm very careful."

Jazzy handed the bag back. "And your family just gives you this stuff?"

"More or less." She put it back in her purse.

"You know you're not supposed to take other people's medication?" Jazzy said.

"Yeah, I know. I hardly ever use it, but when you need it, you really need it."

Jazzy nodded in agreement, while Marnie listened, horrified. She'd never in her life taken medication prescribed for someone else and she never would. Didn't Laverne know that doctors and pharmacists carefully calculate drug usage based on weight and other health considerations? It was a good way to get herself killed, this cavalier attitude toward drugs. Some people were unbelievable.

As they drove the next hundred miles, Marnie watched as Laverne's eyes closed and then her head drooped, her curly head pressed against the car window, wire-rim glasses askew. Odd to think the woman lived right below her for months and she'd never caught sight of her until now. She wanted to know what Laverne's problem was—why had she been so reclusive? And why come out now? She didn't ask though. Marnie had learned that people tell you what they want you to know all in good time. It would come out eventually or not at all. The choice was Laverne's. If there was anything she learned from Brian, it was not to push things. She got better results with a soft approach.

Iowa was lush and green with gently rolling hills that leveled out deeper into the state. The sun was ahead of them now, but in the backseat, Marnie was in the shade. Rita had turned on the air-conditioning long ago, and it seemed to do a good job cooling the whole car. It was comfortable in the back, anyway. Jazzy fiddled with her iPod and made an occasional comment, but otherwise, things were quiet.

They'd stopped for a bite at a McDonald's at one point, and made regular bathroom stops along the way. Halfway through the afternoon, Rita had insisted on stopping for gas, even though the tank wasn't that low. She'd filled up at a place called "Kum & Go," a name that Jazzy had said was wrong "on so many levels." Even though Jazzy didn't like the name, she got out with the rest of them to use the bathrooms and buy some junk food and a magazine in the attached convenience store. Now that they'd spent a good amount of time together, Marnie was starting to get a read on everyone in the car. Jazzy was a cheerful free spirit, Rita was a prim and proper lady (she rarely went more than five miles over the speed limit, which was so infuriating), and Laverne vacillated between wide-eyed tourist and naïve old-person. Her most defining characteristic was her tendency to blurt out whatever came into her brain. The woman had no filters. At all.

It was going to be a long trip.

Chapter Nineteen

They were still in Iowa and it wasn't even dark yet, so Jazzy was surprised when Rita said, "What do you say, ladies? Should we stop here for the night or no?"

Laverne, who had been dozing, lifted her head and rubbed her eyes. "Where are we?"

"Coming up on Des Moines."

"We're stopping in Des Moines?" Marnie said. Jazzy could tell she was disappointed and wanted to keep going, but Rita was the driver, so she couldn't really object. Rita said she was tired, and that they'd gone a respectable distance for a first day. "Tomorrow we'll be almost entirely on the interstate and we can really put some miles behind us," she said. "There seem to be plenty of hotels. Let's find a place for dinner first."

Rita veered off the expressway, and Jazzy fiddled with the Garmin to find restaurants close by. "There's a steak house a few blocks down," she said, scrolling through their choices. "And a Chinese restaurant and a pizza place."

"Anything but pizza," Laverne said. "It tastes good, but it sits like a brick in my stomach afterward."

"I've heard good things about the steak house," Jazzy said. "I really think we should go there."

Rita turned to Jazzy. "Where did you hear good things about the steak house?"

"Oh, just around," Jazzy said evasively. "I have some relatives who go to Des Moines fairly often." She could tell Rita wasn't buying it, but she didn't want to elaborate. Because they'd talked about it, Rita knew about the voices from beyond the grave, but Jazzy hated giving details. She could elaborate if she wanted to—say things like sometime spirits gave her tips: when she should avoid a certain road or which restaurant to go to. It wasn't like getting a personal recommendation from a friend. More like an inkling. Not too different from what other people experienced when they had a hunch. Jazzy's hunches were more reliable. But she didn't want to get into it. She knew from experience that people were initially fascinated but very soon would start to treat her differently. They wanted things from her, things she couldn't always give. It was a cursed blessing, or blessed curse, depending on your point of view.

They were in the city now. The steak house was a box of a building, set on the corner. Rita was able to get a parking spot half a block away. An easy walk on a summer evening. Outside the restaurant, standing on the sidewalk, a group of three men, paunchy guys in their sixties, smoked cigars. The men said, "Good evening, ladies," as they approached, and Laverne gave a wave like she was brushing away a fly. Inside, the place was dark wood with brass accents. Potted ferns hung in the corners. The guys at the bar watched CNN and drank from tall mugs of beer.

A young man with spiked hair and a nose ring greeted them as they walked in, then grabbed some menus and escorted them to a booth in the bar area, the last available table in the place. "Maybe we should have gone somewhere else," Marnie said, frowning over the menu. Jazzy had noticed that Marnie had a tendency to second-guess decisions. For someone her age she didn't seem very sure of herself.

"Nope," Jazzy said firmly, "we picked just the right place."

"It smells good in here," Rita said.

They were eating their dinners when they first noticed three people at a table on the other side of the room staring at them. A woman and two men. The guys were young—in their early twenties. The woman, pudgy but attractive with red shoulder-length hair and an abundance of sparkly jewelry, looked old enough to be the mother of the group, but she wasn't. None of them were related, Jazzy knew. The woman wasn't even pretending not to look at Jazzy—she stared until Jazzy became uncomfortable and looked away. Marnie was the first to say something about it. She leaned in to the table and subtly pointed. "We're being watched by three people across the way," she said. "They've been—"

Laverne's head whipped around way too conspicuously.

"Don't look," Marnie said sharply, but it was too late. The woman noticed and raised a hand in acknowledgement, then picked up a fork and started eating as if nothing had happened. Marnie continued. "Those three in the corner have been staring at us for the last fifteen minutes."

"Distracted by our beauty, would be my guess," said Rita, which made Laverne laugh.

Laverne said, "I can't remember the last time anyone looked my way. You get past fifty and you're darn near invisible, especially to men."

"I noticed that too," Rita said. "Every now and then an elderly man will hold the door for me and I'll think to myself, *Well, I guess I still have it*. How sad is that? It makes my day when an old guy does me a small courtesy."

"Some older men are very distinguished looking," Marnie said.

Rita laughed. "I'm not talking distinguished-old. I'm talking geezer. One of them had his oxygen tank with him."

They continued talking about men and the lack of admiring glances women got as they aged, and all the while Jazzy snuck glances at the men and the older lady. While she watched them, they watched her. She felt a jolt of fear rise up her spine as she sensed the reason they had picked her out of the crowd. They could tell she was different. They knew it in the same way a dog senses fear. She felt vulnerable. She picked up her fork and speared a mushroom, hoping she was wrong about being scrutinized. Except she was rarely wrong when it came to this kind of stuff.

By the time the waitress took their plates away, the other table had been looking in their direction for half an hour. Jazzy felt them honing in on her. The obvious solution—confront the group and ask if they had a staring problem—was not what she wanted to do. She wanted to sneak out, to get far away from there. As soon as possible. Of course, Laverne had to order dessert.

"Dessert is one of life's greatest pleasures," she said. Jazzy's heart sank as Laverne discussed all her options in detail with the waitress. Cheesecake was too heavy, sherbet not a real dessert. Pie might be good, but was their key lime pie *real* key lime pie? Laverne knew the difference. If it wasn't real key lime pie, it wasn't worth bothering with.

Come on already, Jazzy thought impatiently. To make matters worse, Laverne talked Rita into getting something too.

When the strawberry cheesecake arrived, Laverne and Rita exclaimed over it like two women who hadn't had a decent meal in years. While Marnie debated aloud whether she should order dessert herself, Jazzy had a visceral reaction. She felt herself getting lightheaded and uncomfortable, like she was wrapped in something she couldn't shake off. The booth became confining and the background noise assaulted her senses. She pulled some money out of her wallet, enough to cover her share and then some, and put it on the table. "I'll wait for you guys outside," she said, slinging her purse strap over her shoulder. "I need to get some air."

Outside the restaurant, Jazzy filled her lungs with the warm evening air. The group of smoking men had gone, and she had the space to herself. With every passing minute her sense of panic dissipated along with the trapped feeling. The three people at the table weren't going to follow her out. She was fine for now.

But now what? She could go for a walk—the other women had her cell phone number and could meet up with her when they were done. But she was in a strange city and it was getting dark. Maybe not the best idea. *Patience*, said a voice. *It will all work out.* She closed her eyes and aimed her face at her feet, shaking off her tension, relaxing in the moment.

The front door to the restaurant opened, and she heard a slice of conversation mixed with up-tempo music. "Jazzy?" She looked up to see Marnie, a worried look on her face. "Are you okay?"

Jazzy pushed her hair out of her face. "Yeah, I'm fine." She smiled in what she hoped was a convincing way.

"You looked like you were going to be sick." Marnie had such a caring look on her face Jazzy almost felt like hugging her. It occurred to Jazzy that she was in the company of women old enough to be her aunt, mother, and grandmother.

"No, I'm okay."

"What is it, then?" Marnie was next to her now, her arm around her shoulder. "Tell me."

Jazzy hadn't planned on spilling the truth. She'd been ready to spin a tale of stomach issues or menstrual cramps. The words were there, willing and able, but different words came out instead. "I couldn't deal with those three people staring. It was freaking me out. I had to get away."

The traffic light at the closest intersection changed from red to green, and a black Mustang screeched away from the intersection, trailed by a line of cars. Marnie said, "Usually I find that people stare because they think you look like someone they know. In your case, though, I think it's because you're so pretty."

"I'm not so pretty," Jazzy said. "I look like most everyone else."

"Youth has its own beauty," Marnie said, sounding wistful. "You are completely perfect, every bit of you. Someday you'll look back and realize that."

Jazzy gave her a faint smile. "Your theory is really nice, and I appreciate you trying to make me feel better," she said, slowly, "but I believe the reason they were staring is that they could sense something about me."

"Which is what?"

She sighed. It was official—Jazzy was tired of denying who she was. If people couldn't accept her oddities, then the hell with them. It was better to know what they thought right from the start. She turned to meet Marnie's gaze. "I don't usually tell people this, but I've already told Rita, so the rest of you might as well know too. You might think I'm crazy or woo woo or whatever. I can't help that. But the fact of the matter is that I'm psychic."

Marnie raised an eyebrow in surprise. "Do you see dead people?"

"Something like that."

"Wow."

"Does that change what you think of me?" Jazzy asked.

Marnie shook her head.

"Really? You don't think I'm crazy or lying?"

"No, I don't think you're crazy or lying. If you believe it, that's good enough for me," Marnie said. "It must be nice to know you have a special talent."

They were both quiet for a minute or two. "You're a really good cook," Jazzy offered.

"Anyone can do that," Marnie said glumly.

"I can't. Believe me, not many people cook anymore."

They stood there in companionable silence. The door to the restaurant opened and closed and a middle-aged couple came out laughing. The woman said, "Stop it. I already said you were right." She playfully slapped his arm. "What more do you want?" Jazzy would have liked to hear the answer, but the couple had their backs to them now and they were heading toward their car; his response was muffled.

"So," Marnie asked, slowly, "if I wanted to communicate with someone specific, someone dead I mean, could you like, call them up?"

Jazzy shook her head. "It doesn't work like that. It's more like I get messages out of the blue. It almost always happens when I'm not expecting it. I'll get a thought in my head that's not mine, or I get an impression of something."

Marnie said, "So can you actually see the person, or is it like a hologram?"

Jazzy sighed. How to explain this? "You know how sometimes at the grocery store you'll be holding a box of something, maybe checking the ingredients or reading the label?" When

Marnie nodded she continued. "And out of the corner of your eye you see someone approach, maybe a woman pushing a cart? You might even move to make room for her to pass. If someone were to question you about the woman later, you could give a general description—female, age range, maybe an idea of her size, whether or not she was in a hurry, or whatever. But you couldn't really say exactly what she looked like. It was more of an impression."

"That's what it's like for you?" Marnie looked fascinated.

"Pretty much. And when I get messages it's like the person whispered something as they went by. I usually only get like seventy percent of it, and most of the time I don't even know what it means or what I'm supposed to do with it."

"Wow."

"And some of the dead people are *so* persistent. They get frustrated with me when I can't figure it out, so they keep coming back, and back, and back." She rolled her eyes at the thought. So many times she wished it would all go away. It would be so nice to curl up with a good book or take a nap without being interrupted. Having no control over her private time was frustrating. Closing doors didn't keep them out. Nothing did.

"How often does this happen?"

Jazzy tilted her head and considered. "At least once a week. Sometimes every day."

"Maybe it's not such a cool thing after all," Marnie said.

"It's not always so bad," Jazzy said. "Sometimes I help people. Once I saw a woman eating at the food court at the mall and I kept hearing, 'Tell her to check the inside pocket. Tell her to check the inside pocket,' and I knew it was connected to this quilted bag she had sitting on the table. I went up to her and said I liked her purse, where could I buy one, and she said I couldn't buy it, her mother had made it. She said her mother was a quilter and very talented seamstress and it was the last thing she made before she passed away. I told her I wanted to make one like it, did it have an inside pocket, and she said yes, but she didn't use it because it was in an inconvenient place."

She had Marnie's full attention now. "Then what happened?" Marnie said.

"I asked if I could see the pocket. She was starting to think I was loony, I think, but she opened the purse and showed me this zippered pocket way at the bottom of the bag. I said, oh that would be the perfect place to hide something valuable. When I said that, her expression changed but she didn't say anything. I thanked her and went back to my table and pretended to eat my sweet potato fries, but I kept sneaking peeks in her direction."

"And then she looked in the pocket," Marnie said.

"Yep. And she pulled out a ring," Jazzy said. "Her face lit up like you wouldn't believe."

"And you never told her how you knew?"

"Oh no," Jazzy said, drawing back in horror. "I've had bad luck with that. If I had told her, she would have thought I was crazy or faking it or mean. Or else she would have pestered me to do it some more. Believe me, you learn pretty quick what people will accept."

Marnie looked thoughtful. "Those people staring at you in there." She pointed. "What tipped you off? Did a spirit tell you they knew you were psychic?"

Jazzy had almost forgotten about them. Almost. "No. I have very good intuition. I think it goes along with the psychic thing. I can tell when people are lying or when they think I'm lying. I can tell when people are covering up something. And I know when they know things."

"So if they knew, so what? What's there to be afraid of?"

Jazzy exhaled. "I don't know. I got this creepy feeling, like they could see me with my clothes off. Usually if people find out I'm psychic they want things from me. Or they treat me differently. I hate that."

"You have a lot of burdens for someone your age," Marnie said. "At this point in your life you should be carefree. Going to college or traveling. Going out with friends."

"I'm okay," Jazzy said. "My grandma was the same way as me. When I was growing up, she did a good job explaining all about our *special gift.*" She put the last two words in finger quotes. "Grandma died a few years ago, but I still feel her sometimes. And Dylan understands and is supportive, so that's good." The truth of it was, Jazzy mused, that if you had at least one person who believed in you, you could tolerate almost anything. "I just wish I knew what to do with it all. I always feel like I'm falling short somehow."

"You're young," Marnie said. "You have all the time in the world."

The door to the restaurant opened, and out came Laverne and Rita. "You gals missed one heck of a dessert," Laverne said. "Strawberry cheesecake. The cheesecake was the baked kind and the strawberries were fresh. It was to die for." She came up to Jazzy and patted her on the back. "You should be indulging at your age. That slim figure won't last forever, you know. At some point you'll have to watch your weight. Enjoy it while you can. Yep, that was a heck of a dessert."

Behind her, Rita smiled. "I have to agree. The cheesecake was outstanding." She pulled her car keys out of her purse. "What do you say we head to the hotel? We have a lot of driving to do tomorrow."

Chapter Twenty

Marnie couldn't help but think that if you'd seen one Marriott Hotel, you'd seen them all. Rita expressed a preference for the chain, though, because she had some kind of rewards card thing. Funny how one person could dominate a group. Well, it was hard to be irritated with her. Rita was a true lady, one of those women who set a lovely table, did volunteer work, and talked about their church friends. The type who quietly did good work, visiting people in the hospital, going on mission trips, planting flower beds, making the world a better place. Not asking for credit or praise, or getting it, for that matter, just doing what needed to be done. Like offering to drive on this trip. That was nice of her. Marnie never would have had the guts to drive across the country on her own, but with Rita driving, and the other two women in the car for support, anything seemed possible. She'd have her own posse when she went to confront Kimberly. The thought comforted her.

The hotel's front desk was busy tonight. When it was finally their turn, the clerk apologized for the delay, saying it was because of a wedding.

"We don't have a reservation," Rita said. "What is your room availability?"

Laverne nudged her way in and said, "I don't know about you gals, but I don't think the four of us sharing a room is gonna work." She leaned on the counter and turned to get their reaction. None of them seemed to have thought through the sleeping arrangements ahead of time, but one by one they all agreed that four women in one room was too many. No one wanted to share a bed or wait too long for bathroom time.

When Rita suggested doubling up, Marnie quickly claimed Jazzy, leaving Rita stuck with Laverne. Even Laverne thought Rita got a raw deal. She poked her in the arm and said, "Looks like you drew the short straw! Hope you brought your earplugs. My family says I snore loud enough to wake the dead. Like a buzz saw, they say."

Rita smiled. "Don't worry about that. Glenn has snored for years. I'm used to it."

— — —

Marnie and Jazzy's room had two queen-sized beds on either side of a nightstand. The large flat-screen TV was bigger than the one Marnie had at home, but she was too tired to watch it. Jazzy was efficient in her bedtime routine, coming out of the bathroom in pink pajama bottoms and a camisole top. Marnie was suddenly embarrassed by her nightshirt with the panda on it. All of her clothing, she realized, was juvenile or old-lady-ish. When had she stopped caring how she looked?

That night as they lay in bed in the dark, Marnie couldn't help herself. "Jazzy? Are you asleep?" Over the hum of the air-conditioner, she heard Jazzy shift under the covers.

"No, I'm still awake."

"Can I ask you a question? About being psychic, I mean?"

"Sure."

"If you heard from my Brian, would you tell me? Please? You'd know him, if he came through. He's kind of a burly guy, brash, confident." Marnie was sure Brian's true personality would shine through even after death. Sometimes when he was alive she sensed his energy in the next room even when he was silent.

"Yes, I'd tell you. But please don't count on it. I don't want you to be disappointed."

"No, I know. I'm not counting on anything."

Jazzy cleared her throat. "What is it you're hoping you'll find out? Was there something left unsaid between the two of you?"

Marnie had to think. There really had been nothing left unsaid. First he had loved her (or seemed to), then he was distracted, and after that only intermittently affectionate. The last few years he seemed barely aware of her existence. Being ignored was the worst of all. She'd bring up the subject of his inattention, and he'd promise to do better, even meet her halfway for a time, but eventually he'd lapse again. After a while she got tired of wondering why she wasn't good enough. All of the anger and tears never changed a thing. He was never going to change. She went through all the stages of grief, and when she got to acceptance, a few years into the relationship, it was a relief. They reached a sort of unspoken agreement and carried out their part of the bargain.

At least he was there. When she was unsure of what to do in a situation at work, or she needed to talk to someone about how to handle the landscape company's screwup, she could always consult him. Never short of an opinion, that was Brian. And he was smart too. That's what she'd initially admired about him. But she didn't miss him really, just missed the way her life had been. So what was she hoping to get from Brian? She mulled it over for another second, and finally she had an answer for Jazzy. "There was nothing left unsaid, really. I would just like to know if I'm doing the right thing going out to see Troy. I need his advice."

Jazzy said, "Oh, Marnie, you don't need his advice. You made a decision from the heart; that should tell you you're doing the right thing."

Her words had a calming effect on Marnie—a verbal hug. She let out a sigh of relief. A minute before she'd been too keyed up to sleep, but now her eyelids grew heavy and she felt herself sink into the mattress. "Thanks, Jazzy. I needed to hear that."

"Good night, Marnie."

"Good night."

— — —

When Laverne had fallen asleep and was snoring like a three-hundred-pound man, Rita got out of bed and fumbled her way through the dark until she found her purse next to her suitcase. In the bathroom, she turned on the light and searched for her phone so she could call Glenn. He answered after one ring, which made her smile. He'd been waiting up to hear from her.

"How's it going, sweetie?" he asked. "Are you girls having a good time?" She could picture him on the couch, his feet up on the coffee table, the remote within easy reach on the armrest, the cat curled up next to him.

Are you girls having a good time? That's what he'd always asked when she and Melinda used to call home from their trips. He'd either forgotten or didn't realize. A month ago the words would have been a stab to her heart; today she let it pass. "I am having a good time," she said, looking at her reflection in the harsh light of the bathroom and taking note of her flattened hair and the dark circles under her eyes. She looked tired, but she felt wonderful. Traveling with these three ladies was unexpectedly invigorating. "You won't believe what happened today. One of the women I'm traveling with, that young woman named Jazzy—I told you about her? Anyway, it turns out she's psychic." She paused to let him digest this information. "And the most incredible thing happened. I've been thinking about it all day, and I think, no I *know*, that I've received the sign I've been praying for."

Even in the silence she heard his hesitation. She knew Glenn would be supportive, even if he had his doubts. By nature, he wasn't as open-minded as she was. Still, he wanted her to be happy, and he shared her hope of finding out the truth of their daughter's death. There would be no making sense of it; it was a senseless act. The most she could hope for was a resolution to the crime and to gain some peace for her wounded heart. Glenn wanted the same things, but he didn't believe in signs or answers to prayers. He was practical. Things just happened. She couldn't abide that kind of thinking, and so they agreed to disagree. But she wanted to share this with him. She needed him to see things her way, even if he didn't agree. He must have heard the urgency in her voice because instead of trying to talk sense into her, he simply said, "Tell me about it."

When she was done telling the story, Glenn agreed that it was odd, maybe even significant, but he wasn't ready to say it was a sign or a miracle. "So are you going to stop at this place in Colorado, that Preston Place or whatever?"

"I'd like to," Rita said. "But the problem is that I don't know where it is." She and Jazzy had tried programming it onto the GPS and looking in the atlas. No luck. There simply wasn't a city, town, or village called Preston Place or anything resembling it in the state of Colorado. Jazzy tried looking it up on her phone, but her search came up empty.

At one point in their discussion, Laverne had perked up and asked, "What are you gals looking for?" and Rita had given Jazzy a look that said, *Let's not tell her.* Nothing against Laverne, but Rita felt strongly that she'd been given a sign just for her and she didn't want to share it. And the fact that it might turn out to be nothing made it too disheartening to talk about. So she made up a story to tell Laverne, said she was looking for a place she'd visited with her parents when she was a kid.

Thinking about this made her pause on the phone for so long that Glenn said, "Rita, are you still there?"

"Yes, I'm sorry. I'm just tired."

"Do you want me to do some digging online for this Preston Place? Maybe it's a historical site or a park or something. I can look, anyway." His suggestion made her feel better. When Glenn was on a mission, he was extremely effective. If anyone could find Preston Place, he could.

"Oh, Glenn, would you? That would be great."

When they ended the conversation, she said, "I love you," and he said the same, and then the only thing left was to say good-bye. After she closed the phone and snuck back to bed she felt better about the whole thing.

Chapter Twenty-One

The next morning, during a late breakfast in the hotel restaurant, the group compared notes about the night before. "I slept better than I have in years," Rita said, salting her eggs. The waitress walked around the table to top up the coffee cups of the three older women; Jazzy alone had opted for orange juice. "Like a rock."

"It's the driving," Laverne said. "Having to be constantly on the lookout wears a person out. One of you other gals should take a turn at the wheel today."

"I don't mind it," Rita said. "Really, I prefer to drive."

They ate for a few minutes, saying nothing, but aware of conversations at the other tables in the dining room, all of them occupied by middle-aged married couples. Marnie thought back to her conversation with Jazzy. She did find Jazzy's words reassuring but still wondered if going to Las Vegas unannounced was a good idea. Maybe she should let Troy and Kimberly know she was on her way. What if she showed up and the house was empty and they were gone? Wouldn't she feel stupid then! And disappointed. Since they started this road trip Marnie had pulled out her cell phone a half dozen times with the intent to call, but she never went through with it. Something made her stop. It would be worse if she called and Troy told her not to come. She didn't know if she could handle the rejection.

While Rita checked her phone for the weather forecast, and Laverne nattered about the drawbacks of sausage first thing in the morning, Marnie noticed a look of alarm cross Jazzy's face. Under her breath, Jazzy said, "Oh no." Marnie turned to see a woman walking determinedly into the dining room. She didn't so much as glance at the other tables but headed straight toward them. Marnie recognized her as the red-haired woman who'd been staring at them at the restaurant the previous evening. Last night she'd been flanked by two young men. This morning she was alone.

As she approached, Marnie noted the woman's expression of delight upon seeing Jazzy. Yesterday Marnie had gotten the impression the woman was in her fifties, but on closer inspection, she realized she was off by a decade or more. This woman moved like a younger person, but her wrinkled face gave away her age. She wore a knit tank top, a pleated knee-length skirt, and gladiator sandals. A small purse swung off a strap looped over her shoulder. The whole ensemble would have been a cute look on someone younger, preferably someone with toned upper arms.

"Excuse me, ladies," the woman said, resting her palms on the table. Marnie couldn't take her eyes off Jazzy, who had a trapped look in her eyes. "I hate to interrupt your meal, but I was hoping to talk to you, if you don't mind."

"Welcome," Rita said, and then gesturing, "Please join us." *Oh, Rita,* Marnie thought, *how can you be so clueless?*

"Thank you," the woman said, dragging a chair from an empty table and inserting herself between Jazzy and Rita. "I saw the four of you last night at the steak house and would have introduced myself then, but the timing didn't seem right. I'm Scarlett Turner." She said her name as if they would recognize it. When no one reacted, she opened her purse and pulled out business cards, then dealt them out on the table.

"Are you selling something?" Rita asked.

"Oh no, not at all," Scarlett said. "I'm a psychic. World-renowned. Perhaps you've heard of my book, *Messages from Beyond*? It was a *New York Times* best seller. Thirty-two weeks on the list."

"Hey!" Laverne snapped her fingers. "I think I read that. Did it have a tunnel and light on the cover?"

"No."

"Never mind then. I must of been thinking of a different one."

"I've heard of you," Jazzy said, her face serious. "I've read your book."

"Oh good," Scarlett said brightly. "I was hoping that would be the case. Your name is?"

"Jazzy."

Scarlett repeated the name. "Jazzy." She clucked approvingly. "Very good. I like it. It conveys a certain energy."

Breaking into the conversation, Laverne said, "I'm Laverne," and stuck out her hand.

Scarlett politely shook it and then, peering intently at her, said, "Laverne, I'm getting that your life is on the brink of a major change. You're going through something life-changing."

"You got that right," Laverne said. "This is my first time out of state."

As Rita and Marnie each introduced themselves, Scarlett nodded in acknowledgment, but Marnie got the impression the only one she was interested in was Jazzy.

"There's a convention here in town next weekend," Scarlett said. "It's a worldwide gathering of all the most talented psychics, intuitives, and mediums alive."

"I'd hope they're alive," Laverne said, chuckling.

"I arrived a few days ahead of the rest," Scarlett said, continuing, "because I'm taking part in a documentary about my work. Two photographers from the Discovery Channel have been filming me." She looked around the table, inviting questions, but the group was silent.

"What do you want from me?" Jazzy asked, in a calm tone. The waitress came to clear plates, but Rita waved her away.

"I got a very strong vibe from you last night," Scarlett said, smiling. "My spirit guides told me some time ago that I would meet someone who would be very important to me on this trip, someone who has a great psychic ability. I've been waiting patiently to meet that person."

"And that would be me, you think?" Jazzy asked.

"Yes, I think it's you. I think you have the talent. Or am I wrong?"

Jazzy fiddled with her napkin before looking up, her blue eyes bright. "No, you're not wrong."

Scarlett nodded. "Now that we've met, I'll cut to the chase. I have something to offer you. I'd like to see if you'd be interested in my full-time mentorship. I can help you in a way not too many others can. It's a unique journey you're on. If we spend some time together, I could teach you how to refine your abilities, and how to signal the spirits so they won't bother you when you need time to recharge."

"Oh," Jazzy said slowly, tucking a shining lock of blonde hair behind her ear. She looked like this was not what she'd been expecting. "So you're offering me some kind of apprenticeship?"

Something shifted in the room. Like a telescope coming into focus, all Marnie saw was the exchange between Jazzy and Scarlett—Jazzy becoming intrigued, Scarlett holding back a little, but clearly excited to have found the person she'd been looking for.

"I'm so confused, I can't even tell you," Laverne said to Rita. "What in the heck are they talking about?"

Rita put a finger to her lips. "I'll tell you later."

Jazzy shook her head. "I think you might have mistaken me for someone else. I do have some of the tendencies you're talking about, but not even close to what you have. And I have no control over any of it. Things just happen to me."

"As I said, I can help you with that," Scarlett said. "With my guidance you could reach your full potential. Believe me, you have a rare gift. This is what you should be doing with your life."

Laverne whispered to Rita, "What should she be doing?"

Rita leaned over and softly said, "Working as a psychic."

"Wait, wait, wait," Laverne said, sputtering. "Jazzy is a psychic? How come I didn't know this?"

"I don't tell too many people," Jazzy said.

"But you two knew?" Laverne asked, pointing. Rita and Marnie both nodded. "Well, shoot, just because I'm a tagalong on this trip doesn't mean I want to be left out of things."

Scarlett held out a business card, which Jazzy took. "You don't have to decide right this minute," the older woman said. "When you're done with your trip, give me a call and we'll talk."

"What would we talk about?"

"We'll talk about what I have in mind for you."

"Which is what?"

"You'd work as my assistant at first, traveling with me, and helping me with administrative details. In return, I'd help you develop your talents."

"I already have a job," Jazzy said. "I'm pretty good at it too."

"Believe me, you'll be better at this. And you can change people's lives. If you accept my offer, every day from now on will be an adventure."

"And would I have to move?"

"Where do you live now?"

"Wisconsin."

Scarlett laughed. "Wisconsin? Yes, you'd have to move. But trust me, it won't be a sacrifice. I promise you'll like where I live better than Wisconsin."

Jazzy held the business card between two fingers. "I'll think about it. Really I will." Then she reached out her hand. "It was nice to meet you, Scarlett Turner." Polite, but noncommittal.

Scarlett took her hand and still grasping it said, "It was nice meeting you too. I look forward to hearing from you." She stood up, pushed her chair away from the table, and then retraced her steps out of the restaurant.

The women silently watched her leave. "Well, that was certainly interesting," Rita said. "I never would have seen that coming."

"I can't say I like that slur against Wisconsin," Laverne said. "What's wrong with Wisconsin?"

Jazzy looked at the card. "She's from New York."

"That explains it," Rita said. "There's a lot of East Coast elitism. They look down on the Midwest."

Laverne snorted. "What's there to look down on? Heck, I can think of a hundred things that are right with Wisconsin."

"They think we're rubes," Rita explained. "And if we had anything going for us we'd be smart enough to live in New York."

"So are you going to take the job?" Marnie asked Jazzy.

"I don't know," Jazzy said slowly. "I have mixed feelings about this. I'd like to wait and see if my grandmother has some thoughts on the subject."

Her grandmother. That must be the dead one, Marnie thought. It must be reassuring to be able to keep a connection with loved ones even after death. If everyone could do that, there would be no atheists.

"How did that Scarlett Turner know we were on a trip?" Laverne asked.

"We're in a hotel," Rita said. "It only makes sense."

Chapter Twenty-Two

Most of the songs Jazzy selected had a bright, bouncy beat. Laverne didn't find any of it to be too obnoxious; in fact, most of the time she found herself humming along.

That morning, as they drove out of Des Moines, Jazzy turned around and faced Marnie and Laverne to say, "Hey, you guys! Do you ever pretend like you're in a movie and the music that's playing is the soundtrack?"

"No," Marnie said, and returned to reading her magazine.

"Never? Oh, that's too bad. I do it all the time," Jazzy said, not deterred at all by her lack of enthusiasm. "It's really fun to do, once you get the hang of it."

Laverne didn't want to be rude, so she said, "What are you talking about?"

"I'm talking about life with a soundtrack." Jazzy vibrated with excitement. "I'll show you what I mean." She held up a finger before turning to her iPod to look for a song. "Ooh, I have the perfect one." The music began and she turned the volume up.

"I know this one," Rita said, glancing over.

Jazzy smiled. "Everyone knows this one. It's an old song. A classic. Queen."

To Laverne it sounded familiar, but she couldn't have put a name to it. She didn't want to look stupid though, so she said, "Oh yes, Queen. I love that song."

"This is the perfect background music for four new friends on a road trip heading toward new horizons," Jazzy said, grandly waving toward the windshield. "If this were a movie, we would see Rita at the wheel and each of us looking out our window searching for our future. And then the camera would focus on the car barreling down the highway, and as the music built to a crescendo, our faces would reflect new hope." She turned and beamed at Laverne.

"A crescendo," Laverne repeated, trying it out. What a beautiful word. She'd never said it aloud before, could have gone her whole life without saying it, if not for Jazzy. She leaned forward, grasping the back of Jazzy's seat, trying to capture the happiness rays that came off the girl. Oh, to have that much energy again! It would be so wonderful.

"Can you imagine it?" Jazzy asked. She made an L with each hand, connected them, and peered through the opening.

"I can. Sure," Rita said, while Laverne nodded.

Jazzy turned around and drummed on the dashboard, her head keeping time with the music. Laverne could see it now. They were in a movie about four women, complete strangers bonding as they traveled from Wisconsin to Las Vegas. A week ago her daily routine included scooping out the cat litter and going through the mail. No way could she have imagined this turn of events.

Laverne thought of her son's reaction when she called to tell him she was going on this trip. The word *astounded* didn't begin to cover it. "Are you kidding me? Last week you wouldn't go out to eat with me because it seemed like too much, and now you're going on a road trip with people I've never met?" It was the way he phrased it that cracked her up—that she was going on a road trip with people *he'd* never met. As if she needed his approval. He'd continued, "I don't think this is such a good idea." If she'd been even the least bit on the fence about going, this comment would have put her right over. She wasn't asking his permission; she was a grown woman. More than grown, Laverne mused. She was closer to the end of her life than she'd ever been before, and if she didn't take some risks now, she never would.

What she didn't and couldn't explain was the way everything aligned perfectly in an instant: the very day she decided she was ready to end her reign of solitude, Jazzy showed up at her door and invited her on a road trip to the very place she'd always wanted to go—Las Vegas! What were the chances of that happening?

Jazzy sure had a persuasive way about her. She had leaned against the doorframe, a bag slung over her shoulder and a big smile on her face. Enthusiastically, she told Laverne about the trip, and how they were coming together to help Marnie out. "This trip is going to be life-changing for all of us," she said, her eyes shining. Jazzy also said that every woman should go on a road trip with friends at least once in her life. At that moment, Laverne felt a flush of joy. It was then that she made the split-second decision to go on the trip; she went to pack before she could change her mind. Later she realized the phrase "with friends" didn't apply to the group at all. But by then, it was too late. They were already on the road, heading west.

And now she was in Jazzy's pretend movie about four friends on a road trip, with a soundtrack and everything. Coming on this trip had been the right thing to do.

"This is the good part," Jazzy said, turning up the volume and singing a line about how they were all champions. She raised her hands like she was conducting. "Attention, everybody. I need you all to join in. Let's rock this car."

Rita laughed and started singing along. She had a good voice. Laverne didn't really know the words, but Jazzy kept gesturing wildly for her to join in, so she faked it. Luckily, Jazzy was so loud and off-key that nobody noticed Laverne's mistakes.

Finally Marnie couldn't ignore them any longer. She put down the magazine and looked disapprovingly at their shenanigans.

"Don't be shy, Marnie," Jazzy yelled out. "Join us, my friend. Come over to the dark side."

Marnie shook her head and for a moment Laverne didn't think she was going to cave, but it turned out that the allure of the song was just too strong. Right at the end she opened her mouth and belted out the last verse with the rest of them.

They were champions of the world.

— — —

Iowa had seemed to go on forever, cornfields as far as the eye could see. It felt like it would stretch on endlessly, so it was a shock when Rita announced they were close to switching states. "After Council Bluffs, we'll be heading into Nebraska."

Laverne sat up to take it all in. She was noticing a trend with rivers delineating state borders. No wonder the lines on maps were all squiggles. Upon reaching the bridge, she fidgeted in anticipation. When a semi pulled up alongside them, she felt the vibration of the big truck first and then it was a wall between her and the view. "Dang it," she said and motioned with her hand. "I wish he'd move." She finally contented herself with looking out

Marnie's window. The Missouri river wasn't as wide as the Mississippi, but it was still impressive. "This is the first time in all my life that I've ever been in Nebraska," she announced.

Marnie didn't look up from her *People* magazine. You'd think she was riding the bus down the block, the little interest she took in what was going on outside the car. Laverne had waited a long time to see America, and she didn't want to miss a minute of it. While Jazzy played with her iPhone and Marnie read, Laverne kept her eyes aimed at the window. Minutes turned into hours. Nebraska went on forever it seemed, and the view didn't vary much, but she didn't care. Even the interstate signs and the passing cars interested her. After a lifetime of seeing Wisconsin license plates, she found the variation in state plates fascinating. She noticed other things too: that the blue signs were for rest areas, the brown ones designated tourist attractions, and the green ones listed cities. When she pointed this out, everyone else in the car seemed to know it already.

So much was new to her. And here she thought she knew so much of the world, having raised three kids, being married for forty-two years, and having a long career as a payroll clerk in the accounting department for Duffy's Food Service. But really, all those years and all those experiences were only the tip of the iceberg compared to everything that was beyond the state line. Why hadn't she ever taken a road trip before? Probably because when the kids were growing up, they vacationed up north, like everyone else she knew. A rental cottage on a lake was heaven. There was something relaxing about being on the water, and the kids loved fishing and swimming. No, she didn't regret it. What she regretted was spending the last three years cooped up at home. After her husband died she'd come undone. It happened without her even realizing it. That first winter was cold and snowy, and she started skipping church and stopped meeting friends for lunch. She insisted on having family gatherings at her place. No one minded much. All the kids worked, and it was nice to have her cook and take care of all the details. After a while her driver's license expired and the car had some mechanical problems and she just let it sit in the garage unused. Eventually she stopped going out except for walks to the corner grocery store right after it opened first thing in the morning. She was always tired. People exhausted her.

Laverne looked up at the puffy white clouds off in the distance. She imagined being up above looking down at the car and seeing her own face peering out. Younger people saw her as old, ancient even. She could tell by the way they called her ma'am and offered to help her out with the groceries at the supermarket. No denying she looked older with her curly white hair and weathered face, so it was odd that she felt the same as ever. Her joints *were* a little stiff when she first woke up, but after a warm shower and a few stretches she was good to go. Looking in the mirror was the biggest shockeroo. When she was younger, she'd been forewarned about wrinkles and arthritis, but no one told her that someday she'd have a turkey neck and age spots. Or that her skin would lose all its elasticity. Everywhere. Places she didn't think *could* droop, did. Even her elbows looked saggy. Elbows! A part she never gave much thought to, and now the skin over the bend of her elbow looked like a bulldog's face. She couldn't remember exactly when all her body parts had dropped. One day she just noticed things had changed. Life sure went by quick when you weren't paying attention. It took forever to go from a child to a grown-up. The middle-aged years went by at a steady clip, and everything else after that just sort of whizzed by.

She vowed to pay more attention to things going on around her, like the fact that Rita seemed to be driving with a new sense of purpose. The first day they'd just been easing in, she explained. "Now we're going to do some serious traveling. We're only stopping for meals and *necessary* bathroom breaks."

"And the meals can be quick too," Marnie said. "Fast food would be fine. I need to be in Las Vegas like yesterday." Laverne wished there was something she could do to help Marnie feel better. The rest of them were on vacation. Marnie was on a heart-stomping, nerve-wrenching, fact-finding mission. At one point Laverne had said, ever so gently, "Worrying about it will just make things worse." Marnie had agreed but didn't seem to take it to heart.

Nebraska didn't have many restaurant options along the interstate. At lunchtime they dove into the sandwiches and grapes in Marnie's cooler. They'd made a few stops for gas and bathroom breaks, but they kept to the schedule and didn't dally. The speed limit was seventy-five miles per hour, but the traffic clipped along at eighty-five. Surprisingly, Rita kept up with the other cars and even commented, "Traveling in Wisconsin is going to seem slow after this." They were making good headway, but it was starting to get tedious. Where Iowa had farm fields, Nebraska had cattle. Jazzy started to sing "Home on the Range" but stopped when Laverne said she thought the song was about Kansas. It had been a long day of driving, but Rita was determined to get through the state before stopping.

Laverne found it interesting to look out the window, even with the sameness of it all. The cows in the distance, most of them with their heads down to graze, reminded her of the plastic livestock from a toy farm set. Soon, though, she found herself lulled into sleep. She rested her head against the seat, closed her eyes, and drifted off.

Chapter Twenty-Three

Rita found it trying to drive due west at the end of the day. As the sun lowered in the sky, the glare intensified. She adjusted the visor and wished for darker sunglasses. At times, when the road curved, she got a break from the bright light. Even so, she still found her temples throbbing with the start of a headache.

"Do you want to get off at the next exit and let me drive for a while?" Jazzy asked. "I don't mind." Jazzy was proving to be a good travel companion. She kept Rita informed as to how far they'd gone so far, and calculated how many miles they needed to log before their final destination. She also proved to be astute at looking up food stops on her cell phone or Garmina and handing over the water bottle at just the right times.

"How much more to the next hotel?" Rita asked, weighing the offer.

"About two hours," Jazzy said.

"I'm fine for now. I might take you up on your offer later, though."

Jazzy opened the flap over the visor mirror and inspected her face, then turned her attention to the backseat.

"Are they both sleeping?" Rita asked.

Laverne's snoring answered half her question, and then Marnie shifted slightly and said, eyes still closed, "I'm awake. Just resting my eyes."

They were hurtling toward Colorado, but the landscape was flat and fairly barren. Not much to see, which made driving monotonous. Rita might have nodded off herself if not for Jazzy, who occasionally made a comment or asked her if she wanted a sip of water or stick of gum. Now she asked a question, but lowered her voice so the backseat peanut gallery wouldn't hear. "Did your husband ever find Preston Place?"

For a split second, Rita was startled. She hadn't remembered telling Jazzy about her conversation with Glenn. Had she mentioned it and forgotten, or did Jazzy just *know*? This girl was scary amazing. "No," she answered, eyes still on the road. "He gave it his best, but couldn't find anything."

"Even if we miss it on the way there, there's always the way back," Jazzy said.

"Or maybe you'll get another message that will clarify?"

"I wouldn't count on it."

They continued on, the interior of the car insulated from the rest of the world. They hadn't encountered another vehicle in a while, and it was starting to feel like they were in some weird *Twilight Zone* episode. The last living people on earth going on a road trip to nowhere. Jazzy had turned the music down earlier, just when the sun started to set. Now it was barely audible, more of a background hum than anything else. It only seemed right. They were all tired. On the expressway, the traffic had abated somewhat. All day Rita had maneuvered around larger vehicles: semis, SUVS, and cars pulling campers. Now they had the right lane to themselves.

When they entered Colorado, Jazzy read the sign: "Welcome to Colorful Colorado." She looked back to see Laverne's reaction, but she was zonked out, dead to the world.

Rita said, "Not so colorful at night." She felt better now that they'd crossed the state line. Nebraska was not awash in hotel accommodations right off the interstate. Colorado offered more options, based on what Jazzy had found online. Plus, there was something satisfying about having driven through three states in one day. She had accomplished something.

They noticed there was something wrong with the car when the music stopped. Jazzy and Rita exchanged puzzled looks, but before they could speak, the dashboard lights dimmed.

"Oh no," Jazzy said, as if she knew where this was going.

"What?" Rita asked.

"Pull over," Jazzy said, her voice rising frantically. "Pull over now!"

"But we're not near an exit."

In the backseat, Marnie came to life. "What's going on?"

Laverne, barely conscious, groaned.

Before anyone could answer, the car faded. It was like, Rita thought, a huge windup toy grinding to a halt. She was able to coast to the side of the road before it died completely. The car thudded over the line that delineated the edge of the lane and came to a complete stop.

"You can't stop here," Marnie said. "Someone's going to hit us."

"I don't have a choice," Rita said sharply. It wasn't like her to snap at someone, but the circumstances forced it out of her. She'd driven all day, while the rest of them slept and read and looked at their phones, and suddenly they were criticizing what she was doing? "I lost power."

"Is it a dead battery?" Marnie said.

"I don't know. I don't think so. The battery is fairly new."

"It's the alternator," Jazzy said with conviction.

"What makes you so sure?" Rita asked, wondering if Jazzy's psychic messages included mechanical mishaps.

"This exact same thing happened once to me and a boyfriend when I was in high school," Jazzy said. "I wound up being like three hours late getting home. Man, was my dad mad. I was grounded for like a month." She shook her head at the memory.

"So now what do we do?" Marnie said.

Rita turned to Jazzy. "Do your spirits have any suggestions?"

"No, I'm not getting anything."

Marnie said, "Speaking of spirits, it would have been nice if they warned us about this ahead of time. We could have had the alternator replaced before we left."

Jazzy said, "You know, this is exactly why I hate telling people about being psychic. I swear to you that I don't have any control." The mood in the car changed. Jazzy, who was usually upbeat, looked irritated.

"Oh, never mind," Marnie said. "I just thought I'd mention it."

But Jazzy was on a tear now. "The spirits—they come, they go. It's not usually convenient. And they nag at me and sometimes I don't know what in the hell they want. Some days it feels like being spiritually stalked, if you want to know the truth."

"Whoa," Marnie said. "I'm sorry to have upset you."

"I'm a little sensitive about it, is all."

Rita reached over and gave her a motherly pat. "Don't worry about it. We're all tired."

"And I really have to pee," Marnie said, something that surprised no one.

"So what are we going to do?" Jazzy said.

Rita ticked off a mental list of strikes against their situation: it was late at night, dark, they were from out of state and not entirely sure where they were. What did someone do under these circumstances? Call the state trooper or 911? Look up towing services in the area? She wasn't sure.

In the lane next to them, only inches away, a pickup truck roared past. To make matters worse, the driver blasted his horn in one continuous scream as it went by. As if they were at fault for being stranded by the side of the road.

The noise woke Laverne, who raised her head in confusion. "What's going on?" she asked groggily. She rubbed her eyes like a child and blinked.

"The car broke down," Marnie said. "The alternator is shot, we think."

"Did you call Triple A?" Laverne asked, the first good suggestion they'd heard yet.

Rita groaned. "I used to have it, but I didn't renew my membership." There had been no need to have it; she only drove locally and always had her phone with her, so she had let it lapse. But maybe it could still be helpful. She knew from experience that AAA covered the driver, not the car. "Does anyone else have it?"

Jazzy and Marnie shook their heads. Laverne said, "I don't even drive."

Marnie said, "I thought about getting it after Brian died, but I never got around to it."

"It would come in handy right about now," Rita said, her voice weary.

A few cars whizzed past in quick succession, perilously close. "You should put the four-way flashers on," Laverne said.

"We. Have. No. Power." Rita didn't know how to make it any clearer.

"Oh," Laverne said, and sank back in her seat.

"I don't know about any of you," Marnie said, "but I have to go so bad I'm about to explode. Jazzy, do you still have those napkins from McDonalds?"

Jazzy opened the glove compartment and handed a wad over the back of the seat. Marnie grabbed her purse, opened the door, and headed into the darkness.

"What in the world is she doing?" Rita said.

"Going to pee would be my guess," Laverne said.

With no lights on the expressway and no headlights, the only illumination came from the almost full moon and Jazzy's cell phone. They watched Marnie maneuver her way down the embankment and through the tall grass until she merged with the darkness beyond and they couldn't see her anymore.

"If this was a horror movie, we'd never see her again," Jazzy said, brightly.

"Don't even talk like that," Rita said.

Jazzy turned her attention to her phone. "I'm going to start Googling emergency roadside service in Colorado. Someone will come." She sounded confident, but Rita wasn't so sure.

Chapter Twenty-Four

Marnie hadn't urinated outdoors since Girl Scout camp when she was twelve, but in retrospect she was grateful the scout leader had covered the subject. She walked far enough that she was certain she was out of view of the expressway, but she could still sort of see the car on the incline above by the glow of Jazzy's phone in the front seat. Every now and then a car drove past. Should they be flagging one down? Maybe the rest of the group would figure out a solution in her absence.

She was more upset about the car problem than she let on. It seemed personal, this delay in the trip. Like the universe was conspiring against her. Or maybe it was Kimberly. She didn't even know the woman, but over the years she'd given Kimberly a lot of power. Brian talked fondly of her and still sang her praises years after they'd been divorced. How often did you hear that from a divorced man? She always wondered if he secretly pined for Kimberly, if he'd take her back in a minute, tossing Marnie out to the curb without a second thought. Even though the idea was ridiculous, she felt like Kimberly chose to live in Las Vegas knowing full well that Marnie would never set foot on an airplane. It made Kimberly untouchable and unreachable for Marnie.

When Brian and Troy went to visit her, always flying, Marnie was left behind. Brian insisted it was just for Troy, that the boy should see his parents together. But why was it that Kimberly hardly ever came to Wisconsin? And when she did come to visit, why was it she never came to the house (which was probably just as well)? Instead, Troy and Brian met up with Kimberly at her hotel.

Marnie would have suspected that Brian was still romantically involved with Kimberly, if not for the fact that Troy was there. Nothing got past that boy. Brian always said that including Marnie would make Kimberly uncomfortable, something Marnie at first thought was flattering. Later she wondered, though. Was it that Kimberly felt replaced by Marnie, or that she just didn't want to deal with her? She speculated that Kimberly, having moved to Las Vegas, now felt superior to her and the entire state as well. She probably told her new friends that Midwesterners were dull and shapeless. That all they ate was potato salad and bratwurst. That weekends were spent going to gun shows and monster truck rallies. Kimberly was all about glitz and glam. Marnie had never seen a bad photo of Kimberly, and she'd looked at all of them, trying to find one, just one, that was even a little bit unflattering. No luck. Brian took plenty of photos on their summer trips, and in every one—it didn't matter if Kimberly was eating or talking or laughing—she looked beautiful. It was unnatural, really, for a woman to be that photogenic.

Marnie finished her business and then zipped her shorts and tossed the damp napkins off to the side into the tall grass. Biodegradable, thank God. No need to feel guilty about littering. She opened her purse and took out her antibacterial hand sanitizer and squirted some into her hand, then rubbed her palms together. Once she was done, Marnie walked slowly back to the car, feeling her way back so as to avoid the odd rock or bump in the ground, not wanting to add the tragedy of a fall on top of everything else. She had enough problems already, although it occurred to her that showing up in Las Vegas in a cast might be a dramatic way of illustrating her emotional pain.

She heard the rumble before she saw the lights; over the embankment and behind the car she saw a group of motorcycles, no, a gang of motorcycles pull up to Rita's car. Marnie froze. There were four bikers, and now they were on both sides of the vehicle, two of them having pulled around to the front. Their machines were loud—*athumpa, athumpa, athumpa.* The smell of exhaust filled the air. A bug flew in front of her face and she swatted at it, suddenly aware that her legs had a few itchy spots.

The motorcyclists shut off their machines, and one of the men came around to the driver's side. Marnie craned her neck. He was a big man with broad shoulders and a confident stride. He wore a dark-colored jacket and had a red bandanna wrapped around his head, his helmet tucked under his arm. He leaned against the car, his face aimed down at the window. She couldn't make out the words, but his voice sounded more calm than threatening. She walked up the incline, the weight of her purse pulling at her shoulder. One of the men did a double take when he spotted her walk up over the berm. It must have looked like she'd appeared out of nowhere. Before she could get back into the car, Jazzy opened her door and came out the passenger side. "Hey, Marnie," she called out, waving her arm. "Guess what? Help has arrived."

The men got off their cycles and clustered around the front of the car. One of them turned on his bike's headlights for illumination; another gestured to Rita to pop the hood. Jazzy stood next to

the group, telling the story of the car failure with exaggerated gestures. She said, "And the next thing you know, we had no power
and the car was dead by the side of the road. I mean, it was dead.
Nothing worked. I think it's the alternator."

Laverne came out now, eager to see what was going on. She
slammed the car door and came up to Marnie and grabbed her
arm. "Isn't this exciting?" she said. "I think they're Hells Angels
or something."

Marnie took a closer look at the men, their heads bent over
the engine conferring among themselves. It was true their bikes
were huge—Harley-Davidsons if she had to guess—but nothing
about them said they were part of a gang. Three of them looked
to be in their forties or fifties. Only one wore a leather jacket. The
youngest of the group, a man of about twenty-five, wore a T-shirt
under a tattered denim vest with khaki shorts. His right forearm
sported a prominent skull tattoo, but it looked more cartoony
than menacing. He looked up at Marnie and smiled as if he knew
she'd been sizing him up. "It's a good thing our dart tournament
was tonight or we wouldn't have been out this way."

"Good thing," Marnie said, not entirely convinced.

"Don't worry, ma'am," he said. "My dad knows all about cars."
He gestured to the big guy, who had his head ducked down under
the hood.

"Glad to hear it," she said, giving him the thumbs-up. Marnie
leaned down and whispered to Laverne, "I hate to disappoint you,
but I don't think they're Hells Angels."

Laverne craned her neck to see. "They look like Hells Angels
to me."

The big man shut the hood of the car and said, "I think you're
right in saying it's the alternator, although we won't know for sure
until morning." Now Rita got out of the car to talk to the men. She

waved Marnie and Laverne over to join the conversation. All for one and one for all.

"Thank you for taking a look," Rita said. "Are you familiar with the area? Is there a mechanic shop we can call for a tow?"

"You're not going to get anyone to come out here tonight, ma'am," said the younger man. "It's late and there's nothing open at this time."

"How about a hotel?" Marnie asked. "We'd pay for a cab, if we could get one."

Another man, a bald-headed guy with a goatee, said, "We live in the area, and I can tell you there's no hotel and no cabs."

"Well isn't this a fine how-do-you-do," Laverne said.

"I've got a thought," said the big guy. "My wife and I live fifteen minutes away, and we have plenty of room. If you ladies would like to be our guests, you're welcome to stay overnight and we can take care of the car in the morning." Seeing their hesitation, he added, "I'm Mike Kent, by the way, and this is my son Carson." The other two men—Bob and Charlie—gave their names too. It was good to know who these men were, but that didn't mean they could be trusted. Even serial killers had names, after all. Mike Kent said, "It's entirely up to you. I know my wife wouldn't mind having you ladies stay over at our house."

Just as Marnie was about to say they couldn't possibly accept his invitation, Jazzy said, "Thanks so much, we'd love to."

Chapter Twenty-Five

Sitting on the back of the motorcycle, her arms wrapped around a strange man's waist, Laverne thought she'd never been so terrified or so exhilarated. Her heart pounded as all of her senses peaked beyond anything she'd ever experienced. The vibration of the bike, the smell of exhaust, the ear-splitting thrum of the engine, the feel of the wind whipping against her face, the sensation of hurtling at top speed with nothing between her and the road but two wheels and a place to sit. That's how it felt, anyway. One of her sons had a motorcycle, but he'd never offered her a ride and she wouldn't have thought to ask. Too dangerous. And now she was on one, hanging onto a complete stranger. Her kids would have thought she was a complete birdbrain, if they knew. But maybe she wouldn't tell them. At least she had a helmet—each of the men had insisted the women use theirs, something about it being state law for passengers.

The men had suggested they give them a ride to Mike's house, each lady getting a ride with one of the men, and then they'd come back later with a truck for the suitcases. Rita had been reluctant;

Laverne could tell by the way she clutched her purse tightly to her side and kept coming up with different ideas of things they could do.

None of her ideas was workable, that was the problem. No taxis, no mechanic, no hotels in the area. They'd landed in the boonies and everything was closed for the night.

"Maybe we could call the highway patrol?" Rita said.

"You can do that ma'am," said one of the men, "but you'll have quite a wait, and I think they'll just tell you the same things we did." Rita looked a little frantic then, and Marnie had patted her arm and whispered something to her. The expressway looked like it stretched endlessly on, just the pavement and them.

They'd probably still be standing there debating their options if Jazzy hadn't charged over and climbed onto the back of Carson's bike, gesturing to the others to do the same. "Come on, it's going to be fine. This is all good."

Rita went up to her and said something Laverne didn't catch, but she heard Jazzy's reply. "Trust me; this is the way it's supposed to be. I'm getting that this is absolutely okay." Her tone was positive and firm. Lately it seemed like Jazzy was the default setting for the group. Her cheerfulness gave everyone a lift; backing her decisions was now a given.

Rita and Marnie must have felt the same way, because Laverne saw them consider it for a moment before exchanging shrugs of resignation. The next thing she knew, they'd locked up the car and each of them was on the back of a motorcycle roaring down the road. It occurred to her that these men might be leading them to some kind of lair, an underground pit where they robbed and killed trusting women, but this thought came to her only after she was already on the bike. Luckily, her purse, which was draped around her neck and pressed to her front, contained the handgun still in its secret compartment.

Laverne closed her eyes at first, but after a minute or two, curiosity got the best of her and she lifted her head to see where they were going. The moon and the headlights did a fairly good job illuminating the other vehicles, and she could see Marnie and Rita on motorcycles ahead of her. After a minute or two her fear turned to pleasure. She didn't feel like she was going to fall off at all, which was odd. She felt fairly secure. Who knew riding on a motorcycle could be this much fun?

Another motorcycle pulled up in the lane next to them— Jazzy and Carson. Laverne snuck a glance in their direction, and what she saw made her grin. Jazzy had her head resting against Carson's back. Her long hair rose out of the bottom of the helmet, swaying and twisting in the wind.

Laverne was almost disappointed when they exited the expressway and slowed down to turn onto a country road. Her driver, a man of about forty, turned slightly and said something she thought was, "We're almost there." Sure enough, a minute later they slowed and turned into a long driveway. At the end of the drive was a two-story farmhouse with a wide porch. Lights dotted the ground leading from the driveway to the house. Shining light fixtures on either side of the door cast a clear view of the porch with its wicker furniture and potted flowers. The whole setup reminded her of something she'd see in *Country Living* magazine.

The motorcycles came to a halt. With the engines off it was eerily quiet. "Nice house," Laverne said.

Chapter Twenty-Six

Jazzy got off the bike, removed her helmet, and smoothed her tangled hair. Carson hopped off the bike and propped it up, then faced her, his thumbs in his belt loops. "I hope the ride was smooth enough," he said, almost shyly. "I tried to avoid the bumps."

Jazzy tucked her hair behind her ears. She'd done the best she could without a comb. Good enough for now. "It was great," she said. "Really great, thanks so much." She gave Carson a long look, trying to size him up. On the motorcycle ride, resting against him, she'd tapped into something profound. He was an interesting guy, this Carson who rode a Harley, lived in the country, and who, at the age of twenty-five, enjoyed hanging out with his dad and his dad's friends. He was good-looking in a rugged way, like a cowboy in an old movie. He loved animals and small children, and read good books. Every day, he tried to do at least one nice thing for someone else, a habit he'd started in college. He felt that if everyone did it, the world would be a better place and that he was obligated to lead by example. Carson never told anyone about this particular belief of his, but Jazzy picked up on it. She got all that and more in the fifteen minutes they'd been on the bike together. As usual, she had no idea why some spirits felt compelled to share this information with her, or what she was supposed to do with it.

Around Jazzy and Carson, the rest of the group dismounted their respective motorcycles and pulled themselves together, adjusting their clothing and smoothing their hair. Rita straightened the front of her shirt, while Marnie nervously glanced around. Only Laverne appeared completely at ease. Delight bubbled out of her. "Woo hoo, that was one heckuva ride," she said, lightly punching the arm of the bald-headed man who'd driven her. "I mighta missed having that kind of adventure completely, if not for you all."

"Glad you liked it," her driver said.

"Mike?" The screen door opened, and a woman dressed in jeans and a T-shirt stepped out. She was slim, with dark hair pulled up in a bun. Not the stereotypical biker babe shown in the movies. More like a mom who did Pilates. "Oh, hello." She came down the steps, seemingly unfazed by a gaggle of women in her front yard.

"I brought us some overnight guests, honey," Mike said. "These ladies were stranded on the expressway."

"Oh, you poor things," she said, striding forward and extending her hand to Rita. "I'm Beth, Mike's wife." She shot her husband a chastising look.

"Sorry, hon." He turned to the others. "I'm always forgetting to introduce my wife."

"Twenty-seven years he's been forgetting," she said. "I'm starting to take it personally."

Mike explained about the alternator and his invitation to stay overnight at their house. Beth didn't seem the least bit disconcerted that her husband and his friends had brought home four strange women. As soon as he was done telling the story, Mike got the car keys from Rita, explaining that they would put the motorcycles in the barn, and then he and his son would take their truck to get the ladies' luggage from the stranded car.

After all the men left, the group of women followed Beth into the house. She led them past the front entryway into what Jazzy supposed was the living room, a welcoming space softly lit by Tiffany-style lamps. The tan couch and two matching chairs were plump and inviting. After they exchanged names and settled into their seats, Beth said. "So where are you all from?"

"We're from Wisconsin," Laverne said, and then, as a preemptively defensive measure, added, "It's a really great state."

Beth said, "Oh, we've been to Wisconsin many times. I have a cousin who lives in Lake Geneva. It's gorgeous there." She gestured for them to sit.

"We're from north of there," Marnie said.

Beth stood up suddenly. "Oh, please excuse my manners. I haven't even offered you something to drink."

"I don't need anything to drink," Laverne said. "But I would like to use your bathroom."

Here we go again with the bathroom, Jazzy thought. Next it would be Rita, if the pattern held true.

"Of course," Beth said, getting up to direct her down a hallway.

While they were out of earshot, Rita leaned forward and hissed at Jazzy, "What were you thinking, getting on that motorcycle and making the decision for all of us? I can't believe you. This is insane."

To Jazzy the words were static in the background. She was focused on a different kind of communication, a voice in her head demanding attention. She held up a hand, but Rita, not understanding her signal, continued. "We have to figure something out. I'm not comfortable staying here overnight."

Marnie murmured something that Jazzy didn't catch, but it was clear she was trying to smooth things over. Marnie didn't like conflict of any kind.

"Jazzy? Did you hear what I said?" Rita said, waving her arm.

"Well, why did you get on the back of the motorcycle, then?" Marnie said to Rita. "I took that as a sign you were fine with it."

Rita gestured at Jazzy. "I couldn't just let her go off with a group of strange men. I had to make a split-second decision. I figured there was safety in numbers."

Beth came out from the hallway. They hadn't heard her coming, but the look on her face said she had heard plenty. "Is there a problem?" she asked in a kind way.

"No," said Jazzy. "Everything's fine."

"Actually there is a problem," said Rita, with a forced smile. "While I appreciate your hospitality, you have to understand that I'm not completely comfortable accepting your offer."

Marnie interjected, "It's not that we don't appreciate—"

Rita continued, steamrolling right past Marnie's attempts to make nice. "I'm sure you know what I mean when I say that although you seem like lovely people, you don't know us and we don't know you. For us to sleep here would be awkward. If there's some way we could call a cab to take us to a hotel, even if the cost is great, or the wait is long, I think—"

Jazzy couldn't hold back any longer. She'd finally interpreted what the voice was trying to tell her. Now it all made sense. She leaped to her feet, startling everyone in the room. "No, Rita, no," she said firmly. "We have to stay here. I have it on very good authority that we're supposed to stay here." She emphasized the words *on good authority* hoping Rita would get it, but she clearly didn't since she just looked bewildered.

"What are you talking about?" Rita asked, irritated.

"It's the message from Melinda," Jazzy said. "This is where we're supposed to stop." She turned to Beth. "Have you ever heard of Preston Place?'

Beth gave her a bemused smile. "Well, of course."

Rita sat up straight, the blood draining from her face. "Where is it? Where is Preston Place? Is it far?"

"No, it's not far. It's right in town on the main drag. Next to the hardware store and across from the gas station," Beth said, as if that would make it clearer. "You can't miss it."

"But what is it, exactly?" Jazzy asked. "What is Preston Place?"

"It's the name of the restaurant Mike and I own."

"You own a restaurant called Preston Place?" Rita's tone was incredulous.

"Yep."

"An actual business?" Rita said.

"We think it's an actual business," Beth said, amused. "It's my pie shop, but we serve soup and sandwiches too."

"Why doesn't it come up on Google?"

Beth looked sheepish. "It's only been open for about six months. We've been meaning to get a website going, but it's one of those things we haven't gotten to yet. Most of our customers are local, so it's not a huge priority."

Marnie said, "I feel like I walked into a movie halfway through. Will someone please tell me what this all about?"

"I was wondering the same thing," Beth said. "How do you know about Preston Place?"

Rita said, "Jazzy got some messages—"

Jazzy interrupted, not wanting to explain the whole psychic thing. "I overheard some people talking about it when we stopped for gas the last time. Preston Place in Colorado."

"Must be us," Beth said. "As far as I know, we're the only Preston Place in Colorado."

"In Colorado?" Laverne said, walking in on the conversation.

"We're in Colorado," Jazzy said. "Didn't you know that?"

"Right now we're in Colorado?" Laverne pointed to the floor.

"Yes," Rita said. "We drove over the state line an hour ago."

"Shoot, I can't believe I missed the end of Nebraska. You gals shoulda woke me up."

Jazzy said, "You'll see it on the way back."

Beth said, "So are you staying here tonight or are you thinking you might not be staying? Because if you want to go to a hotel we're talking fifty miles away and it's going to take some doing to get you there."

"No, we're staying," Rita said. "That is, if the offer still stands, we'd appreciate the hospitality. And tomorrow, after we figure out what to do with the car, we'd like to see your restaurant, if that's possible."

Beth said, "We're open for lunch at eleven thirty, and we always welcome out-of-state customers. Or any customers, for that matter."

Chapter Twenty-Seven

When Mike and Carson returned with the suitcases, the women got the tour of the house and discovered that of the three bedrooms, they'd be occupying two of them. Carson chivalrously gave up his room to sleep on the couch. Rita quickly nabbed Jazzy as a roommate, which left Marnie with Laverne. It was only fair, because Rita had been stuck with Laverne the night before, but that had been in a hotel room, a space with far more personal barriers than this room with the queen-sized bed. "What side do you want?" Laverne asked, and Marnie inwardly groaned. Jazzy and Rita's room had two twin beds in a sports-themed bedroom. Upon seeing it she'd graciously let them have it, not knowing of course what the setup in Carson's room would be.

"I'll take the side by the wall," Marnie said. "As long as you don't care."

"Whatever you want. I never sleep a wink, so it really doesn't matter to me." They'd been hearing about Laverne and her trouble sleeping for most of this trip. Ironic, because she was the only one who dozed in the car. "Getting caught up," is how she put it, as if she'd gone days without sleep.

When they were washed up, teeth brushed, and in their sleepwear, the two women climbed under the covers. It had been a long time since Marnie had shared a bed with anyone. It felt odd. Laverne must have sensed her reluctance, because she took the pillow shams, punched them into cylinders, and positioned them down the center of the bed. "Now I have my side and you have yours."

"Thanks, Laverne," Marnie said. Maybe she was too hard on the woman. Laverne could be a little bit annoying, but she was a good soul. It wasn't her fault that Marnie was a nervous wreck about this trip and that Laverne's excitement about traveling out of the state rubbed her the wrong way. "Laverne," she said after they'd turned off the lights and settled under the covers. "What do you suppose is the deal with Preston Place?"

Laverne yawned. Marnie heard the bed creak as she shifted position. "I don't know."

"It has something to do with Rita and her daughter, I got that much from what they said when you were in the bathroom."

"Okay."

"I find it kind of upsetting that they're keeping things from us. I mean, we know that Jazzy's psychic, so it's not like that's a mystery or anything. I just hate being left out."

"I'm sure they'll tell us tomorrow." Laverne's voice trailed off at the end. "I wouldn't take it personally."

"I guess you're right." Marnie pulled at the edge of the sheet until the smooth cotton was against her chin. She took a deep breath, drawing in the clean smell of fresh laundry. "I just hate secrets. I guess it's just a thing with me. Brian used to keep me out of so much. It made me feel like I wasn't worthy. You know what I mean?" She waited for a response, but there was only the sound of loud breathing from Laverne's side of the bed. In another minute, the breathing turned to snoring, an odd snoring like the popping of air from between closed lips. And then a gasp, and a minute later a muted snort. A barnyard of human snoring. It was familiar to Marnie, who'd heard the male version of these sounds every night for the first few years she'd been with Brian. She wasn't a doctor, but she felt confident diagnosing this one.

Laverne had sleep apnea. No wonder she was always tired. Marnie would tell her in the morning.

— — —

In the other bedroom, Rita was too keyed up to sleep. She'd questioned Jazzy once they were alone, but wasn't entirely happy with the answers.

"So, this voice you heard—you're absolutely sure it was the same as the one you heard at the rest stop with the deer?"

"Yes, it was one and the same," Jazzy said. "And yes, she said this was where we needed to be to find Preston Place."

"And you got the impression it was Melinda?"

"Yes, absolutely."

"Did she say anything about me?" Rita said, pressing on. "Did you get any other details?"

"Rita," Jazzy said sternly, and for a second her tone reminded Rita of the way Melinda spoke when she thought her mother was prying into her business. "I told you what I know. If there was anything else, believe me, I'd tell you."

When Jazzy was in the bathroom washing up, Rita called Glenn, thinking he'd find the news of the actual existence of Preston Place astounding. Instead, he reacted calmly. "I hate to say it, hon, but it could just be a fluke." He didn't want her to get her hopes up just to get them dashed, she knew that, but would it have killed him to have mustered a little more enthusiasm?

She tried to explain how uncanny it was that Jazzy heard a voice say the words "Preston Place" and had Beth confirm them, all in the space of a few minutes. "If you had seen it happen, Glenn, you would have been in awe. It was mystical. Jazzy and I are both convinced it's Melinda. There's something going on here, something bigger than anything I've ever experienced."

He agreed then, but she sensed he was placating her. He was more concerned about the car. "I don't like the idea of you staying with strangers," he said. "Do you want me to fly out there tomorrow? I can rent a car at the airport, come get you, and deal with the mechanic myself."

She said of course not, but then on second thought, told him maybe. She'd let him know. Car problems could be so frustrating. She always felt like an idiot when mechanics explained what was wrong, and she was never sure if she should nod like she understood or confess her ignorance and ask them to explain. Either way, the repair bill was the same. Having Glenn fly out and take charge might be comforting. He'd always handled anything with moving parts in their household. But it also might feel like a failure on her part. Her role in this trip, right from the start, was that of leader. It felt good to be in charge of something outside of her normal life. She needed to do this and do it well. Seize the day, and all that. "I'll call you tomorrow when I know more about the car," she repeated.

"All right, hon," her husband said. "I love you."

"I love you too. Good night." Rita turned the phone off, feeling much better about being stranded somewhere in Colorado, in a house with complete strangers. She would sleep well tonight now that Glenn knew where she was. She knew that no matter where she was in the world, if she needed him, he would come.

Chapter Twenty-Eight

That night Jazzy was awakened by the sound of her grandmother's voice calling her name. She sat up in bed and looked around, having momentarily forgotten where she was. She rubbed her eyes, let them adjust to the dark of the room, and listened intently, but only heard Rita breathing softly in the other bed, her sleeping form lit by the moonlight coming through the slats in the blinds.

"Grandma?" She said the word aloud, more out of habit than necessity. The dead could hear her thoughts as well as her voice. She verbalized the word more for herself than her grandmother, having learned from past experience that thoughts are slippery things. To the living, spoken words had shape and meaning.

She knew her grandmother had arrived when she sensed a familiar energy enter the room a moment later. Jazzy felt a sense of happiness and completion at being reunited with the one person who truly understood her. At times like these she was glad to be psychic.

She pushed the covers away and pulled her knees to her chest, hugging herself physically. "Hello, Grandma." It came out as a whisper, but the truth was, she was holding back; if she were alone, she'd have shouted the greeting. Ever since Scarlett Turner offered her a job and said she'd serve as her mentor, Jazzy had yearned for her grandmother's advice and hoped she'd have the opportunity to ask. She never took these spiritual meetings for granted. Each one was a gift because she never knew if it would be the last.

Jazzy, my darling.

Jazzy felt a light touch on her head, a typical affectionate gesture from her grandmother when she'd been alive. "What should I do, Grandma? Should I take the job with Scarlett Turner in New York?" she asked quietly, getting straight to the point. In the other bed, Rita turned over in her sleep. Jazzy hoped she wouldn't wake up. She didn't want anything to break her concentration.

Do you want to work for Scarlett Turner?

"Maybe, but I don't know anyone in New York and..." Why was Grandma answering a question with a question? Jazzy needed her opinion. "I'm not sure. I just want to do the right thing."

For someone who's psychic, you don't use your intuition nearly enough. Grandma conveyed the words in a teasing manner, but Jazzy wasn't in the mood for being teased.

"Grandma, seriously, tell me what to do."

I can't tell you what's right for you. You have to decide that for yourself.

"Really? You won't tell me?" Jazzy said, frustrated. This was especially out of character for her grandmother, who, when alive, loved to give advice. All of Jazzy's life she'd instructed her on everything from how to make a bed (hospital corners!), to how to shake hands (look the person in the eye), to the best way to keep a house tidy (put things away as you go along). And now, for something this important, she was totally bailing on her?

Oh, darling, only you know what will make you happiest. Follow your heart.

Again with the fortune cookie advice. Jazzy sighed. "Okay, Grandma, if you say so."

Remember, when the universe aligns it does so for a reason. There are no coincidences.

What in the name of all that is glorious was *that* supposed to mean? Jazzy opened her mouth to ask, but even as she did, realized that their time together was over. The hazy form that was her grandmother was dissipating. Jazzy felt her spirit retreat in the same way you feel someone get up from the seat next to you on a bus, even if you're engrossed in a book and don't look up. "Wait, Grandma!" she whispered frantically.

Follow your instincts, Jazzy. You'll do fine.

And then she was gone and Jazzy was alone, sitting in the middle of a bed in a strange house. What did it all mean? A pressure headache began to form behind her eyes, and she ran her fingers through her hair to try to relax. Tears welled up in her eyes and a small sob escaped her throat.

From the next bed, she heard the rustling of covers followed by Rita's voice. "Jazzy? Are you okay?"

She drew in a deep breath before answering. "Yeah, I just can't sleep and I'm getting a headache. Sorry if I disturbed you." She leaned over and ran her fingers over the space above her ears in small circles. The motion alleviated the pressure, but as soon as she pulled her hands away the pain was the same as before.

— — —

Jazzy hadn't really disturbed her. Rita had been awake the whole time, and had caught snatches of her whispering. The girl was talking to her grandmother, from the sounds of it. It wasn't such an odd concept to Rita. She talked to Melinda on a regular basis.

"I have some Excedrin PM in my purse." Rita sat up and turned on the nightstand lamp. Jazzy blinked from the sudden brightness.

"Oh, you don't need to—"

"Nonsense. I have it right here." Rita grabbed her purse off the floor and rummaged through it for a minute before pulling out a white plastic container. "This will fix you right up." She handed it over and Jazzy accepted, opening the lid and shaking it until a blue pill popped out.

"One?"

"The directions say two, but one usually does it for me. How bad is your headache?"

Jazzy considered. "Not too bad. It just started."

"Take one," Rita advised. She reached back in her purse and pulled out a small plastic bottle of water. "It's lukewarm, but unopened."

"Thanks." Jazzy took it from her outstretched hand. "I'm sorry for waking you up."

"Not to worry." Rita waved a hand to indicate it was nothing. "I was a mom for twenty-three years, I'm used to it."

"You're still a mom," Jazzy said. "Nothing can take that away from you."

Rita sighed. "That's nice of you to say, and I know you're talking in a spiritual sense, but the truth is someone took it away from me. Davis Diamontopoulos killed my daughter, and all I have left is her memory and the sad thought that her life was not fully lived. He not only took Melinda's life—he destroyed mine and my husband's too." She could tell she'd upset Jazzy, but she couldn't help it. The platitudes no longer worked. Rita didn't want to hear that Melinda was an angel who would never grow old, or that at least she and Glenn had the blessing of a daughter for twenty-three years. Some people never have children; that's what one well-meaning woman told her recently when they'd met up at the post office. Well, too bad for those people, but how dare someone minimize her loss. "That's just the way it is," she said. "She's gone."

"I'm sorry."

"Me too."

Jazzy handed back the bottle of water. "I think we should both get some sleep. I have a feeling tomorrow will be a big day."

Chapter Twenty-Nine

Marnie had a particularly vivid dream about Troy that night, so in the morning, while waiting for Laverne to get out of the bathroom, she pulled the cell phone out of her bag and called Troy's cell phone number. When she got his voice mail, she hung up without leaving a message, and punched in the numbers for Kimberly's house. As the phone rang, she pictured it ringing on the other end in Las Vegas. From the photos she'd seen, Kimberly had a modern house decorated with sleek, uncomfortable-looking furniture and blindingly white walls. According to Brian, Kimberly prided herself on her New Age sensibilities and thought indoor fountains added positive energy to a house. Something about flow. Kimberly also had oddly shaped chrome sculptures randomly displayed in cutouts in the walls. To Marnie, the house looked like it had been designed by a decorator who did the lobbies for hotel chains. Not that it was a bad look. Just not very cozy.

She clutched the phone to her ear, ready to hang up if Laverne came back into the room. It rang once, twice, three times. She wanted to hang up, but didn't.

"Hallo, Berringer residence." A female voice, older, with a slight accent. The housekeeper maybe?

"Good morning," Marnie said, her voice all business. "May I speak with Troy, please?"

"He is not here at the moment. Can I take a message?"

Marnie hesitated. She wanted confirmation that Troy was fine. The dream had been so disturbing. "Troy—is he okay?" she finally asked.

"He is out shopping with his mother. Can I take a message?"

"Shopping?"

"Yes, yes, shopping." The woman said yes so it sounded like the word *ease*. The silence hung for only a second, and then she filled the gap. "Shopping for his camp. What is the message?"

"Could you please tell Troy that Marnie called?"

"Marnie?"

"Yes, Marnie." Marnie slowly spelled her name, but she still wasn't sure the woman quite got it. "Could you tell him I'm driving to Las Vegas right now? To come see him?"

"Yes, yes, I tell him," the woman said.

"Thank you *so* much." Marnie hung up, relieved to have gotten a Troy update. If he was out shopping with Kimberly, he was alive and healthy. Dying people didn't go to the store. And in the dream he had been dying. She dreamt that she'd come to visit him, but it wasn't at Kimberly's. It was somewhere else, somewhere not quite as nice, rustic even. She'd found him stretched out on some kind of gurney, groaning in pain. Heartbreaking. She'd brushed away his floppy bangs and rested a hand on his damp forehead. Troy opened his eyes, those beautiful dark eyes of his, looked up gratefully and said, "Oh, Marnie, I've been wishing for you to come. I'm dying." She'd sat down next to him and sobbed in the dream, knowing that he was, in fact, dying. The dream had been so real that waking up was discombobulating. She still could feel the heart-wrenching agony of knowing she would lose him. There were actual tears on her face. Clearly she'd been crying in her sleep.

But it was just a dream. Troy was okay.

When Laverne got back to the room, her head wrapped in a towel-turban, Marnie gathered up her cosmetic bag and headed to the bathroom. So weird to shower in someone else's house. She couldn't imagine extending the same hospitality to strangers. Did that make her cautious or repressed? Inhospitable, anyway. She'd been so closed up, so careful, and for what? It hadn't really gotten her anywhere.

When Marnie came down for breakfast, Laverne and Rita were at the table eating eggs and toast. Rita motioned her toward a set place at the table and went over to the stove.

"Good news," Rita said, returning with a plate of food and cup of coffee for Marnie as if this were her kitchen. "Mike went to meet his mechanic friend so they could tow the Crown Vic back to his shop." Marnie accepted the plate and mug, and Rita slid back into her chair to get back to her own breakfast.

"That is good news." Marnie took a sip of the coffee. Strong, but not too bitter. Just what she needed. "Where is everyone?" she said. The house was unexpectedly quiet.

"Beth and Mike and Carson went to open the restaurant. Jazzy went with them to help."

"And they just left us here?" Marnie asked, astonished that the Kent family was so trusting. She looked around at the well-kept house and wondered if she would trust strangers not to steal or break anything if the situation were reversed.

"If you hafta work, you hafta work," Laverne said. "They said we should make ourselves at home in the meantime. One of them will come pick us up before lunchtime so we can eat at the restaurant."

"Preston Place?" Marnie asked. "What's the story with that anyway?"

"Yeah," Laverne said. "Why did you and Jazzy make such a to-do about it?'

Rita added more creamer to her coffee before answering. "Do you really want to know?"

"Of course. We asked, didn't we?" Laverne said.

And Rita proceeded to tell them about the deer in the wayside, a spectacle that Marnie had missed because she'd been getting a 7UP and couldn't get the vending machine to accept her bills. While Marnie was inside, smoothing her single dollar bills over and over again, Rita had been getting some kind of sign from heaven. Or at least that's how she saw it. Marnie didn't want to burst her bubble, but she'd seen deer and goats act somewhat like that at the petting zoo. And she knew that so often people desperate for signs see things that aren't there.

"So I immediately knew it was my daughter, Melinda." The story finished, Rita got back to her plate and picked up a corner of buttered toast.

"Because she collected deer," Laverne said, proud that she'd put it all together.

"Exactly. And Jazzy heard something about how we had to stop in Colorado at Preston Place. And here we were led right to it." She took a nibble of her toast, a satisfied look on her face.

"So was the failed alternator part of this? The universe made the car break down?" As open-minded as Marnie was, it was a lot to process.

Rita raised one eyebrow. "Who can say? Stranger things have happened."

Chapter Thirty

Earlier that morning, Jazzy had woken early and dressed while Rita slept on. When she went downstairs, she found Carson already up reading and drinking from a large mug of coffee. "Good morning!" he said, closing his book and greeting her warmly. "Jazzy, is it?"

"It is," she said, pulling up a chair as confidently as if this were her house. As comfortably as if she and Carson were old friends. The night before had been so harum-scarum that she hadn't had a chance to really look at him. He was good-looking, she could see that now. Not pretty boy good-looking, but definitely above average. He had wavy dark hair and intense blue eyes, not a very common combination. His smile was wide and showed straight, white teeth. His short-sleeved button-down shirt covered his skull tattoo. Without it he looked more like a college student than a biker dude.

They were the first ones up, he said, and he offered her coffee and juice and whole wheat toast, which was what he was having. The house was quiet except for the ticking of a wall clock. Even in the cool of the kitchen, Jazzy felt summertime press in from out-side. The sun was just above the horizon and rays of light grazed the window. The June air had a lightness to it. Jazzy let him serve her, and she ate with appreciation, not having realized how hun-gry she'd become. Maybe that was the reason for the headache last night.

Carson rested his elbow on his book. It was a novel she'd read last year when it first came out. She was about to ask about it when he said, "So how is it that you know the other women? Friends or relatives?"

"Neither, really." She hadn't planned on getting into it, but he seemed so interested, and since they had all the time in the world, the entire story spilled out. A half hour later, their plates were empty and Carson knew nearly everything about the road trip.

"So you just up and decided to go on a road trip with three older women you didn't know at all?" Carson said.

"Basically."

"But weren't you worried about traveling with strangers? One of them could have been a complete psycho and then you'd be stuck."

He made a valid point, despite the irony that he had also started out being a stranger. Jazzy said, "No, I wasn't worried. I have very good instincts about people. A sixth sense, you could say."

"A sixth sense? That would come in handy." He leaned back in his chair, the front legs rising up off the floor. "My aunt has a real sixth sense. She even sees ghosts sometimes."

"I get that too, on occasion." She'd blurted it out without giv-ing it much thought. Her usual policy of keeping it to herself had been shot to hell on this trip. In short order she'd told all three of her car companions and now Carson.

"Interesting," he said.

She stopped talking and waited for the questions, the ones that inevitably came after someone found out she was psychic, but he just gave her a curious look.

Finally she had to know what he was thinking. "What's on your mind?" she asked.

"I was just thinking..." He trailed off and then looked around the kitchen to make sure they were still alone. When he did speak, what he said surprised her. "I was thinking that I didn't know someone like you existed in the world."

"Psychic, you mean?"

"Not that. I was thinking how nice it is that you go out hunting for people who need your help. Most people go out of their way to avoid having to put themselves out there. But you do the opposite."

"Well, I don't know about that..."

"Think about it this way—how many people would just meet someone and take off work and go on a road trip to help them?"

"Three of us did, actually," she said, smoothing her hair back.

"But it's different for you," he said. "Those other ladies are older. They didn't have anything better to do. For you, it was a sacrifice."

False praise. She didn't really have anything better to do either, but she didn't contradict him. Watching him watching her had an addictive quality. He gave her his full attention. His eyes crinkled at the corners when he smiled. She had a sudden flash, an image of him in ten years, then twenty, then thirty. His hair would be somewhat thinner and gray would creep in along the sides above his ears, but he would still have that gorgeous smile and it would still be aimed right at her. Right at her because they would still be together. The thought gave her a jolt.

He was really looking at her now, his eyes studying her face in an intense way. "I like your laugh."

She got another flash of images, this one involving future children and grandchildren. An involuntary shudder overcame her, the shock of seeing a future image pertaining to her own life, something that had never happened before. Her flashes had always involved other people. This was intense. "Whoa," she said.

"Are you okay?" he asked, concerned. "I didn't mean to freak you out."

"You didn't freak me out," Jazzy said. "I'm fine." She was fine, but it was still a relief to hear Beth and her husband coming down the stairs right at that moment. It was enough of a shock to meet someone who had no questions about her psychic ability, but then to get the message that this man was the one who would be by her side for the rest of her life? She needed some time to process this.

— — —

With others in the room, the spell was broken. Jazzy caught Carson looking at her out of the corner of his eye, but when she met his gaze he looked away, shy in front of his parents. In the next hour, the kitchen got busier, so she and Carson weren't able to talk anymore. After Rita and Laverne came down for breakfast, Mike arranged to meet a tow truck at Rita's car, and the family planned their day.

"Unfortunately, we have to get to the restaurant," Beth said, explaining about the setting up that needed to be done before the lunch crowd arrived. "So you'll be on your own this morning."

Jazzy, who'd just finished helping Carson do the dishes, piped up. "Can I come too? I'd love to help you work." She was feeling antsy, but there was more to it than that, of course. She felt this magnetic attraction to Carson and to his parents too, for some odd reason. She had an odd compulsion to follow them around, to see what they were all about. The idea of staying behind with the three older ladies had no appeal.

"Well, sure, hon, if you don't mind," Beth said. "We can always use another set of hands."

Later, when they arrived at the restaurant and pulled into the back lot, Jazzy lost the feeling of being on vacation that she'd had since leaving Wisconsin. Walking from the lot to the building, waiting while Big Mike fumbled with the keys before getting the door unlocked, and walking into the restaurant kitchen, every step of the way, it all felt familiar, she thought, but even as the idea floated across her brain she knew that wasn't quite right. It wasn't familiar because she'd been there before. It was familiar because she could see ahead. Past memories were getting confused with future memories.

Beth flipped on the fluorescent lights. They flickered for a moment and then burst into full power, illuminating a large room with large stainless steel counters, a sink deep enough to bathe a Labrador, a row of industrial stove tops, and several glass-fronted coolers. "Welcome to our world," she said. "My main job is baking pies. We open at eleven thirty. Carson cooks, my husband puts the orders together, and I take care of the front of the house. Our part-timer, Sherry, is waitressing today, but she won't come in until eleven."

Jazzy looked at Carson. "You cook?"

Carson nodded. "Don't be too impressed. It's a pretty limited menu. Mostly sandwiches and soup. And the soup is already made. A lot of times people just order pie and coffee." He looked down modestly for a second before adding, "I'm actually just filling in for the regular cook. He's in rehab."

"Really?" she said, one eyebrow raised.

"Poor Burt had a double knee replacement," Beth said. "We're lucky Carson could cover the restaurant while he's recovering."

"You don't have a job?" Jazzy asked.

"I just graduated. I don't start my new job until fall," he said, and before she could ask where he graduated from and what he was going to do, Beth handed her an apron and put her to work slicing cheese and filling tiny paper cups with coleslaw.

Getting the restaurant ready to open required a series of repetitive chores that Jazzy found both mind-numbing and soothing. Eighties rock music poured out of speakers cleverly hidden throughout the place, and she found herself working in time to the beat. After she was done with the coleslaw, she sliced rolls, and after that she folded napkins. Before she knew it, they were done, and Mike had gone to pick up the other ladies. "Don't open until I get back," he said to his wife.

"You can bank on that," she said.

Chapter Thirty-One

Rita couldn't help but notice Marnie was in a grumpy mood that morning. When she asked about it, Marnie said, "I just don't like this whole setup. I operate better when I know what to expect. I didn't count on the car breaking down and us staying at someone's house we don't even know. I wish we could just get in the car and leave right now."

"None of us wanted this to happen," Laverne said. "It just did." Laverne's attempt to make Marnie feel better only seemed to make things worse. Out of the four of them, Rita decided that Laverne and Marnie seemed the least compatible. Jazzy found Laverne's lack of tact adorable, and Rita was unfazed by it. Only Marnie had no patience for it.

"None of you seem to grasp the urgency of this trip," Marnie said, through gritted teeth. "I need to get to Las Vegas as soon as possible."

"If you wanted to go faster we could've flown, but you didn't want to do that," Laverne said, to which Marnie gave her the kind of look Melinda would have called "killer death ray eyes." To Rita it looked like Marnie was on her way to a meltdown.

"Now, now," Rita said. "We're all tired, and this little bump in the road was upsetting to all of us. I know it's been rough on you, Marnie." She patted Marnie's arm in a motherly way, which seemed to calm her down. Impulsively she opened her arms. "Do you need a hug?"

Marnie shrugged and started to walk away, but then seemed to think better of it and turned back. She surprised Rita by throwing her arms around her neck and resting her face in the crook of her shoulder.

"Oh, it'll be okay," Rita said. "Everything's going to be fine."

"Much ado about nothing," said Laverne. "You'll see." Rita gave her a stern look that went unnoticed. Laverne was not one for subtleties.

Marnie leaned into Rita, who patted her back and made soothing noises.

"I just really miss Troy." Marnie's voice quavered. Rita heard the words and could have sworn she felt the pounding of the younger woman's heart—or was it her own? Missing a child had connected them in some way, even if their circumstances were vastly different. "Sometimes it seems like I'll never see him again."

"Don't be silly, of course you're gonna see him again," Laverne said.

"It's just I'm not used to being away from him. I've spent nearly every day with him since he was four years old. And it's been so long already."

"Trust me, no one understands missing a child as well as I do," Rita said.

Marnie pulled apart abruptly. "I'm sorry, I wasn't thinking—"

"It's all right. Just put it in perspective. Troy is in a safe place, and you'll be there by tomorrow," Rita said. "You'll see. I'll drive through the night if we have to."

Marnie wiped her eyes. "That was so insensitive of me. Please forgive me. I'm so, so sorry."

Rita waved it away. "You're entitled," she said. "Don't worry about it."

Marnie clearly felt bad about complaining to Rita, but neither of them spoke of it again. Instead they spent the rest of the morning cleaning up the breakfast dishes and getting their things together so they'd be ready to go as soon as the car was ready.

By the time Mike arrived to pick them up, their suitcases were packed and piled by the door in preparation for their departure. Mike filled the doorframe with his imposing build and in a booming voice called out, "Hello, ladies! Are you ready for lunch?" He wore a white cook's shirt with a loose bandana around his neck. It looked out of place with his khaki shorts, white socks, and hiking boots, but presumably it was practical.

"I am," Laverne said. "I'm starving." She looped her purse over her shoulder and gestured to Marnie and Rita. "Let's get a move on, gals."

"Should we take our suitcases along?" Marnie asked eagerly. "So we can go to the garage from there?"

The expression on Mike's face changed. Rita sensed bad news coming. "Um, about that. I'm sorry to have to tell you this, but there's been a little glitch." His mouth twitched into a nervous smile.

"What kind of glitch?" Marnie asked.

"Well, here's the thing," Mike said. "There's more to it than just the alternator. Jason had to order another part too, so it's going to take longer than he thought."

Marnie looked aggravated. "But you told him we have to leave today, right?"

"I did," Mike said. "I'll take you to the garage after lunch and you can talk to him yourself. The last I heard there was a delay. That's all I know."

"Maybe there's another mechanic nearby who has the part?" Marnie's tone was frantic. "Or maybe he could get the part from a junked car. Used parts can still be good."

"Trust me, I told him you ladies need to get on the road as soon as possible, and he's working as fast as he can," Mike said gently. "He's a good guy. I've known Jason for twenty years."

The vein in Marnie's forehead stood out. "But what if he—"

"Marnie," Rita said sharply. "There's no point in arguing about it. We'll go to lunch, and then talk to the mechanic after that. We can find out what our options are at that point."

"I wasn't arguing," Marnie said, miserably. "I was just offering suggestions."

"Let's think positively and take the luggage along," Mike said. "If the car is ready, you won't have anything holding you back." Marnie looked only remotely comforted by this suggestion.

— — —

On the way to the restaurant Rita mentally set aside Marnie's misery and the problem with the car. The anticipation was building. She was going to Preston Place. Was she deluding herself thinking that Melinda had guided her here? No, she didn't think so. It felt right.

Rita never used to think in terms of spirits or the world beyond this one. She'd accepted what she'd learned in Sunday school as a kid. Everything happened for a reason, and when you died, if you were good, you went to heaven. Really, really horrible people went to hell. She never questioned any of it, not even when her own parents died. Living in the real world had seemed like plenty. She had Glenn and Melinda, friends and family, her beautiful home. She loved to garden and sing in the church choir. So much to do, she didn't have time to dwell on anything that wasn't in front of her.

And then Melinda was murdered and life as she knew it was over.

At the funeral, surrounded by friends and family, Davis's absence stood out. And when Glenn finally reached him on the phone a few days later, he was abrupt and didn't want to talk. They were puzzled and hurt, but figured Davis was grieving as well. When Davis left town without notice, they didn't know what to think. And when Melinda's friend, Tiffany, came to their house shortly thereafter, what she had to say confirmed what they'd suspected, but didn't want to believe. "I think Davis killed Melinda," she said, tears filling her eyes. She told them that Davis's alibi, his brother, had told her a different story of what happened that night. Davis hadn't spent the night at his brother's apartment, as he told the police, but actually left the bar around midnight to go home. The brother said that Davis had left enraged that Melinda kept calling his cell phone. "Melinda was going to break up with him," Tiffany said. "She told me so. She was tired of his jealousy and the fighting." Rita and Glenn listened, horrified. They reported this new information to the police of course, but Davis's brother stuck to his original story, and Davis, by then, was long gone.

After that Rita found herself on a spiritual search—looking for meaning in all the pain. She studied the Bible looking for references to death and the hereafter. She read up on near-death experiences. When she broached the subject, an amazing number of friends confessed to having mystical experiences. One friend, a widow, woke up with the feeling that her husband was snuggling up against her. She even felt his breath on her neck. It wasn't a dream, she said. Another friend's son fell off a scaffold and felt something catch him halfway down, slowing his fall. A drop that could have been fatal left him with only a broken arm. Her own cousin swore that she'd been looking through photo albums, thinking about their grandmother, when she spotted something out of the corner of her eye. "It was Grandma," she said emphatically. "Standing in my dining room watching me."

"What did she look like?" Rita had asked, fascinated.

Her cousin had shrugged. "Like Grandma, but like a hologram of her. It was only for a few seconds, and then she was gone."

When she told Glenn about it, he was skeptical, but Rita believed it. Her cousin had always been truthful.

She considered all of this on the drive to Preston Place and tapped her fingers on the window in anticipation. In the front seat, Marnie, also deep in thought, stared out the window, although Rita guessed they had far different things on their minds. They passed other houses on the country road and eventually made it onto a highway where they saw the first sign of civilization—a gas station with an attached convenience store.

"Is that the mechanic place that has our car?" Marnie asked.

"What?" Mike glanced over. "Oh no, that's just a gas station. Jason's place is west of here. When you see it, you'll know it's an auto shop. All he does is repairs and tires."

They drove the rest of the way in silence. When they pulled onto the asphalt parking lot, Rita's heart sank. There was nothing special about the building. It had been a converted something or other, most likely a small warehouse, and not much had been done to disguise that fact. The front door was covered by a small striped awning. Above the awning a large wooden sign spelled out "Preston Place" in painted letters. To one side of the door was another sign: "HOMEMADE PIES." Why would she be led here? It wasn't even the type of place Melinda would have liked.

As they pulled up in front of the restaurant, Rita saw Beth flip the window sign so that the word "OPEN" faced outward. Beth opened the door with a smile. "Welcome," she said, ushering them in.

The restaurant was empty, except for Jazzy, who wore a white apron and had a bunch of menus clutched to her chest. She rushed toward them. "Look, guys, I totally work here now!"

Normally Rita would have responded, but she was busy looking for meaning in this restaurant. Her eyes searched the room, finding nothing of significance. Overall, it looked comfortable and clean, but somewhat worn and old. The scuffed floor was dark hardwood. The light fixtures were hanging bulbs dangling beneath metal cones. A glass-fronted refrigerated case held at least a dozen varieties of pies. The floor space was filled with tables covered in checkered oilcloth and topped by glass candle-holders encased in some kind of netting. Three booths sat along one wall, the wood not matching anything else in the room. It was as if, Rita decided, they'd bought the booths at another restaurant's going-out-of-business sale. Some people might think the décor was eclectic, but to her it seemed to be a mishmash of styles.

Carson came out of a swinging door carrying a tray of pies. "Hi, ladies," he said cheerily, before opening the door to the pie case and adding the new arrivals. Jazzy turned her head and the two of them exchanged smiles like they had a private secret.

"Give me one of those menus," Laverne said, motioning to Jazzy. "I'm starving."

"No, no, no," Jazzy said, pulling them away. "You don't get to see them until you're officially seated."

"You do look like you work here," Marnie said. "You fit right in." And she did. Her hair was pulled back in a high ponytail, her T-shirt was tucked in, and the apron was wrapped expertly around her middle. She held the menus like an experienced hostess.

Jazzy said, "I don't just look like I work here. I *do* work here. Sherry called in sick." She rolled her eyes as if to say, *You know how unreliable Sherry can be.* "So I'm covering for her for lunch. Right this way. I'll show you to your table." She called out to Beth, "Okay if I put them at table eight?" When she got the okay, she expertly maneuvered them around tables and straight to a booth.

Laverne slid right in and Marnie did the same on the opposite side, but Rita couldn't stand it another minute longer. She grasped Jazzy's arm and said, "Do you know why we were led to Preston Place? Have you heard anything from my daughter?"

Jazzy shook her head and placed the menus on the table. "Nothing at all, at least not yet." She gave the room a quick glance. "But I think we'll know something before the day is done. This place just feels right, you know? Familiar. Like I've been here before."

It didn't feel that way to Rita. "But don't you think you'd know something, if this is the place? The name matches so perfectly..." She wrung her hands. "I thought you'd know right away."

"It's not always so cut-and-dried," Jazzy said. "Just sit back and go with the flow. If something is meant to happen, it will." She patted Rita's arm in what was supposed to be reassurance.

New Age advice. Not what Rita needed right now. Reluctantly she slid into the booth next to Laverne, who was hunched over the menu.

"Seems like mostly sandwiches," Laverne said, running a finger over the entrees.

"There's soup too," Marnie said.

Rita didn't even look at the menu. She'd seen Marnie and Laverne exchange a glance when she'd asked Jazzy for an update. *They think I'm loony,* she thought. *A grief-stricken mother who can't accept reality.* She couldn't blame them. This whole thing was pretty out there. Still, what mother wouldn't hope for one last message?

And Rita realized that she was suddenly very tired of being in the company of these women. It made no sense at all since they hadn't really done anything to make her feel that way. Each was likable in her own way, and in this short time she'd grown fond of them. She empathized with Marnie's desire to see Troy; she was happy that Laverne, formerly housebound, was getting to see more of the world. And Jazzy, well, she was in her element. Good for all of them. But Rita felt lost. She missed Glenn and their routine at home. Watching the news at night. Eating dinner together and discussing their respective days. It had been only two days, but she felt like she'd been away for years.

Maybe she'd feel better after a good meal. Iced tea, too, sounded good.

Jazzy not only looked the part of a waitress—as the lunch crowd poured in, she acted the part as well. She took orders and delivered food with speedy precision. Amazing, really, the way she bustled around: joking with a table of old men, topping up coffee cups, and clearing away plates with finesse. You'd think she'd worked there for years.

"She's a natural," Laverne observed, dipping a sweet potato fry into ketchup. "And the way she's been cozying up to Carson, I think she's gonna stay."

"What do you mean, stay?" Marnie said. "She can't stay."

Laverne harrumphed. "Seems to me she's an adult woman, she can do what she wants. You heard it here first. We're going to lose our navigator. Jazzy's caught the love bug."

"That's ridiculous. They just met." Marnie looked to Rita for affirmation. "She can't stay. We came here together, we all leave together. As soon as the car is ready, we're out of here, right?"

Laverne swirled another fry into a puddle of ketchup on the edge of her plate. "And did you notice no one knows anything about the car? For all we know it's long gone. They could have sold it for scrap. And then what would we do?"

"Laverne!" Marnie said. "What a terrible thing to say."

"Well, it's true. Once my cousin Marvin lent his Oldsmobile to a neighbor's brother. It was supposed to be just for a day. Guess what? He never saw it again. It was gone, gone, gone. Happens more than you'd think."

Marnie frowned. "Would you stop already?" She snapped her fingers in front of Rita. "Rita! Can you tell her that's not going to happen?"

But Rita wasn't fully present. She hadn't been listening since she saw a man get up from the bar and stop at the register to pay his bill. Her throat dried up along with her voice. She swallowed hard, raised one arm, and pointed.

"What is it?" Marnie asked, turning her head to look. Laverne's fry was halfway to her mouth, the ketchup dripping off one end, but she stopped and squinted in the direction Rita indicated.

Rita's ears were filled with the sound of her heart drumming. She lowered her shaking arm. "It's him." She barely got the words out.

"Who?" Marnie asked.

"Davis." She collected herself then, and spoke just a bit more loudly. "Melinda's boyfriend. Davis." He looked different. His hair, once shaggy, was now so short his head looked nearly shaved. She'd been used to seeing him in polo shirts and neatly pressed pants, but today he wore a T-shirt and mud-splattered jeans. But it was him. The way he walked, the languid way he pulled his wallet out of his back pocket as he exchanged small talk with Beth, who stood behind the cash register. She could almost read her lips asking the standard question. *How was everything today?* She only had a side view of Davis, but it was enough to see his face light up when he responded and handed over the money. Rita knew that smile.

Laverne said, "Are you sure?"

"Yes." Memories flooded her brain. Melinda and Davis at her dinner table. The teasing way they spoke to each other. The smiles between them. And then later, the easy camaraderie between the young couple, reminding her so much of Glenn and herself. She'd been sure they would be married, and that he'd be the father of her grandchildren someday. Her beautiful, beautiful daughter, once so in love, once so happy. Until something went terribly, terribly wrong.

She grabbed her purse and got up out of the booth walking purposefully toward Davis, not sure what she was going to do or say, propelled by some force greater than herself. Behind her, she heard Marnie say, "Rita!" as if to stop her, but there was no stopping her.

A younger woman with short dark hair came out of the bathroom, and Rita momentarily slowed to let her pass, then regretted it because she was also heading toward the front, much more slowly than Rita. The woman wore a dark tank top and form-fitting jeans. Her cropped haircut topped dangling silver earrings;

her tanned shoulders and arms showcased multiple ornate tattoos. Rita tried to look around her to see if Davis was still there, and she saw, with a stab to her heart, that not only was he still at the register, he was now turning to face her and smiling in recognition.

Just a few feet away she hesitated, and in that moment, the dark-haired woman approached Davis and rested a hand on his back. "Are we good to go?" she asked him, and then it became clear to her that he'd been smiling at this woman, not her. He didn't recognize Rita. In fact, he hadn't even noticed her.

"All set," he answered, putting his wallet in his back pocket.

Rita stepped around them, blocking the door. She cleared her throat. "Davis?" she said.

When he looked up and realized it was her, his reaction was one of shock. His mouth dropped open and his eyes widened. "No," he said, taking a step back. And then more firmly, "No." Seeming to get his bearings, he brushed past her, pulling the girl along with him. He made it to the door, with Rita in full pursuit.

"Where do you think you're going?" she said, her voice shrill and loud. "Do you think you can just walk away from me?" The conversation in the restaurant went silent as everyone in the place turned their attention toward her.

"Not here. Not now, Rita. Good-bye." He pushed open the door, making the attached bell jangle. The woman with him turned to look at Rita questioningly before following him outside.

Rita, right on their heels, left the restaurant. "Yes, now, Davis. We need to talk." She followed them to the far corner of the lot, determined not to let him get away.

The dark-haired woman looked from Davis to Rita and back again. "What's going on, Davis?"

"Get in the car, Sophie. I'll tell you later." He shoved her shoulder and she pulled back, glaring at him.

"No, I won't get in the car. Not until I hear what this is all about."

"I'll tell you what this is all about," Rita said, reaching into her purse and pulling out her wallet. With shaking hands, she found the photo of Melinda and Davis she kept underneath her driver's license. Their engagement picture. She couldn't bear to look at it, but still she kept it, knowing it might be useful someday. She handed it to Sophie. "This was my daughter, Melinda."

"It was a long time ago," Davis said.

"It doesn't seem that long ago to me," Rita said, and although she was still trembling with emotion, she had tapped into some inner strength and was now directing her attention to Sophie. "My daughter has been dead for ten years." Sophie's face softened in sympathy, and Rita continued in a rush while she still had the chance. "The murder has never been solved. She was living with Davis at the time, and he was the last person to see her alive."

The restaurant door jangled open, and Rita realized all three of her friends had followed her outside and now stood behind her in a silent show of strength.

"I need to know, Davis. Did you kill my daughter?" She and Glenn had talked about what they'd do if they ever came face-to-face with Davis. She'd played this scene over in her mind a hundred times. And every time she thought about it, she'd spoken these exact words. But it wasn't enough, because he didn't react. She needed him to acknowledge what he did, so she pressed on. "Did you strangle her and leave her in that parked car? Did you leave my baby all alone in that car in the dark in the cold?" She was shaking hard, from anger and conviction.

For one brief moment she saw the horror in his eyes. She hoped he might break down and tell the truth, but he straightened up suddenly as if remembering himself and responded indignantly. "I don't have to listen to this. I had nothing to do with Melinda's death, and you know it, Rita."

"Your brother said you weren't with him all night. And Tiffany Miller told me Melinda was going to break up with you."

Sophie stared at the photo and then up at Davis's face as if trying to connect the image with the man. "Why didn't you ever mention Melinda?"

"Soph, it was a long time ago." He clicked on his car's remote, and it beeped as it unlocked the doors.

"They were engaged," Laverne said, putting her hand on Rita's shoulder, and then to clarify, "to be married."

"You were engaged to her?" Sophie's asked, sounding injured. She handed the photo back, and it was then that Rita saw the diamond ring on the girl's left hand.

Davis bristled. "This is harassment. You track me down here and embarrass me in public. What did you do, hire a private detective?"

"No," Rita said. "I didn't hire a private detective. Melinda sent me to find you."

He opened his car door and slid into the seat. "Are you coming or not, Sophie?"

Rita grabbed at the door. "Melinda knew you would be here, and she knows the truth. Eventually everyone will know."

"You're crazy. Leave me alone." He slammed the door shut and started the engine. Sophie reluctantly went to the other side of the car and got in. Davis backed up without looking at them and furiously drove off, his wheels stirring up dust in the gravel. Sophie's small face in the window tugged at Rita's heart.

"Well, that's that," Rita said, her eyes filling with tears. In all the times she imagined confronting Davis it had ended differently than this. She wanted him to admit he was guilty, to tell her what he knew. This encounter felt incomplete.

"You did real good," Laverne said. "Real good."

Marnie turned to Jazzy. "I can't believe you came up with the name Preston Place and he turned out to be here. Incredible."

"I don't feel like I did good," Rita said. "I had hoped for so much more." A tremble in her chest took over her body, and she began to cry like a child, big tears running down her cheeks. Marnie's face softened in concern, and she leaned in for a hug, followed by Laverne and Jazzy. Rita felt cocooned by their caring and tried to choke back the tears. "So that's it, then."

"Well, it's not over yet," Jazzy said. "Let's just wait and see."

The door opened and Carson stuck his head out. "Everything okay out here?"

Rita knew they must look ridiculous. She smiled and wiped her eyes. She called out, "We're fine. I'm just having a little breakdown."

"Do you want to quit working, Jazzy?" he asked. "My mom can take over your tables."

"No," she said to him. "I'll be right in." And then to Rita, "Just wait. Things will get better."

Chapter Thirty-Two

But things didn't get better. If anything, they got worse.

When the lunch rush died down, Beth drove Rita to the mechanic's shop while the other three ladies stayed behind at the restaurant. They returned a half hour later and Marnie knew it wasn't going to be good. When Rita and Beth walked through the door, the look on their faces said it all.

"Bad news, ladies," Beth said to Marnie and Laverne, who were sitting at a table nursing soft drinks. "The car won't be fixed until tomorrow."

The words hit Marnie like an arrow to the chest. "No," she said, and then as if saying it again would make it true, "No! That can't be right. There has to be a way. We need to leave today. We've been delayed too long already."

Jazzy, who was nearby, intently filling salt shakers, raised her head to listen.

"I'm really sorry," Beth said. "But you have to understand he's a small-town mechanic. He has to send out for most parts. That's just the way it is when you live around here."

"What if we drove to a bigger city?" Marnie asked. "And brought a new alternator back ourselves? If you let us borrow your car and told us where to go, we could leave right now." She couldn't hide the desperation in her voice. Could this get any worse? It was the real-life version of the bad dream where you couldn't get home, no matter how hard you tried. "We could do that, couldn't we, Rita?"

Rita and Beth exchanged a look that said, *Oh boy, here we go.* Beth pulled up a chair, but Rita kept standing.

Rita sighed and said, "Even if we did that, the work still has to be done. The car won't be ready until tomorrow either way." She'd broken the news gently, but it still made Marnie want to fall to the floor keening. Or walk to Las Vegas. Anything rather than sit here and feel helpless.

"But, but…" Marnie accidentally bit the inside of her cheek, the result of stammering like an idiot, which is exactly how she felt. Like an idiot on the verge of a breakdown. The other women looked at her with sympathy. She knew they felt for her, which was one small consolation. "I just feel like we'll never get there."

"I have an idea," Carson said. Somehow he'd materialized next to Jazzy without Marnie having noticed. "Why don't you borrow my car?"

Marnie said, "Seriously?" at the same time that Rita said, "We couldn't possibly."

"Sure, why not?" Carson wiped a hand across his forehead. "I've got my bike. I can do without a car for a week or so."

"That's very nice of you, but I'm not driving anyone's car besides my own," Rita said firmly.

So true to form, Marnie thought. Rita, the perfect lady, would never leave her car behind and borrow a stranger's vehicle. She gave Rita a pleading look. "We could pick it up on the way back," she suggested.

But Rita wouldn't budge. "It's not happening. One day won't make that much of a difference."

But Marnie felt that every minute made a difference. She lifted her Diet Coke and took a sip, her eyes welling with tears. Somewhere Troy was out there without her, miserable and alone. She thought of what Matt Haverman said at the grocery store: *The dude's depressed, that's clear.* And he'd also said that Troy missed her. If he missed her half as much as she missed him, he was in complete misery.

"I got a thought," Laverne said, and Marnie inwardly moaned. Laverne was such an odd duck. Who knew what she was going to come up with? Nothing good, she thought.

"What's that?" Jazzy said.

"Why don't we split up?" Laverne said, glancing at each of them for a reaction. "We're not stuck like glue, are we? Two of us could stay here and wait for Rita's car and the other two could borrow Carson's car and leave right now."

Marnie's eyes widened in amazement. What a brilliant idea! And to think Laverne had come up with it.

"I don't think that's such a good idea," Rita announced. "We came together, we should stay together." She gave Marnie's arm a dismissive pat, a signal that this was the last word on the subject. "The buddy system."

The buddy system. Why was it not surprising to hear Rita quote Girl Scout wisdom? Or was it the Boy Scouts who touted the buddy system?

"I'm not sure I agree with you on this, Rita," Jazzy said, slowly. "I think Marnie needs to leave right now and not tomorrow. I think," and here she smiled at Carson, who grinned right back, "that the universe is giving Marnie a gift. If someone offers you something out of the kindness of their heart, and you need that something, you really have to take it." She spoke directly to Marnie. "Take the car. I'll stay here with Rita, and you and Laverne can leave right this minute."

"I'm ready," Laverne said, slipping down from her bar stool. "Just a quick trip to the ladies' room and we can be on our way."

"But..." Marnie said, watching Laverne as she headed toward the bathroom. She pointed to Jazzy. "I was thinking maybe you and I could go, and Laverne and Rita would stay and wait for the car to be fixed." How many hours from here until Las Vegas? Thirteen or so? She wasn't exactly sure, but it would feel even longer with Laverne right next to her.

Jazzy shook her head vigorously. "No, Laverne should be the one to go. I think this is going to work out fine."

Rita shrugged. "If everyone else wants to do it this way, I can live with it."

From there, everything happened so quickly that Marnie had no time to object. As it turned out, Carson's car was in the parking lot behind the building. "Clean and full of gas," he said. "And believe me, that doesn't happen too often." He loaded their suitcases into the back, showing the women the compartment that held the spare and the jack. Marnie listened politely and wished she'd paid attention when Brian used to talk about the car. She'd always thought of it as his department. Now that he was gone, everything was her department.

Jazzy and Rita stood nearby and listened, like sightseers on a tour. "Don't forget to get out your GPS," Jazzy said to Carson, shading her eyes and peering into the car. "They're definitely going to need one."

"I'm glad you mentioned it," Carson said. "I keep it under the seat."

Marnie had to wonder at the familiarity between the two. They just met, for crying out loud. How was it that they were so in sync? How did she even know he had a GPS? This whole trip was surreal.

After instructions on how to operate the GPS and the radio and everything else, they were finally ready to go. "Hugs!" Jazzy said, throwing her arms wide open. Oh, but she was a sunshine girl. Beams of light practically radiated from her fingertips.

Laverne pushed past Marnie in order to be the first to hug Jazzy good-bye. It was hard to believe she'd been a recluse until recently. Even Carson got into the act, giving Laverne a hug first, and then Marnie. He wished them well. Marnie was struck by the solidness of the young man's sinewy arms and how his embrace smelled like chicken noodle soup.

Marnie reluctantly hugged Rita, who was, comparatively speaking, a little stiff, and then went to Jazzy. Wrapping her arms around the girl, she was struck by how petite she was. Tiny, oh so tiny. Hard to believe such a little rib cage held Jazzy's big heart. The rest of her body was made up of crackling energy, slim limbs, and a big smile. "It's going to be fine," she whispered to Marnie. "Wait and see."

Such reassuring words. Gratitude coursed through Marnie's veins. She had a funny, random thought, the kind she didn't usually say out loud. Except now she did. "Jazzy," she whispered into her ear, "I've decided that you are my scarecrow."

Jazzy pulled apart and regarded Marnie with a puzzled expression. "What did you say?"

"You're my scarecrow." Marnie paused to come up with the best explanation. "Like in *The Wizard of Oz*? When Dorothy says good-bye to all her friends? She's nice to all of them, but she says to the scarecrow…" She leaned in conspiratorially and said, "I'm going to miss you most of all."

Chapter Thirty-Three

Marnie adjusted the visor to block the glare, and turned out of the parking lot. Carson had programmed Kimberly's address into the GPS for them, so they were all set. It felt odd to be driving someone else's car. Heck, after the last two days of being a back-seater, it felt weird to be up front like a grown-up. One nice thing about having Rita drive, Marnie never had to pay attention, but could look out the window and let her mind drift. There would be no more of that. Now she had to be on top of things. Watching for turnoffs, looking out for the semis that often changed lanes indiscriminately—all of that fell to her now. Laverne wouldn't be much help. Of the other three women, Laverne would have been her last choice as a travel companion, but having her here was better than being alone.

As if she'd read her thoughts, Laverne said, "Kind of bizarre having it be just the two of us, huh?" She pronounced the word like *bee-zarre*.

"Yes. It does feel strange." Marnie turned onto the highway. They'd be on the expressway soon. "I'm not used to this car either, so that's another thing to get used to." A cardboard pine tree dangled from the rearview mirror, clearly the source of the Pine-Sol-like scent.

"My son has a Toyota Corolla like this one. Never had a lick of trouble with it. No siree, that thing runs like a top."

"Hmmm." Marnie wondered if she'd be able to stand listening to Laverne for the rest of the day. She'd have to, that's all there was to it.

"Yep, it runs like a top." Laverne opened the glove compartment and gave the contents a poke.

"Are you looking for something in particular?"

"Nope, just fishing around. You can tell a lot about someone by looking through their stuff." Laverne rooted around some more. "No drugs or contraband. Insurance info, Kleenex, a five-dollar bill, a Triple A card. This boy is responsible."

"That's good. I'd like to think he's a good person, because I'm pretty sure he's sweet on Jazzy."

"Yeah, for sure he's sweet on her, and it goes both ways," Laverne said, shutting the glove box. "That girl took to him like they were meant for each other."

"They connected awfully fast, don't you think?" Marnie said, craning her neck to look at the GPS.

"That's how it is a lot of the time. You know how that goes."

"Yes." But Marnie didn't really know. Looking back, it almost seemed like Brian had craftily picked her, like he'd been looking for just the right gullible woman and she'd wandered into his net, all wide-eyed and innocent. Lured in by the promise of love. Which is basically how it worked out, seeing as she segued from babysitter to girlfriend to live-in lover. And after all of that she got demoted to the guest bedroom. How had she not realized that this was probably the plan all along? It was because of Troy, she realized. At some point she *had* realized how little Brian valued and loved her, but by then, it was all about that little boy and what he needed. And he needed her just the way she needed him. And that was enough.

Laverne broke into her thoughts. "Bet you can't wait to see Troy. It'll be a real good reunion."

"I hope so," Marnie said. Despite what Matt Haverman had said, some part of her still worried that her appearance on Kimberly's doorstep wouldn't be a welcome sight.

"It will be," Laverne said confidently. "That mother-to-son bond is strong."

"Except I'm not technically his mother."

Laverne snorted and waved a hand dismissively. "That's not important. Everyone says blood is thicker than water, but I'm here to tell you that that's a load of crap. I'm speaking from personal experience here. I got three kids and my oldest boy is technically my stepson. Not that I think of him that way. I raised him from little on. Just like the rest of 'em, I fed him, taught him to tie his shoes, took care of him when he was sick, helped him with homework, and so on and so forth. Didn't make a bit of difference that he wasn't born to me."

"And do you feel the same way about him as you do about the others?"

Laverne's head bobbed up and down. "Heck, sometimes he's my favorite. Depending on the day."

"That's good to know." The voice of the GPS spoke up then, directing her toward the freeway on-ramp.

"There's no stopping us now," Laverne said, exuberantly hitting the dashboard with her palm. "I can't believe I'm going to Las Vegas."

"Me either."

They were on their way.

Chapter Thirty-Four

Rita drank a cup of coffee in the back of the restaurant and thought about her encounter with Davis. She was still shaken up, still wondering what it all meant. She'd had some vague hope that talking to Davis would give her answers about Melinda's death. Instead he'd brushed her off and walked away.

She sighed heavily and Mike, who was nearby chopping onions, paused. "Did you need something?" he asked.

"No, thank you," she said, manners at the ready even when it wasn't her best day. "If anything, I should be helping you. Are you sure there's not something I can do?"

"You ladies are our guests," Beth said, unloading a tray of dirty dishes. "It's bad enough we put Jazzy to work. Although she was a lifesaver, I'll give you that much."

At two thirty the restaurant closed, not to open again until dinnertime. Beth flipped the sign around and locked the front door.

"What do you do now?" Rita asked. "Siesta?"

Beth laughed. "I wish. Generally we prep for dinner. Sometimes, if we're caught up, we leave and run errands. But that doesn't happen too often."

"And you do this day after day after day," Rita said. "I can't even imagine. Having a dinner party for eight people makes me nervous. I can't imagine cooking and serving so many on a regular basis."

"We love it," Beth said, and to her husband, "Right, hon?"

"*She* loves it," Mike said. "A real people person, this one." He jabbed a thumb in her direction. "And if she's happy that's all I care about."

"You are one smart man," Rita said. "You've discovered the secret of a happy marriage."

From the front of the restaurant she heard peals of laughter coming from Jazzy, followed by her saying, "Oh, you!" and the snap of a towel. Rita couldn't help but smile. They were like children, those two.

— — —

Jazzy found washing dishes at the restaurant to be enjoyable. She whistled while hosing off the plates and arranging them carefully in the square plastic rack. She didn't even mind being surrounded by steam and the smell of detergent. "I've never seen anyone do dishes so joyfully," Carson had said.

"I'm happy most all the time, as long as I'm doing something helpful," Jazzy said.

"Yeah, I'm getting that," he said. He looked pretty pleased himself, the way he wrapped up trays of food to store in the cooler. There was a simplicity to restaurant work that appealed to Jazzy.

People came in wanting food and drink, they got food and drink. Everything else existed to support that need. Customers had to be seated, drinks required ice, food needed to be cooked, and dishes had to be cleaned. Getting the timing right was the trick of it all.

After helping serve lunch, she welcomed the mindlessness of cleaning up. As she scraped and rinsed and stacked, she was startled by a sudden flash of vivid images. She saw a police station and a lady in uniform, clearly a police officer. She paused and closed her eyes, bidding whoever it was to send more. *What does this have to do with me?* she thought, questioningly. In a moment, she had her answer when she saw an image of herself at the station with Rita. Together they sat across the desk from the female officer who was listening intently to what Rita had to say. They were, she realized, filing a report. The police officer came into focus now. She was in her late forties or so, with brown shoulder-length hair threaded with gray. Not the kind of woman to pay much mind to her appearance. Still, she looked kind. She saw this police officer writing something down, and she heard the word *ditz,* which made her smile. Melinda was coming through forcefully today. A name came into her head as clearly as if someone had spoken it. Davis. It was rare for her to experience that kind of clarity in a psychic message. Again: Davis. And then, after that, she sensed the spirit of Melinda receding. It was over.

"Got it," she said aloud. "Will do." Certainly, she was now talking to herself. Still, you never knew for sure. Her grandmother had told her that spirits lurked even when they couldn't be felt.

— — —

Rita was finishing her coffee when Jazzy came through the swinging door ten minutes later, holding up a ring of car keys. "Look! I got permission to use the car. We're free to go."

"Where are we going?" Rita asked, bemused.

Jazzy said, "Beth and Mike said we can borrow their car for the rest of the day, because they're staying anyway. They'll call later when they need a ride home."

"Honestly?" Rita said. These people were the most trusting souls she'd ever met. They'd picked up strangers stranded on the highway, let them use their cars, and opened their home to them. Amazing.

"Yep." Jazzy went back behind the prep counter and retrieved her purse.

As they made their way to the car in the parking lot, Rita said, "I was hoping we could talk about my encounter with Davis and what you think it all meant. I was pretty rattled by it."

"We can talk, if you want," Jazzy said, unlocking the car door with a beep. "But I tend to think action speaks louder than words. And there's something we have to do."

Chapter Thirty-Five

Once they'd cleared the on-ramp and were back on the express-way, Marnie gunned it. Traffic was moving briskly enough, but she felt the need to be the front-runner. Anytime she approached a cluster of vehicles, she maneuvered deftly to the front of the pack until she had the lane to herself.

"Whoa there, Nellie," Laverne said, shielding her eyes from the sun. "I know you're in a hurry, but it's better to be late than dead." She fumbled down by her feet until she located her bag, then reached in and pulled out wraparound sunglasses. "I hate wearing these dad-blamed things, but the older I get, the more my eyes bother me. You'll see; it happens to everyone."

"So much to look forward to," Marnie observed dryly. "I can hardly wait."

"Heck, you're only in your thirties," Laverne said. "You don't need to worry about it. You're good for a while."

They traveled in silence for a few minutes, passing landscape flatter than Marnie expected, for Colorado anyway. She'd some-how imagined crossing the state line and coming smack-dab into a mountain range. Wasn't that what Colorado was all about? Skiing and mountain climbing? Clear running water and views to die for? She was still waiting for that.

"It doesn't bother you?" Laverne asked.

"Excuse me?"

"The sunlight. Doesn't it bother your eyes?"

"Only a little." Marnie shifted in her seat and adjusted her visor.

"It wears on me, I can tell you that much."

"Hmmm."

"Sometimes it gives me a headache too."

Marnie said, "If you don't mind, Laverne, I'm not feeling much for small talk."

"Oh. Sorry."

"I'd like to drive as far as possible today, and it's easier for me to concentrate if we don't talk."

"Fine by me."

Marnie glanced over and saw Laverne stiffen, noticed the way her mouth set in one grim line. She said, "It's not that I don't like to talk, it's just that I'm very focused on getting to Las Vegas."

"And talking will slow the car down?" The way she said it made Marnie's point sound ridiculous.

"Well, no." Marnie came up behind a semi and then veered wildly into the left lane. Assertive driving. This is what they should have done right from the start of the trip. They could have put so many miles behind them if Rita hadn't been so slow and cautious the first day. "I just don't multitask well."

"I don't think that's it at all," Laverne said. "I think you just don't like me."

"Don't be ridiculous. That's not true."

"Yes, it is. I can tell. You always sit next to Jazzy or Rita, if you have a choice. And you act like I annoy you, which is a bunch of hogwash, because I've been nothing but nice to you this whole time." On the word *hogwash* she slapped the dashboard for emphasis.

Marnie winced. Where did this come from? The truth was that Laverne wasn't really her favorite, but they'd just had a nice conversation about Laverne's stepson. She'd thought they were good. "I do like you," she said, in measured tones. "Honestly. If I gave you the impression I don't, I apologize. I'm having a tough time and I'm not completely myself."

"Everyone is having a tough time," Laverne said. "Everyone has something. You're not alone here. Having problems is something all people have." She turned away and made a pretense of looking out the window.

"I know," Marnie said, miserably. "You're right." Laverne said nothing. This last stretch of the trip would be very long if they continued like this. She imagined the pained silences going on for hundreds of miles. And it wasn't going to get any better when they arrived in Las Vegas. Speaking of which, how was she going to explain the old lady when she went to see Troy and Kimberly? How would she even introduce her? They weren't friends. Until three days ago, she'd never laid eyes on Laverne, even though they lived in the same house. But they were the only ones in the car, and they needed to get along. For the sake of peace, she said, "I guess talking would be fine. I'm sorry I was grouchy."

Laverne didn't answer, which just killed her. Marnie hated it when people were mad at her. The quietness between them, which had seemed peaceful a few minutes ago, was now toxic. A void of hurt feelings. When the car went over a bump, they both bounced slightly upward. Marnie felt the pressure of her seat belt on her shoulder for that instant and Laverne must have too, because she finally turned to face forward. "I sure felt that one," she said. "You really know you're alive when your head practically hits the roof of the car."

To Marnie's relief, she didn't sound mad. "That's one thing you can say for Wisconsin. We've got good roads, for the most part."

"We should," Laverne said, grumbling. "We pay enough taxes." Now they were back on familiar terrain. Laverne had an opinion about everything. Marnie listened politely as she griped about taxes and road construction. Ironic, since Laverne didn't even have a driver's license. Marnie wanted to mention that fact, but Laverne was in the flow now. She moved from tirade to tirade without a transition. "And that bed at Beth and Mike's last night? I swear it was filled with sawdust. I barely slept a wink!"

This barely sleeping a wink was one of Laverne's favorite expressions. Which reminded Marnie of something she'd meant to tell her. "Laverne," she said. "Are you familiar with a medical condition called sleep apnea?"

Chapter Thirty-Six

The police station turned out to be a nondescript brick building with a flat front and large glass doors. Jazzy pulled the car into an empty space near the entrance, next to a parked squad car. After the last two days, Rita found having someone else drive comforting. "Are you ready for this?" Jazzy asked, shifting into park.

"As ready as I'll ever be." Rita pulled her purse tight to her side but made no move to open her door. "You know, seeing Davis again was not what I thought it would be. Somehow I thought it might bring me answers. Or maybe a sense of something? I'm not even sure what that something might be."

"Closure?" Jazzy's face was thoughtful.

"No. Not closure." Rita shook her head. "I can't tell you how much I hate that word. It's such a Lifetime movie channel word. There is no closure when you lose a child." A lump formed in her throat, but she pushed past it. "No closure at all. The pain lessens with time, but the loss is always there."

"Of course."

"There's no getting her back, you know? It's not that I don't appreciate all you've done, but somehow I wish it could be so much more. And I'm jealous of you too, and I hate that I feel that way."

"Jealous of me?" Jazzy pulled an elastic off her wrist, lifted her hair up in back, and expertly wound it into a ponytail. "How come?"

"Because you get to feel Melinda's presence and communicate with her. I'd give anything to see her and talk to her for one minute. Anything."

"I know. It's hard. If it makes you feel any better, what I experience isn't the same as talking to a person."

"Still."

"And you know, the times you feel like she's with you, she is. You don't need a psychic to feel her love. My grandmother said everyone has the ability to varying degrees. It's just a matter of developing it."

"Sometimes I look at the front door expecting her to come through it. Out of nowhere, it happens. I won't even be thinking about her, and it happens. Even after all this time, I feel like she might come home."

Jazzy turned off the car and they both sat quietly and stared straight ahead at the building.

"It's not much of a police station. It almost looks deserted," Rita said. "Why are we here again?"

"Your daughter wants us to file a report." Jazzy jangled the keys. "The police lady we're going to meet is really nice, but she's kind of a ditz."

"You saw her being a ditz?"

"No, Melinda told me she was a ditz. Words don't always come through clearly, but this time there was no mistaking it."

Now that the car's air-conditioning was off, the front seat was getting warmer. "I guess we need to do this," Rita said. "But I'm not sure what we're reporting. Davis isn't wanted by the police back home. They questioned him as a person of interest, but he had an alibi for that night. The detective in charge of the case told me that it's not against the law to move out of the state. Suspicious maybe, but not criminal. I think they thought I was a hysterical mother. But both Glenn and I were sure he killed her."

"He did," Jazzy said, opening her car door. "The guilt poured off him in waves."

The heat of the day radiated off the pavement as they walked toward the building. The first set of glass doors led them to a second set just inside. When they entered the station, a blast of cool air hit them. There was no reception area or cubicle dividers. It was just one large room made up of a few desks and some random chairs. Display cases filled with plaques and framed photos lined one wall. In the back, a hallway led to parts unknown. One lone police officer, a trim man of about thirty, sat at a desk in front. His hair was just long enough to be parted neatly to one side, like a small boy just returned from the barber. When they walked in he was on the phone, but he acknowledged their presence by raising a hand. "I gotta go, Roger," he said. "A couple of ladies just walked in." He turned away and lowered his voice, but Rita still heard him. He chuckled in a wicked way, glanced back at them, and said, "One is and one isn't." She could imagine what that was all about. "Well, that's the way it goes," he continued. "You win some, you lose some." After he finished the call, he gave them his full attention. "You girls look lost," he said, with a knowing grin. "And I'm betting you want directions back to the interstate. Am I right, or am I right?"

Jazzy stepped forward and leaned against his desk. "We're not lost. In fact, we're as far from lost as we can be. We're here to talk to a police officer."

He held out his hands. "You came to the right place, miss."

"Another police officer. A lady with brown hair. Older than you. Very nice. A kind face." She glanced up at the back of the room toward the hallway. "Is she here?"

He tapped a pencil against his desktop. "Officer Dietz is out right now, and I'm not sure when she'll be back. I can help you though."

A voice popped into Jazzy's head. *No!* "We'll wait for her to return," Jazzy said.

"Look," he said impatiently, "there's nothing she can do that I can't."

"I very much doubt that," said Rita, put off by his condescending tone. "We'll wait."

"It could be an hour or more," he said, irritated. "I'm telling you, I'm more than qualified to handle any problem you might have." He waved away a fly circling his head before staring at them intently, his close-set eyes narrowing in disapproval.

"Where can we wait?" Rita asked, and when he gestured to some chairs off to the side, she went to take a seat.

Jazzy, however, held her ground. "Would you mind calling Officer Dietz and telling her we're waiting to speak to her?" She smiled sweetly, putting one hand on her hip. "I'd really appreciate it."

"Well," he said, softening. "I'm pretty busy today, but just because I'm a really nice guy, I'll help you out."

"I'd be so grateful, Officer...?"

"Mahoney." He reached over the desk and awkwardly shook her hand. "Bruce Mahoney."

"Thanks, Bruce. That would be great." Jazzy gave him a big smile and sashayed over to where Rita sat.

"Oh brother," Rita said under her breath. "You are unbelievable, missy."

"My grandmother used to say you catch more flies with honey than vinegar." She fluttered her fingertips in Officer Mahoney's direction and he smiled back.

"Mine used to say that there's a sucker born every minute."

"Maybe so, but look, he's calling right now."

And so he was. Jazzy shifted on the vinyl padded chair until one leg was tucked underneath her. Officer Mahoney lowered his voice, but in the quiet of the room they could hear him describing them as mother and daughter. He turned away when he saw them looking, but Rita caught the words, "cute blonde." She was sure his description of her wouldn't be nearly as flattering, not that she cared. She had a sudden thought and nudged Jazzy. "The woman we'll be talking to is Officer Dietz."

"Yes."

"Her last name is Dietz." Rita stretched out her legs and rested her hands on her knees.

"I know, I heard him."

"No, I mean she's not a *ditz*. That's her name: *Dietz*."

"Ahhh," Jazzy said. "You're right. I guess I misunderstood." Then she added, almost apologetically, "It's not an exact science, you understand."

On the other side of the room, Officer Mahoney finished his phone conversation and called out to them, "She's on her way. Be here in a jiffy," and Rita thought how odd it was that he used that expression: in a jiffy. It sounded like something an older person would say.

"Thank you kindly," Jazzy said.

Rita could have sworn Jazzy had picked up a Southern accent somewhere along the way. "You are really something," she said, giving the girl's arm a squeeze.

— — —

In a jiffy turned out to be about fifteen minutes. When Officer Dietz finally came into the building, Rita and Jazzy stood waiting.

Officer Dietz turned out to be the opposite of her younger, male coworker. Less prickly and more welcoming. Just as Jazzy had described, she was in her forties with shoulder-length brown hair laced with strands of gray. She needed to lose a few pounds, but on her it looked more solid than fat. Officer Dietz had a trustworthy air about her. Rita had felt a rush of dread at the thought of having to tell the story of Melinda's death all over again, but this woman had a warm smile, which made it easier. She ushered them over to her desk, which was covered in paperwork, framed family photos, and a houseplant Rita recognized as an African violet. A mahogany nameplate identified her as "Judy Dietz." Rita thought she looked like a Judy, down-to-earth and no-nonsense.

They sat across from her. After the introductions, Officer Dietz said, "What can I help you with today?" On the other side of the room, Officer Mahoney shifted in his chair. Even without looking, Rita knew his ears were poised like antennas to hear what this was all about.

Jazzy looked to Rita, who drew in a deep breath before beginning. "My daughter, Melinda, was murdered ten years ago in Wisconsin, where we live. It happened in December, right before Christmastime. She was twenty-three." Her voice cracked a little, but still she kept going. "A beautiful girl and such a good daughter. Everyone loved her. She was our only child."

"I'm sorry," Officer Dietz murmured, her forehead creased in concern. She opened a drawer in her desk, pulled out a box of Kleenex, and offered it to Rita, who gratefully took a tissue.

"Her live-in boyfriend had an alibi, but my husband and I always believed he did it. He didn't go to the funeral, and he disappeared right after that. We never knew where he went. His own family had no idea where he was," Rita said.

"I can certainly understand why you would think that." Officer Dietz took out a pen and flipped open a small spiral-bound notebook. "And what brings you to Colorado?"

"I'm…" This was a question she wasn't expecting. "We're…"

She glanced at Jazzy, who jumped in to help. "We're on a road trip," Jazzy said. "A group of us are driving to Las Vegas to help a friend meet up with her stepson."

"Oh," Officer Dietz said and jotted something down on her pad.

Rita took a deep breath. "We stopped here because we had some car trouble. And while we were eating lunch at Preston Place, I saw my daughter's fiancé."

"Rita talked to him and he acted defensive and guilty," Jazzy said. "And his car had Colorado license plates, so we figured he must live here now."

Rita had been too upset to notice the plates. Good thing Jazzy never missed a thing.

"I'm sympathetic," Officer Dietz said, "but legally there's not much I can do if he doesn't have any outstanding warrants. I can certainly check and see." She glanced down at her paper. "What's his name?"

"Davis Diamontopoulos."

Officer Dietz's pen dropped from between her fingers. "*Davis Diamontopoulos?*" Her voice was incredulous.

"Yes," Rita said. "Do you know him?" Clearly she did.

"You think Davis Diamontopoulos killed your daughter?"

"I know he did it." Rita's throat had a heavy feeling that radiated down to her chest. Something was happening here, but she didn't know what. Judging from Jazzy's expression she was equally clueless.

Officer Dietz said softly, "How did you daughter die?"

"She was found sitting in the driver's seat of her car, strangled by her own scarf. The car was parked a few blocks from her apartment. There were no witnesses, and the murder was never solved." Rita had said these words many times, but it never got any easier.

"And why are you so convinced it was him? Just because he didn't go to the funeral? People grieve differently. He may have found it too difficult. And leaving town without a forwarding address isn't a crime either." Her voice was still soft, but not as sympathetic.

"I understand that," Rita said. "But the thing is, his alibi didn't hold up. He said he and his brother were out drinking and he crashed on his brother's couch until morning. But the brother told a friend of Melinda's that they actually parted ways around midnight."

Judy Dietz tapped her pen thoughtfully against the desk. "I've found that people who've been drinking aren't always clear on their facts."

"His brother was pretty definite," Rita said. "He said Melinda kept calling Davis at the bar and Davis was furious when he left."

"Did you tell the police this?"

"The brother stuck to his original story when the police questioned him. And then, a few weeks after Melinda's death, some of her other friends came to us. They said she was going to break up with him, that he was too moody and difficult. She was tired of his jealousy." Rita looked down at her hands. "I was close to my daughter, I thought, but she never told me any of this. I would have stepped in and helped her if I had known."

Jazzy placed a hand on her arm. "It's okay. You didn't know."

Rita looked up at Officer Dietz. "I never had a clue. Davis was always wonderful when he was around us. Like part of the family. He helped Glenn grill and offered to help with the dishes. He loved to look through our old photo albums and see pictures of Melinda when she was a little girl. He'd say, 'You know I'm addicted to your daughter.'"

"He said he was *addicted* to your daughter?"

"All the time. I know it sounds creepy, but he'd say it sort of jokingly while he was playing with her hair or holding her hand—"

"I'm sorry, but—" Officer Dietz stood abruptly, her chair scraping against the linoleum. "I need a few moments." She pushed away from the desk and walked briskly away. Just before she reached the hallway in the back of the room, her muffled voice came from over her shoulder: "Please don't go. I'll be back."

Officer Mahoney, clearly concerned, got up from his desk and walked to their side of the room.

"We were just—" Rita started to explain, but he held up a hand to stop her.

"I heard the whole thing," he said, looking somehow younger and yet more self-assured than he had before. "The whole conversation. You were right. She does know Davis. If it's the same guy, we all do." He sat down opposite them, picked up one of the framed photos on the desk, and then turned it around so they could see. "Is this him?" he asked.

Rita gasped in astonishment. There was no mistaking him. It was Davis all right. In the photo he had his arm wrapped tightly around the dark-haired girl they'd seen in the restaurant parking lot. Sophie, he'd called her.

"That's him," Jazzy said. "No doubt about it."

Rita stood up, took the picture out of his hands, and studied it. The couple in the photo wore formal clothing and stood under an archway covered in flowers. Like they were guests at a wedding. Sophie looked up at Davis and beamed, while he looked straight ahead, giving the camera his million-dollar smile. She knew this tableau oh so well. She had similar photos of Davis and Melinda. "The girl is Officer Dietz's daughter?" she said, venturing a guess.

"Yes, they're engaged. They live together."

"Oh my." Rita ran a finger over the glass. Another lovely young woman, someone else's daughter. He probably made Sophie feel loved and special too.

"Everyone really likes Davis," Officer Mahoney said. "I've met him several times myself and he's never said or done anything that makes me suspicious. I'm a pretty good judge of character."

"Yes, he's a fooler," Rita said.

"He lives with Sophie?" Jazzy said.

"Yes, and he works for Judy's husband."

Rita's eyes didn't leave the photo. She couldn't get over that all the time she'd been looking for him, he'd been here. She'd pictured him living on the lam, sleeping in flophouses and begging for handouts. It only seemed right that he'd suffer. But her vision of him was all wrong. He hadn't suffered at all. Instead he was up to his old tricks—charming people with his looks and personality and getting what he wanted. He hadn't changed at all; he just changed his location.

When Judy Dietz returned, she went straight to Rita and took the picture out of her hands. It was hard to read her face. Rita wanted to say something significant, something wise that would convince her that Davis wasn't as charming as he seemed and that Sophie was now in danger. She was wary of sounding like a hysterical mother. It would be her word against Davis's. Everything she thought to say seemed inadequate, so she said, "Your daughter is gorgeous."

"My daughter is everything to me," Judy Dietz said, gently setting the photo back on her desk. "Everything in the world." She turned to where Officer Mahoney sat in her chair and made a shooing gesture. "Bruce, we need some privacy. Could you leave the building, please?"

Startled, he said, "Why sure, I guess. I mean, if you think that's best."

"Yes, I think it would be best."

He went back to his desk to get his keys and hesitated a moment before heading out. He rested his hand on the door and looked back one more time, questioningly.

"Go," she said, pointing, and kept her eye aimed in that direction until both sets of doors had clicked shut behind him. "Now," she said, giving Rita her full attention, "I need you to tell me everything."

Chapter Thirty-Seven

Sleep apnea? Laverne had never even considered such a thing, but Marnie seemed pretty certain she had it. It made sense, anyway. Something had to explain all these years of feeling so dragged down. She was barely up for an hour in the morning when she felt like taking a nap. Her kids thought she was depressed, her grandkids assumed it was because she was old, her friends thought she'd turned antisocial, but really she was just tired. Bone-weary exhausted. Putting one foot in front of the other was the most she could manage some days. There was no joy in anything.

Marnie explained how Brian had gotten diagnosed at the sleep clinic right in town. He'd gotten a referral from his doctor and then spent the night with electrodes fastened to his head and chest. "They have a camera on you all night, and they monitor your oxygen level," she said. "It's not a difficult test to have done. If you decide to get checked out I can drive you. I mean, if you want me to," Marnie said, which Laverne thought was a downright nice offer.

If Laverne did have sleep apnea, the cure would be a sleep mask with a hose thing attached to a machine. She'd have to strap it to her face and have it on all night, every night. "It's not as bad as it sounds," Marnie said. "Brian got used to it right away, and he felt better than he had in years."

"Did he have more energy then?" Laverne asked. "Was he happier?"

"Definitely more energy," Marnie said, one finger tapping the steering wheel. "But I wouldn't say he was happier. Brian was not a happy man. At least not when I was around. He was dour and irritable." Dour and irritable, that's what she said. What a combination. And then, without Laverne even asking any more, Marnie had a mini-breakdown as they were driving west on I-70. She started to cry so hard, Laverne worried they'd get in an accident. She fished the Kleenex out of the glove compartment and handed it to over. Without saying a word, Marnie took it, dabbed her eyes, and blew her nose. "Brian never loved me." She choked out the words in machine-gun-like spurts. "No matter what I did. I tried everything. I showed interest in his work, I took care of the house, I made all of his travel arrangements. I did this for years, but none of it meant anything to him."

"Some men are just like that," Laverne offered. "They're jerks."

"No, but you don't understand. He wasn't a jerk. Everyone else thought he was great. He had golf buddies and work friends and college friends. Every time I turned around he was meeting someone for drinks or going out for happy hour. I'd hear him in the den on the phone, and he'd be laughing and telling jokes, and then he'd come out and it was like he was a different person with me." She stepped on the gas and hooked a quick lane change around a minivan full of kids. They were so close when they passed that Laverne saw that the little boy in the middle seat wore a New York Mets baseball cap and regarded her with solemn eyes. "He said I was clingy." Marnie blotted her nose with the wadded-up tissue.

"Ha!" Laverne said. "That's jerk talk if I ever heard it."

"He said I had unrealistic expectations."

"Jerk, jerk, jerk." Laverne drew in a sharp breath as the car veered slightly into the other lane. "Hey there. Watch it there, Marnie. I'd like to live another day."

Marnie wiped at her eyes. "I'm sorry for blubbering like this. I thought I'd gotten past all this. I mean, it was my choice to stay with Brian…"

Laverne shrugged. "You're entitled to feel any which way you want."

In this light, Marnie's profile with her blotchy nose and downturned mouth were even more pronounced. It wasn't a good look for her. "Maybe I should have tried harder."

Laverne said, "You know what, Marnie? We could go round and round on this all day, but why keep torturing yourself? It is what it is. There's no going back, so you might as well remember the good stuff and move on. It's time to let it go."

"I just feel like an idiot. I wasted ten years."

"I wouldn't call it a waste. You helped that little boy grow up, didn't you?"

There was a long pause and then the beginning of a smile crossed Marnie's lips. "Well, that's true. Troy was the one good thing that came out of all of this."

"And now think how happy he's gonna be when you show up on his doorstep. It'll be one heckuva reunion!"

"I hope you're right, Laverne."

They drove another hundred or so miles in complete silence. Laverne was starting to doze when Marnie said, "You know, I thought I could drive straight through, but I think we're going to have to stop for the night."

"We're going to have to stop sooner than that," Laverne said. "I drank a whole Mountain Dew and I'm ready for a bathroom break."

Chapter Thirty-Eight

Rita told Officer Dietz the whole story, from the time Melinda and Davis met, to the horrible day she'd gotten the phone call saying her daughter's body had been found. And then she told about meeting Davis and Sophie at the restaurant and Sophie's reaction at hearing Davis had been engaged before.

Judy Dietz said not a word but listened quietly, twisting her hands and looking sicker as the minutes ticked by.

Rita said, "You might find it hard to believe that Davis was responsible. I know he's very charming—"

"No, I believe it. When you used the word *addicted* it struck me. He tells us he's addicted to Sophie," Judy Dietz said. "I've always thought it was an odd thing to say. I've had a feeling about him for a while. Nothing I could put my finger on, just a niggling sort of feeling…"

"Mother's intuition," Jazzy said, startling both women. It was like they'd forgotten she was there.

"My husband adores him, thinks he's tamed our daughter," Judy said. "She used to be a wild thing, partying all the time, but she's stopped since Davis came into her life. It's always bothered me that Davis is so domineering, but she goes along with it." Rita nodded. It had been the same with Melinda. Judy continued, "I have to think about how to handle this." She raked her fingertips through her hair.

"You've got a gun," Rita said. "I would just shoot him if I were you." As soon as the words were out, she wished she could take them back. Even though she did feel that way, it was an inappropriate thing to say. "I'm sorry. I'm not normally a violent person."

"I understand," Judy said. "I would feel the same way. Still, I need a solution that won't put me in jail." She sighed and looked up to the ceiling. Her eyes went back and forth like she was in a wide-awake REM state. Finally, after a few minutes she said, "I think I've thought of something. Do you have a picture of your daughter with Davis?"

Chapter Thirty-Nine

They ate dinner at a truck stop in Utah. It was a bustling place whose customers consisted mainly of large men with booming voices. From their table, way in the back corner near the kitchen, the smell of battered chicken and pan-fried potatoes filled the air. When the food arrived, Laverne was delighted to see the piled-high plates and the beverages served in tall glasses filled with crushed ice. "You can always tell where the good food is by seeing what place is busy," Laverne said, digging into her meatloaf. Marnie nodded in agreement even though she wasn't as in love with the BLT she'd ordered. The bacon was nice and crisp, but the tomato was an anemic pink, and the iceberg lettuce was fringed with brown. Still, most everything else was fine. The waitress, a peroxide blonde of about sixty-five named Shirley, was friendly, and everything on the laminated menu was cheap.

When they finished, Shirley brought a handwritten bill on a scrap of paper the size of a postcard. "You can pay up front at the register," she said, slapping it on the table. "You drive safe now." Marnie imaged that she had said these words a thousand times or more. They had to be etched into her mouth, her vocal cords, the very core of her.

When Laverne went to get her wallet, Marnie stopped her and opened her bag. "It's my turn to pay. Remember?" They'd taken to trading off now that it was just the two of them. It seemed easier.

Laverne nodded. She put down her napkin and said, "I'll make a pit stop then, while you pay." She trundled off with her purse clutched to her side and greeted the truckers sitting at the counter as she went past. Marnie opened her wallet until she found a twenty and then got in line behind a man at the pay station. It was there she noticed the boy sitting on a folding chair behind the cash register, his ankles tied to the chair legs with twine. He wore ripped blue jeans and a sleeveless T-shirt and had a red bandana wound around his floppy black hair like he was from a 1990s boy band. He looked to be about Troy's age, maybe a little older. From the look on his face he was in complete misery; he kept shooting glances at the parking lot and nervously chewing his lip. Marnie found herself strangely drawn to this kid. "Are you okay?" she asked him, and when he looked up, she saw intense gray eyes fringed with dark lashes.

"Don't worry about the likes of him," the heavyset man behind the register said. Without Marnie realizing it, the line had shortened and it was now her turn. "The kid's getting what he deserves."

"I told you that my dad was going to come back for me! He has my wallet," the teenager said, and it was part wail, part indignation. Marnie knew that tone well. She'd heard it from Troy many times.

She moved closer to the counter and handed the man her bill and money. "What did he do?" she asked, looking over sympathetically. The kid looked like he needed a good hug. She was tempted to scoop him up herself.

"He ordered food and now he can't pay. And if that's not bad enough, he tried to pickpocket one of my waitresses. He had his damn hand right in her pocket. If another customer hadn't noticed, he'd have walked off with her money." The man shuffled through some bills, double-checking before handing them over the counter. "The police are on their way." He raised his eyebrows menacingly at the kid. "Or at least they will be as soon as I call. I'm tempted to just inflict some punishment of my own."

"That's kind of harsh, don't you think?" Marnie said. "He's just a kid." The boy raised his head and gave her a grateful look. With his hair poking out of his bandana he looked heartbreakingly young. She could imagine him standing in front of the mirror in the morning, trying to get the bandana angled just right and then unwrapping it and doing it over again. Image was everything at that age.

He shrugged. "I run a business, not a soup kitchen. And the girls who work here deserve every penny they make. They don't need some punk ripping them off."

Marnie took her change, and when the man's beefy hand brushed hers she got what felt like a cosmic jolt. Suddenly she saw the whole thing as if she were looking down on the scene. The repentant boy on the bench, the unyielding diner owner, and even herself, Marnie, formerly a mouse, but now someone who took charge. They were all pieces in a real-life board game and it was her turn to make a move. Behind her another customer, a large trucker, said, "Are you finished?" and she turned to see beefy shoulders, tattooed arms, and a handlebar mustache.

"Just a minute," she said to him, and then to the owner: "I would like to pay the boy's bill."

"Lady, I know you're being a Good Samaritan, and that's real nice and all, but in the long run, you won't be helping him. I know his type. He needs to learn."

"I insist," she said. "Just tell me how much and I'll pay it right now."

The boy leapt to his feet and moved forward, dragging the chair with him. He was taller than she'd thought, maybe three or four inches taller than herself. Still, something about him made him look small. Maybe it was the untucked T-shirt two sizes too large for him. "I swear I'll pay you back, miss. I mean it, I'll do anything—"

"Hey! Get back there and sit down," the owner said, swatting him with an outstretched arm. "*I will kill you.*" The way he said it made the hackles on Marnie's neck rise and stopped conversation in the diner. Customers paused mid-chew to see what the ruckus was about.

The handlebar mustache guy standing behind Marnie said, "Eh, Scooter, if the lady is willing to pay, let the kid go. Why be such a hard-ass?"

Scooter? Was there ever such an unlikely pairing of man and name? Marnie watched this drama play out while still aware of Laverne returning from the ladies' room. Marnie held up a twenty-dollar bill and raised it in the air. "Let's just settle up, sir." She added the *sir* as a courtesy. "If you let him go, I'm sure this young man will never bother you again."

"That's for sure," the kid said, frantically. "I'll never come in here again."

"Damn right you won't." The owner plucked the twenty out of Marnie's hand. "This should cover it." He stuck the bill into his drawer and slammed it shut. Furious, he took scissors and cut the twine holding the kid hostage. "Now get the hell out," he yelled at the boy, who didn't wait but hastily dashed out the door. "Good riddance," the owner muttered loudly. An unnecessary show of authority, Marnie thought. With the disturbance now over, the other customers resumed talking.

Laverne came up alongside Marnie with a puzzled look on her face. "What happened?"

"I'll tell you outside," Marnie said.

— — —

"Well, that was real nice of you to pay for him," Laverne said in the car, after Marnie had explained. They were still in the parking lot, the engine idling. Marnie felt it necessary to have the diner in sight, almost as if it would help illustrate the story. "Not too many people would have done that for a kid they didn't know."

"Oh, you would have done it too, if you saw him," Marnie told her with certainty. "The look on his face would have broken your heart. Poor kid. All I could think was that I'd want someone to help Troy if he was in the same situation."

"You were looking at him with your mom eyes," Laverne said.

"I couldn't help it," Marnie said, adjusting the angle of Carson's GPS, which was suction-cupped to the windshield again. "I guess we should hit the road. I want to get another two or three hours in before we stop for the night."

They circled the building and turned onto the frontage road that would take them to the freeway. Marnie couldn't believe her eyes when she saw a familiar figure in the distance. Like a mirage, the kid in the red bandana stood on the shoulder of the road, his thumb held up hitchhiker-style. "That's him," Marnie said, excitedly, "the boy from the diner."

"Looks more like a man than a boy to me," Laverne said, but Marnie disregarded her comment and slowed the car until they were alongside him.

"Hello," she called out. "Remember me? I'm the lady who paid your bill."

"Yes, ma'am," he said. "I know." He shuffled his feet in a way that struck her as being modest. "Very nice of you. Thank you."

"Do you need a ride?"

Laverne reached over and gripped the loose skin on Marnie's elbow. "I'm not sure this is a good idea."

What a weird sensation, having someone pull on your elbow. Marnie shook her off. "We're heading west toward Las Vegas."

The kid didn't wait but went to the back door of the car even before Marnie could undo the lock. There was an awkward exchange when he pulled on the latch at the same time as she was releasing it, so it didn't work, but the second time their timing was better, and he got the door open and scrambled into the backseat like he belonged there. "This is great, thanks," he said. "I'm going the same way you are."

"Where exactly are you going?" Laverne asked. "And why don't you have a ride?" She sounded downright mistrustful.

To counteract Laverne's rudeness, Marnie said, "My name's Marnie and this is my friend Laverne. We're from Wisconsin."

"I'm Max," he said, fastening his seat belt in one smooth motion. "From Colorado. I'm heading to California. I'll go as far as you'll take me."

"I have a stepson about your age," Marnie said. "His name is Troy. I haven't seen him in quite a while."

"You have a last name there, Max?" Laverne's forehead furrowed in disapproval.

Marnie could have clunked her on the head for being so abrupt. "There's no need to interrogate him," she said primly. "He's had a rough day." She steered the car back onto the roadway.

"Yeah, it's been a rough day. My dad abandoned me at the truck stop. He has a powerful bad temper and he randomly got pissed off and just stormed out."

"What was he so mad about?" Laverne asked.

"I said I wanted to live with my mom. That I was sick of taking his abuse."

"Well, good for you!" Marnie said, hoping her enthusiasm would set a tone and encourage Laverne to be a little more welcoming. "And is that why you're going to California? To see your mom?"

"Yeah, that's why," Max said. "She has custody, but my dad took me for a visit and wouldn't let me go back. He wouldn't let me call her or anything. I miss her so much."

"Oh, you poor thing," Marnie said. She wished she could turn around and give him a smile, but she had to settle for a glance in the mirror. He didn't meet her gaze though; he was too busy looking out the window. "Do you want to borrow my cell phone to call your mom?"

"Nah. She's at work right now, so I couldn't talk to her anyway."

"You could leave a message," Marnie said. "I'm sure she's sick with worry."

"I called her from the restaurant and said I was on my way. She knows I'm fine."

"Oh," Marnie said. Something about that didn't ring true. Hadn't he said his father wouldn't let him call his mother? She was sure of it. So how had he called from the restaurant? The kid didn't seem to have a phone on him. Or anything at all for that matter—just the clothes on his back. And there's no way the owner would have let him call. That maniac was an inch away from killing the kid. And over what? Twenty dollars? Although now that she thought of it, that must have been a heckuva lunch. The total combined for her and Laverne's lunch came to less than fifteen. Clearly she'd been ripped off.

"What are you going to do once we drop you off?" Laverne asked. "With no money and no phone?" She'd turned around so far her body had twisted out from underneath the shoulder portion of the seat belt.

He shrugged his shoulders defensively. "I'll figure out something. People are nice. I'm sure someone will help me out. You did."

"Is that a style with the kids now, a scarf wrapped around the head?" Laverne asked, casting a critical eye.

"It's a bandana," Marnie said. "I like it."

Max said nothing. He looked preoccupied, as if watching the passing cars in the left lane fascinated him. With one finger, he pushed the bandana upward, giving it a jaunty look.

"It looks good," Marnie said, but Max's eyes never veered from the window.

"How old are you anyway?" Laverne asked him.

"Old enough," he said, in a bored, disaffected way. "I've been on my own for a long time." Marnie thought he probably meant he was taking care of himself for a long time. She remembered being that age and thinking that adults were extraneous. At fourteen or fifteen she'd been convinced that if her parents suddenly disappeared off the face of the planet, she'd manage just fine on her own. Maybe even better than when they were there.

Laverne turned up the radio, and country music blared out of the car's speakers. She leaned toward Marnie and said something indecipherable out of the side of her mouth.

"What?"

She repeated it, but Marnie still couldn't make it out. Finally, Laverne fumbled through her purse until she found a pen. She wrote on the back of an old receipt and held it against the dashboard, sneaking a look back at the boy. The note said, BOY UNDERAGE TAKE TO POLICE STATION.

Marnie looked from the note up to Laverne, whose forehead was creased with worry. She glanced in the rearview mirror to see that Max now had his head tipped back and eyes closed. His unlined face and long lashes made him look like a small child, and she could see that his tough-guy exterior was just a façade for a sweet, mixed-up kid. Could he be lying to them? Maybe. But she didn't want to believe it. She turned back to Laverne and shook her head.

Laverne gave her a withering look and took pen to paper again. At the bottom of the receipt she added: NEXT STOP. I WILL CALL.

"If you insist," Marnie said, and this time didn't even bother lowering her voice. Laverne underlined the words with a pointed finger for emphasis, but Marnie pretended not to notice and lowered the volume of the radio.

They'd driven for a half hour or more when Laverne broke through the silence. "You can't keep him, you know. It's not like finding a stray puppy." She fiddled with the sun visor, first putting it up, then reconsidering and lowering it again. "He's somebody's kid."

"I know that," Marnie said evenly, but inside she'd bristled. Oh why had she agreed to let Laverne come along? She'd have been better off driving by herself. She was thirty-five years old and capable of making her own decisions. She didn't need a keeper.

Laverne, oblivious to Marnie's irritation, continued. "We could get ourselves in a mess of trouble taking that kid over state lines. We could be charged with kidnapping or something."

Now that was something she hadn't considered. Marnie massaged her forehead and deliberated. She sighed. "At the next stop, I'll have him call his mom and talk to her myself," she said.

"And we never did find out his last name," Laverne said. "Very fishy."

"Kids hate answering questions," Marnie said, remembering how it was with Troy. "If you give them time, eventually it spills out." She knew this from personal experience. Over the last year or so, she'd learned not to ask Troy how his school day had gone. He acted as if she was prying. Instead she gave him some space, both physically and emotionally, trusting that if he needed to talk, he'd come to her. And he always did. Granted, it was often at inconvenient times. She'd be watching a movie on TV and just getting to the climactic part and wouldn't you know it—there would be Troy, a dark silhouette in the doorway wanting her immediate attention. She never let on that his timing was poor, just shut off the movie and made room for him on the couch. Brian never had the knack or patience for it, even after she explained it to him. Troy would want to talk and his father would say, "Does it have to be now?" and Troy would lower his head and duck out of the room. She knew there would never be a better time. Moments like that pass, and then they're gone.

"I know kids hate answering questions," Laverne grumbled. "I raised three of my own, so I know full well, but jeez, I don't think asking his last name is prying."

— — —

On this leg of the trip, Marnie developed a new appreciation for Jazzy and Rita. When those two had been in charge, she'd never had to worry about getting lost or how far it was to the next stop. Between the GPS and her phone, Jazzy attended to every detail. Laverne had the same equipment at her disposal but failed to keep up. Marnie saw the sign for the rest area a full thirty seconds before Laverne announced they were approaching one. Really, she wasn't much help at all.

It was late when they arrived at the rest stop and not a moment too soon, according to Laverne, who swore her bladder was fit to burst. It was so late, Marnie wondered if the place would be closed, but when she said as much, Laverne said, "Rest stops never close," in a way that implied Marnie was clueless. This from a woman who'd never left Wisconsin until recently.

The rest stop was lit up, and as they got closer, they saw a few other cars. "We're here," Marnie chirped, shifting into park and shutting off the engine. Stepping out of the car, the warm, thick air greeted her like a vaporous blanket. It was so easy to get used to air-conditioning, to think that comfortable temperatures were a given.

Standing on the other side of the vehicle, Laverne pointed and said, "Are you going to wake up Johnny Depp, or should I?" When Marnie said she would, Laverne added, "Good, 'cause I'm late to a meeting." And off she went, her short legs scissoring quickly up to the building.

Marnie had already decided she'd pay for a hotel room for Max that night. Hopefully they could get two adjacent rooms, so she could keep an eye on him. She'd talk to his mother tonight, and they could work something out. Maybe his mom would want to meet them in Las Vegas? That's what she would do, if it were her son. She opened the car door in back and leaned over Max, who still had his eyes closed. She watched him sleep for a minute or more. He looked so peaceful, she hated to disturb him. "Max?" she said gently, almost crooning the word. "We're stopping now. Do you need to use the restroom?"

"Mom?" His eyelids fluttered.

She wanted to cry for him. Big kids were just little kids at heart. "No, hon, I'm not your mom. I'm Marnie, remember? We're giving you a ride?"

"Marnie?"

"Yes, that's right. We met at the restaurant."

"Oh yeah." Max looked around and then yawned loudly. "What are we doing here?"

"Just stopping to use the bathrooms. You might want to get out and stretch your legs."

"Okay." He unbuckled his seat belt, and she stepped away from the car to let him pass.

On the other side of the building a truck revved its engine and turned on its headlights. Her eyes followed its movement as it turned out of the lot and lumbered toward the on-ramp. Next to her, Max stretched and leaned lazily against the car. She told him, "I'm going to use the ladies' room, and I was thinking we could meet back here in a few minutes and then give your mom a call before it gets too late. I know you said she knows, but I would feel better if I talked to her myself. You understand, I'm sure," she said, apologetically. "It's a mom thing. I can only imagine how I'd feel if my son was out in the world, being driven by complete strangers. I mean, we're perfectly fine people, but *she* has no way of knowing that." Max regarded her blankly. She opened her purse and rummaged around until she located her wallet. "Now I want to give you some change, and if there's a vending machine, you get yourself whatever you want." She unzipped the coin compartment and stuck two fingers into the narrow opening. She was aware of Max standing nearby, waiting expectantly, but she was so focused on retrieving quarters that she didn't notice he'd moved closer until he was right up against her. When his hand grabbed her arm, and she felt something hard and sharp pressed against her side, she reflexively tried to pull away, but his grip was too tight. "Ow, stop it," she said, twisting but not getting free.

"Give me the keys," he said, and his voice was guttural and deep, not at all like it had been before.

"Max, what are you doing?" she cried out, thinking this had to be a mistake. Maybe he'd had a bad dream in the car and was confused. Perhaps he'd become afraid and thought she meant him harm. Anything but what she saw now—his eyes, once friendly and warm, were narrow and menacing. The pressure of his hand on her arm was unbearable.

"Lady, just give me the damn keys. The wallet too." It was a voice out of a horror movie. "I will cut you. I swear to God I will slice you up."

She glanced down and saw that he held a knife against her side. The reality of the situation hit her all at once, and she talked frantically, pleading with him. "Please, Max, I'll drive you wherever you want to go. You don't want to do this."

Max pushed the knife up against her body and she cried out in pain. He pulled at her purse, yanking it out of her hands. She couldn't believe how strong he was. He shoved her aside and she fell backward against the side of the car, her head snapping back from the impact. He was emptying her purse now, throwing all of her possessions on the pavement. It all came out: her lip gloss, Kleenex, floss, emergency granola bar, some extra earrings, pens, hotel receipts. "Why do you have all this crap?" he muttered, half to himself. She noticed he had the knife under one arm now. It looked to be eight or ten inches, including the handle. A hunting knife? It occurred to her that she could try to rush him and get her purse back but she didn't. It was too risky.

"Please don't," Marnie said weakly. Her side felt wet. Instinctively she touched it with the opposite hand and found her fingertips covered with blood. He'd cut her. "It doesn't have to be like this."

Crazed at not finding the keys, he turned the purse upside down and shook it. Out came some loose coins, her garage door opener, and finally her cell phone, which skittered and bounced, landing on the pavement eight feet away. "Where the hell are they?" he screamed. He came at her, the knife in hand. Marnie tried to move away from the car, but her legs weren't working right and he had a hold of her again, gripping her with a terrifying ferocity. *So this is how it all ends*, she thought, her heart pounding wildly. What a stupid way to die. And she'd never really lived in the first place.

"I need the keys," he screamed at her, and she felt the tip of his knife against her stomach.

"I don't know," she said. "Honest, I—" A sudden deafening blast like a sonic boom came from nearby, startling her. Max let go of her arm and reared back, and both of them looked over to see Laverne heading toward them, a gun in her hand aimed at the sky.

"You gotta be kidding," he said.

"Get away, you punk," Laverne said, walking so quickly that her purse, looped over her bent arm like she was the Queen Mum, swung madly.

"Lady, mind your own damn business."

Laverne waved the gun with authority. As guns went, it was on the small side, although clearly it made a big noise. "I mean it."

He scoffed. "You're not going to shoot me. Give me a break." Marnie became aware of people peering out from the open door of the building.

"Are you kidding? I've been wanting to shoot someone for the longest time." She gestured to Marnie. "Come over here by me." And Marnie did as she was told, her hand clutched to her side. She stood next to Laverne with relief, the realization hitting her that she wasn't going to die that day.

"Look, old woman, I don't have time for this. I'm taking the car."

"Stop or I'll shoot," Laverne said, and extended her arm so the gun was aimed right at him. He gave her the finger and then leaned over to pick up Marnie's purse. Laverne lowered the gun and pulled the trigger. Boom!

"Jesus!" he screamed, and fell over, almost in slow motion, then rocked back and forth, clutching his leg. "You shot me, you crazy bitch."

"You shot him," Marnie said, dazed. "I can't believe you shot him." How had all of this happened during a quick stop to go to the bathroom? She had the sense that when she turned onto the exit ramp she'd left real life and entered a movie.

Laverne tipped her head to one side. "I warned him. You heard me warn him, right?"

Marnie nodded. Laverne had warned him all right.

"And he gave me the finger. I hate that. There's no reason to be doing that." She leaned over Max, who was now crying and clutching his leg. "You shouldn't have given me the finger. That was rude." She reached down and grabbed something off the pavement. "Hey, Marnie, I found your phone!"

"I can't believe you shot me. Jesus!"

Laverne reached over to Marnie and tentatively touched her side. "It looks like you're bleeding."

"He cut me." Marnie had to push the words out. Just looking at the blood made her woozy. "With a knife."

A man moved tentatively out of the building and then, deciding it was all clear, walked toward them. "Is everything okay?" he called out. He wore khaki shorts and a polo shirt like a suburban dad about to start up the grill. "Is anyone hurt?"

"We're going to need an ambulance," Laverne said matter-of-factly, putting the gun in her purse. "We got a man who's been shot and a woman with a knife wound."

On the ground Max, angry and in pain, wailed, "I need help here! Someone call 911."

Marnie looked from Laverne to Max, and to the half dozen people rushing toward them seemingly from out of nowhere. Everyone and everything began to spin and blend together. Dizzy, she staggered back against the side of the car, slid to the ground, and landed on her butt with a jolt.

And then everything went black.

Chapter Forty

When Marnie came to, she was on a gurney in the back of an ambulance with an oxygen mask strapped to her face. Even without looking she knew that her shirt had been sliced open to expose her wounded side. A young paramedic who looked like a teenage boy held her wrist and gingerly took her pulse. A woman crouched down next to her was doing something to the cut under her rib cage. Marnie felt the gentle pressure of something soft up against her side. The young man noticed her fluttering eyelids. "Welcome back," he said. "We're taking you to the hospital."

"Where's Laverne?" she asked. She feared the worst, which was that they'd dragged her off to jail, or that Laverne, now that she'd discovered the power of the gun, had shot someone else in the meantime.

The paramedic, his name tag said he was Dave, leaned over her and lifted the mask off her face. "I'm sorry, I didn't quite catch what you said."

She swallowed and repeated the question, and he smiled. "Don't worry about your stepmother. She has to answer some questions for the police. Once that's cleared up, she'll meet up with you at the hospital." Marnie wondered about the stepmother reference, but she was too out of it to pursue the topic. Apparently, someone was mixed up somewhere. It didn't really matter.

The rest of the ride was a blur, as was getting checked in at the hospital. Laverne, at least, had the presence of mind to send her purse along with her, so she had identification and her insurance card. Sitting up in the ER and rummaging through her purse, she unzipped a side compartment and came across her car keys. She'd nearly lost her life because Max couldn't find them, and they'd been there the whole time. Unbelievable.

The cut in her side was not as big as she'd thought. "You lost a fair amount of blood," the doctor who cleaned the wound said, "but it's not serious. You'll definitely have a scar." He advised her to see a plastic surgeon if she wanted that taken care of, but she couldn't imagine that she would. No one would ever see that part of her body again. Although on second thought, having a scar from a knife wound could be a pretty impressive badge of honor. *What I did on my summer vacation,* she thought dryly.

The ER wasn't that big, and she heard snippets of what was happening to Max from the other side of the partition. When she first arrived, she heard him saying loudly, "And then out of nowhere, the old woman took out a gun and shot me. Out of freaking nowhere! I didn't do nothing to her. Crazy-ass old woman." Someone shushed him, and eventually he was wheeled out of that room.

"Is he going for surgery to remove the bullet?" she asked.

"No, it was just a flesh wound," a nurse told her. "The bullet went through his calf and passed through. He'll be treated and turned over to the police."

Marnie was cleaned and stitched, and moved from the ER to a regular room on the third floor. It was a stark room but spotlessly clean and she didn't have to share it with another patient. She had her own bathroom too. Having been given a shot of something, she felt no pain. She rested comfortably in bed, her body relaxed, but her mind racing. Her thoughts were more erratic than they'd ever been. She could barely keep track of all the people coming in and out of her room, checking her chart, asking her questions. At one point, a young man whom she'd noticed mopping outside her door earlier came in with a woman's V-necked T-shirt. She thought he was Filipino or maybe Hmong, she never was good at differentiating different ethnicities, not that she'd admit that to anyone. It would make her sound racist, and she wasn't. His name tag, which identified him as "George" didn't narrow it down. He was, she decided, just another American originally from somewhere else. George held up the gray T-shirt and said, "For you?" She shook her head, thinking he was trying to find the owner. "Not mine," she said.

"No," he said and gestured in a searching way. "From Lost and Found. You keep. To go home."

Now she understood. From the paramedics, to the doctors and nurses—all of them had been so concerned, so caring. They milled around her and fussed over her injury. And now this man, someone she didn't even know, had thought ahead to what she might wear when she left. He had nothing to gain by giving her a T-shirt. She was touched by his innate goodness. It helped to offset the shock of finding evil in Max. People could surprise you. "Thank you," she said, taking it from him. After he left the room, she held it up and gave it a good looking over. It was enormous, and smelled strongly of powdered laundry detergent. But still, Marnie was grateful to have it.

By the time Laverne showed up, escorted by a police officer, a world of things had happened. "Hey there, gal," Laverne said cheerfully, shuffling into the room. "How you feeling?"

"Pretty good," Marnie said, pushing the button on the bed until she was sitting upright. It was true, she felt pretty good, in a loopy and otherworldly sort of way. Since the drugs kicked in, she'd felt herself to be on a different spiritual plane and found she understood more of life than other people did, maybe even in the entire history of the world. The young officer who accompanied Laverne was handsome in a fresh-from-the-academy sort of way. Just a youngster. With her now heightened sensitivity she could tell that he loved the excitement of his job. By the courteous way he led Laverne into the room, she knew he loved his mother and grandmother. His hair was cropped short, even around the ears and base of the neck, leading her to believe he took his role in the community seriously. You could tell so much from paying attention. It wouldn't be much more of a step for her to become psychic like Jazzy.

She'd been staring at the young cop for so long that when he spoke it seemed like a statue come to life. He said, "I'm just going to have to ask you a few questions." He started with the easy things—name, address, date of birth—then launched into questions about what had happened at the rest stop. He phrased those questions so that she only had to confirm Laverne's story. Was it true, he asked, that Max was charging at Laverne with the knife when she shot him?

Marnie hesitated and looked at Laverne, who said, "She was down on the ground, so she might not a seen it happen." The cop nodded and added that to his report. It wasn't technically true, but she didn't correct Laverne. She could tell the police officer needed a different truth, the kind of truth that would put the matter to rest in just the right way.

"It all happened so fast," Marnie said. Her head was muzzy and she wasn't sure about anything anymore. Maybe Max *had* lunged at Laverne when she'd been on the ground. Anything was possible.

"And he said he was going to kill you?" He paused and looked up at her.

Marnie thought. "He said he was going to slice me up." Her ears still held the echo of his voice saying the words. She'd been nothing but kind to Max. How could he have turned on her? Worse yet, how could she have misjudged him so? "He pushed the knife into my side and said he was going to slice me up."

Laverne interjected, "Isn't that the same thing, really? I mean, you felt like your life was in danger, right, Marn?"

She nodded. "I thought I was going to die, right then and there."

"You ladies really shouldn't be picking up hitchhikers. First of all, it's illegal. Secondly, it's very dangerous," the officer said firmly. "At your age, you shouldn't have to be told that."

"Do I get my gun back?" Laverne asked.

"No, you do not," he said. "You're lucky we're not charging you with anything."

"Okay," Laverne said in resignation, and then to Marnie, "Who would have thought I'd go my whole life without even a parking ticket, and today I shoot a guy and help the police catch a criminal?" She pressed a hand on Marnie's knee. "Turns out he's not a kid at all. He's eighteen and he was wanted, can you imagine that?"

"Wanted?"

"There was a warrant out for his arrest," the police officer explained. "It makes the case easier. Between that and the witnesses saying it was self-defense, it's fairly cut-and-dried."

"So we can go?" Laverne said. "Because we really need to get to Las Vegas."

"You can go, but you might be called back to testify at some point in the future. Although it's highly unlikely," he added, more to himself than anything else.

"We can always come back, right, Marnie?"

"Sure," Marnie said, but she had no intention of coming back here ever again. She wasn't entirely sure where she was right now, if the truth be told. All she knew was that she was in a hospital more than a thousand miles from home. She'd dropped down a rabbit hole and into an alternate existence. It had been fun for a while, but now she wanted to be finished. A few days of fast food and gas stops and endless driving had been bad enough, but now, having endured being threatened and cut, she was tired and hurt and shaken to the core. Perhaps the universe was telling her this trip was a mistake. She wanted nothing more than to go home. Once she made it past her front door, she'd drop her suitcase and crawl into bed, not coming out until right before school started. If then.

"You ladies take care," he said, giving Laverne's shoulder a squeeze. "Have a safe trip."

"Such a nice young man," Laverne said, after he'd left the room. They heard the receding click of his shoes as he went down the hall.

Marnie waited until he was out of earshot to ask, "So where did you get the gun?"

"It was my husband's. I always keep it in my handbag." She pursed her lips thoughtfully. "Never thought I'd need it, but boy oh boy, it sure came in handy today."

"I'd say so," Marnie said. "Things might have gotten far worse without it."

"So gal, what's the good word from the doctor?" Laverne asked, settling into the chair next to the bed.

"He said the cut wasn't too bad, although it hurt like nobody's business and it bled a lot. I was lucky that the knife only went through the skin and into a layer of fat," Marnie said. For the first time, she was thankful for having a little extra fat. "They're keeping me overnight for observation. The test results came out fine, but they want me checked out tomorrow morning before they release me."

"Probably not a bad idea, seeing what you've been through." Laverne fumbled through her purse and then handed a phone to Marnie. "You're going to want this."

"Oh, you found my phone! Thank you," Marnie said. The screen was a little scratched, but it looked functional.

"That reminds me. Kimberly called about an hour ago. She wanted you to come right away. I explained about you being in the hospital and all—"

"Kimberly?" Marnie asked, dazed. "Troy's mother?"

"None other."

"She called me?"

"Well, she wanted to talk to you, but since you were here, I answered the phone and she had to talk to me." Laverne said the words slowly, like explaining to a young child.

"You're sure it was Kimberly?"

"I think we've covered this, Marnie," Laverne said impatiently. "Kimberly called. She called you. On the phone. Because she needs a favor. Troy's at camp, but he's sick with a fever. They want her to pick him up, but her flight to Europe leaves tomorrow night, so she was wondering if you'd come out and get him. Of course I said you were in no condition..."

"He's already at camp?"

"That's what she said."

Marnie was so confused. Troy had left already? Matt Haverman must have gotten the time frame mixed up. "You said he's sick?" She swung her legs around the side of the bed and sat up straight. "What's wrong with him?"

"Nothing's wrong with him, he's just got a flu bug or something. You know how it is. Kids get sick." Laverne settled back into a padded vinyl chair against the wall. "She sounded disappointed. Said she'd see if she could make other arrangements."

Marnie stared at her phone in disbelief. Kimberly had called *her* asking for a favor. And the favor had to do with taking care of Troy. Unbelievable. Hadn't she been giving her the cold shoulder ever since the funeral? Every time she'd phoned her in the past, Marnie got the impression that Kimberly was in the middle of something and she was interrupting. This time, though, it would be different. She called Kimberly back.

Even though it was late, Kimberly answered on the second ring. "Hello?"

"Kimberly, it's me, Marnie." There was a long pause.

"Oh, Marnie," Kimberly said at last, her tone friendly. "I'm so glad to hear from you. How are you?"

"I'm just fine," she said hurriedly. "Laverne told me that you want me to come and take care of Troy?"

"Oh, yes, but that was before I knew what you'd been through. I'm sorry to have bothered you. Your stepmom said you'd been rushed to the hospital?"

"I think Laverne exaggerated slightly," Marnie said, holding her side. "I'm barely hurt at all. Just a scratch."

"That's good. I'm glad to hear it."

Marnie said, "So I can pick up Troy tomorrow, if you still need me to." Laverne gave her a disapproving look, which she waved away.

"Really?" Kimberly sounded relieved. "If you can, I'd be so grateful. I didn't know what I was going to do…" Her voice trailed off, and Marnie heard her shushing a dog barking in the background. Troy had always wanted a dog, but Brian didn't want the mess or chaos of an animal.

"Of course," Marnie said. "Just give me the address to the camp."

"You'll have to stop here first," Kimberly said. "So I can give you written permission to pick him up. My house is on the way, though."

"Will do."

"I know this is asking a lot, but could you possibly be at my house by ten?"

"Yes, I can be there by ten." Marnie noticed the digital display of the clock in her hospital room showed it was nearly midnight. She didn't know how many hours they were from Las Vegas. They were still in Utah, she knew that—probably only a few hours away. They'd make it, easy enough.

"I'm so relieved," Kimberly said. "My housekeeper, Natalie, said she'd watch him during the day, but I wasn't sure what I was going to do for the night shift. Then Natalie remembered that in the rush to get Troy off to camp she never gave me the message you had called. It seemed like fate that you were on your way."

"Of course I'll come."

"If you can stay with him for a few days while my assistant works out a long-term solution, I'd be so grateful."

Marnie said, "I'm perfectly willing to watch him the whole time."

"We can talk about that when you get here," Kimberly said. "Just so you know, the camp is about two hours from here. I would have picked him up already, but I've been crazy busy getting ready for my trip. I had to get shots and make arrangements for the dogs, not to mention coordinating my schedule." Kimberly was getting to be talkative. Marnie, by comparison, was getting wearier.

"I hate to cut this short, Kimberly, but I need to get going. We'll talk tomorrow." They exchanged good-byes and that was it. Marnie turned off the phone and turned to Laverne. "Why does everyone think you're my stepmother?"

Laverne cast her eyes down on the bed and poked sheepishly at the blanket. "Oh, that. Everyone assumed we were related somehow, so I just claimed you. It made things simpler." She looked up to see Marnie shaking her head in amusement.

Marnie said, "Well, let's get a move on then, Stepmom. We have a couple hours of driving to go."

"Are you sure this is such a good idea?" Laverne said. "You look whipped."

"Laverne, I'm not staying in this room one minute longer than I have to. Troy is waiting." Knowing she would be able to see him soon gave her a surge of energy. A few minutes ago she was nearly passed out from the drugs and the day's events. Now she was wide awake and ready to go.

"I hear you." Laverne picked up the beige remote tethered to the hospital bed by a thick cord. She studied it for a second and then pushed the red call button.

"What are you doing?" Marnie asked, her voice rising in alarm.

"Letting the nurse know you're leaving."

"No, no, no! Don't ask permission. They'll just say I can't go." Marnie pulled the remote out of her hand, but it was too late. A voice came through the intercom above the bed. "Yes? You needed something?"

"I pushed the button by accident," Marnie said. "I'm sorry."

"No problem." The voice clicked off.

Marnie spoke firmly to Laverne. "If you want to be helpful, start gathering up my stuff while I get dressed, so we can get out of here."

"Okeydokey." Looking around the room, Laverne found a plastic bag with the hospital logo on it. She threw a box of Kleenex into the bag along with a plastic pan the nurse had said Marnie could use if she felt the urge to get sick.

Marnie stood up slowly, her legs unsteady and shaky. She had the sense she was getting a preview of what it would be like to be very old. Every move took complete concentration. She went to the cabinet where her clothes were stowed and pulled them off the shelf. Someone, she noticed, had carefully folded them. Her sandals were at the very the bottom, soles down, side by side. Setting aside her usual modesty, she changed right in front of Laverne, struggling into her bra and putting on the gray T-shirt from the Lost and Found.

When it came time to pull on her shorts and sandals, she sat in the bedside chair. It seemed to take a long time, but Laverne didn't notice. She was too busy scooping up toiletries from the bathroom.

"You lucked out," Laverne said, coming out of the bathroom with the now bulging bag. "There was a whole box of maxi pads and some soap and a little shampoo bottle and some Purell too. That stuff's like gold."

"I don't think you're supposed to take the supplies," Marnie said. "It's not like a hotel."

Laverne scoffed. "Are you kidding? They're gonna charge you for it. You might as well take 'em. You'll be glad later on."

Marnie wasn't in the mood to argue. She let Laverne take charge, gathering up both their purses and pulling the string on the plastic bag and looping it over her wrist. "Now we're ready," Laverne said, after giving the room the once-over. She came to Marnie's side and offered her arm for support. "Easy there, gal. We'll get there, slowly but surely." The empty hall echoed with their footsteps, but no one seemed to notice. They passed the nurses' station, but even that seemed to be deserted, except for one woman, whose back was to them. She was hunched over a keyboard, entering something into a computer, and didn't look up when they went past. When they got into the elevator, Marnie leaned against the wall, while Laverne pushed the button for the first floor. They exchanged a conspiratorial glance. Marnie hadn't felt like this since her teen years. She and some friends used to sneak into the quarry at night to go swimming. She clearly remembered the feeling of triumph when she'd made it over the fence, her towel tucked under her arm.

When they got to the first floor and the elevator door opened, a doctor stood in front of them, his gaze on his pager. They traded places and he never said a word. Laverne turned to look. "Keep going," Marnie muttered. "Just keep going. We're not home free yet."

The first floor was brighter and busier than the third, but the staff didn't question their presence as they made their way to the front door. As they walked out, one man called out, "Good night, ladies," and Laverne flapped an arm in acknowledgment.

Out in the parking lot, Marnie nearly wilted. She'd forgotten the insufferable weight of the heat, the way it pressed against her chest, making it hard to breathe. Even in the dark of night, it felt like they'd walked into an oven. She pushed her hair back off her forehead and looked around. "Where's the car?" Laverne's face had a sudden stricken look that Marnie didn't like at all. She asked again, "The car's here, right? The police brought it over?"

"No."

"Why not?"

"I completely forgot—it's still back at the rest stop," Laverne said, smacking her forehead. "I didn't have the keys, so that nice officer brought me in the police car."

Marnie groaned. Who would have thought car keys could cause so much trouble? "The cop didn't wonder how you were going to leave the hospital without a car?"

"He did say something about it, but I told him not to worry about it, that I'd figure something out."

Marnie had the urge to collapse on the pavement weeping. Her legs felt like Jell-O, and her side, which had ten dissolvable stitches, now felt sore and tender.

"I'm sorry," Laverne said. "I didn't have my thinking cap on." At least she had the decency to look miserable and apologetic.

"Now what are we going to do?" Marnie surveyed the parking lot, as if the dozen or so cars would give her a clue. There were no signs indicating public transportation, and even if there had been, she was pretty sure buses didn't make stops on the freeway.

"Maybe we can call a cab?" Laverne suggested. "Let's see what's on the other side of the building."

Reluctantly, Marnie let herself be led past a row of cars and around the corner of the building. This side had its own parking area, but it wasn't as brightly lit. She had a feeling that if they rounded one more corner they'd be in complete darkness. "It's no use, Laverne, we have to go back inside."

"Wait!" Laverne held up a hand and peered off in the distance. "I see someone."

Marnie rolled her eyes. Yes, there was a man coming out of one of the exits, dragging a plastic bag with him. He moved quickly to the back of the lot to where two Dumpsters stood side by side, lifted the cover of one of them, flung the bag inside, and pumped a fist in the air. They could hear his happy exclamation: "Yes!"

"Yoo hoo," Laverne yelled in his direction, waving the plastic bag over her head. "Sir, can you help us?"

Marnie didn't like where this was going. Dealing with strange men had not turned out well for her lately. "Let's go back in," she said, tugging at Laverne's shirt. But it was too late. The young man jogged toward them in a friendly way. As he got closer, she recognized him as the young man who'd given her the T-shirt. George.

"You need help?" he said with concern, and then a flash of recognition crossed his face upon seeing Marnie and the gray T-shirt. "Oh, hello."

Marnie said, "Our car is parked at a rest stop on the interstate, and we need to get there real quick. Is there a bus or a cab company or something that could take us?"

"Is very late for cab," he said. "Very late. And no buses around here."

"You've got to be kidding." Marnie pictured Troy, feverish and asking for her, and her not being able to get there. She wanted to be there for him. There was nothing she wanted more, in fact. It was unfair. She had been so close. But she was also exhausted. Walking took supreme effort, like swimming against the current.

Too tired to hold back, she wept openly, tears streaming down her cheeks. She felt her nose become itchy and congested, and she wiped at it even though it wasn't running quite yet.

"Do not cry," George said, alarmed. You'd have thought Marnie was his own mother, the way he responded. "No crying." He held up his hands like warding off her sadness. "I take you. I take you. In my car."

"But," Marnie said, swallowing, "don't you have to work?"

"All done now," he said. "Garbage out, then I go home."

"You'll drive us to the rest stop?" Laverne said incredulously, as if she couldn't believe their good luck.

"Oh yes," George said. "I take you ladies now. If you wish."

It occurred to Marnie that one of them should have objected to the idea of getting into a car with a strange man, but neither of them did.

Chapter Forty-One

That night, while Laverne and Marnie were driving toward Las Vegas, Rita slept in the guest bedroom at Beth and Mike's house. For the first time in years, she was able to sink into sleep, completely relaxed, at peace with the world. She dreamt that Melinda was sitting on the edge of the bed, stroking her mother's hair and murmuring comforting words. The dream felt as real as anything that had happened in her waking hours, and when she would wake, nine hours later, she was going to recall every bit of it. In the future, the memory of that dream would sustain her when grief came to call.

— — —

Beth and Mike slept down the hall, their bodies nestled together in the center of their king-sized bed. Near their feet, a gray tabby cat slept, her body curled into a comma. When Mike drifted into a deep sleep, his breathing was loud enough to be considered snoring, but Beth was used to it. In fact, she couldn't sleep without it.

— — —

Downstairs, Jazzy sat on one end of the floral-print couch and Carson on the other end, one cushion between them. She fought a craving to move closer, to touch his face. Just seeing him smile overwhelmed her. So curious, that she was having such an intense reaction. She'd seen attractive men before, but she'd never felt like this. Jazzy couldn't stop looking at him. She was, she realized, completely enamored.

In the dim light, his dark eyes seemed even more intense. "So you aren't seeing anyone right now?" he asked. "There's no guy who's going to come and pound on me for spending time with you?"

She shook her head.

"Unbelievable. A woman like you, unattached. And if your car hadn't broken down at just that spot at just that time, we never would have met. How lucky am I?" he said, flooding her with his warmth.

What to say to that? She wasn't sure, but she felt herself blush, and thought, *Get your act together, Jazzy. You don't want to blow this.* To distract herself from the overpowering urge to move closer and throw her arms around him (a total slut move), she starting talking about what had happened at the police station that afternoon.

"I know the Dietz family," he said, when she got to the part where they'd realized Davis Diamontopoulos was going out with Judy's daughter. "And I've seen Sophie and her boyfriend in the restaurant. I don't know him though."

Jazzy said, "Officer Dietz says she'll do what she can." Offhand, it hadn't sounded like that would be much, but Judy had said she'd have another officer call Davis in to the precinct to question him in an official capacity, broaching it like it was a friendly chat, just a few questions to clear things up.

And Judy had also said she was going to try to talk some sense into Sophie. "She's crazy about Davis," she said. "It's not going to be easy to persuade her he's capable of murder. I have to think about the best way to handle this." Her brow furrowed in thought. Such a difficult situation.

Jazzy paused at that point in the story, and Carson said, "And that's when you made the posters." It was a statement, not a question.

Jazzy curled up and rested her chin on her knees, her eyes never leaving Carson's face. Amazing how he gave her his full attention. He was a man who really listened. She said, "Rita had the photo in her wallet, and we had the posters printed up at the police station. Not officially, of course. Judy said if anyone asked, she had nothing to do with it." The poster, the size of a piece of printer paper, featured the enlarged photo of Melinda and Davis at their happiest. He looked remarkably the same, considering ten years had passed. Beneath the photo, it read: "Please help solve the murder of Melinda Larson. Any information appreciated." Underneath was printed the date and location of the crime and the contact information of the police detective in charge of the case back in Wisconsin.

They printed up a hundred of these posters and spent the next two hours posting them everywhere they could think of: shop windows, store bulletin boards, power poles, and beneath wiper blades on car windshields. The business owners they approached were incredibly nice. No one was able to turn down a woman who started the conversation by saying, "I hope you can help me solve the murder of my beautiful daughter, Melinda." Some of the people they approached recognized Davis in the photo, Jazzy could tell. They didn't say as much, but she knew by the look on their faces.

When they had distributed every last one, Jazzy and Rita were tired and sweaty, but they both felt a certain sense of accomplishment.

Jazzy said, "When we were finished, Rita said, 'Maybe nothing will come of it, but at least he'll know it's not over.'"

"Wow," Carson said, and repeated, "At least he'll know it's not over."

They both were quiet for a minute, and then Jazzy said, "I told her that something would definitely come of it."

"And you know that because you're psychic?" There was curiosity in his eyes.

"No," Jazzy admitted. "I don't really know what's going to happen. I just want to believe that Rita will get some satisfaction, after all this time. She and her husband have been through so much."

"You are a really good friend," he said, tilting his head and looking at her approvingly.

"I try."

"You do more than try. You go all out for people. That's a rare thing."

She was silent. Compliments made her uncomfortable for some reason. And this guy kept lobbing them her way. "Thank you," she said, looking down at her bare feet. "But what about you? Helping out in your parents' restaurant, that's awfully nice of you."

He laughed. "I'm not all that nice. I needed a place to stay until I move and start my new job at the end of summer. I couldn't really stay here and leech off them. Besides, I don't mind. There are worse things to do."

"So what's your new job?"

"My degree is in environmental engineering. I was hired by a company on Long Island. It's not my ideal job, but it pays well and it's a foot in the door, considering I'm right out of college."

"Environmental engineering? And you couldn't get something closer to home?" It seemed to Jazzy that Colorado had to have jobs in this area. Colorado was nothing if not environment—water and mountains and clean, crisp air.

"You're not the first one to tell me that," he said. "But I wanted the adventure of living somewhere different. And I like the idea of being close to New York City. I love it there. The energy, the diversity, the people. It's awesome."

"I actually just got an offer to work in New York," Jazzy said, remembering her encounter with Scarlett Turner and the business card still tucked in her wallet. "If I take the job, I'll be an assistant to a *New York Times* best-selling author."

"Are you going to take it?"

"I'm thinking I will, yes," Jazzy said. On the other side of the room, just past where Carson sat, Jazzy felt her grandmother's presence, and at the same time, a picture of a thumbs-up came to mind—Grandma's way of giving Carson her stamp of approval. Jazzy almost laughed out loud.

Carson tilted his head to one side. "If you're going to be in New York, and I'm going to be living nearby, maybe we could see each other sometime?"

"That's a distinct possibility."

They were both quiet for a minute, the silence wrapping them in a cocoon of intimacy. Finally Carson said, "So you're leaving tomorrow, when the car is ready. Are you meeting up with the other two in Las Vegas?"

Jazzy hesitated. She and Rita had discussed the matter exhaustively but still weren't entirely sure what they were going to do. "I don't know. Rita really wants to go home. She misses her husband something fierce. But she doesn't want to leave Laverne and Marnie high and dry. It's very awkward for her." She stretched her legs out on the couch, stopping just short of touching Carson. "She's not sure what to do."

"And what about you?" He leaned over and trailed his fingertips over the top of her foot. "What do you want to do?"

"I'm in no hurry to go," she said, holding back a shudder of pleasure. Pure bliss.

"No hurry to go." He gave her a slight smile. "Is that the same as saying you'd like to stay?"

"Yes, that's the same as saying I'd like to stay."

Chapter Forty-Two

True to his word, George drove them directly to the rest stop, then waited to make sure the car started. Laverne tried to give him a five-dollar bill for his time and trouble, but he refused. "No money," he said, clearly offended. "I like to help." Laverne liked the boy's pluck. It was the kind of attitude that restored a person's faith in humanity.

After he drove off, Laverne told Marnie to get in the back. "You're all drugged up. You might as well sleep," she said. "I'll take a turn driving."

Marnie said, "But I thought you didn't have a driver's license?"

"Aw pshaw," Laverne said, waving her hand dismissively. "Yeah, it expired, but I still got the skills. It's like riding a bike. You don't forget."

Marnie, who could barely keep her eyes open, didn't argue. They switched spots, Laverne circling the car to get to the driver's side, Marnie exiting the vehicle to get to the backseat. After pulling the door shut, she said, "Thanks, Laverne. You're a lifesaver."

"Aw, it's nothing."

"Wake me up in an hour or so," Marnie murmured, loosely fastening her seat belt and then flopping over and curling up on her good side. "I just need a little cat nap."

"Sure thing." Laverne took her time adjusting the seat and the mirrors, then double-checked to see that the GPS was still set for Kimberly's address. She found an unopened bottle of Mountain Dew on the floor of the front passenger side; she claimed it and stuck it in the cup holder next to her. The caffeine would come in handy if the road got too monotonous.

She hadn't driven in years, but it was amazing how fast it came back to her. She'd forgotten how powerful it made her feel. At home she had let herself become a recluse, but in the last few days that had all changed. On this trip, she was originally a tagalong, the one they invited along out of pity (or so she suspected), but now it all hinged on her. She could tell that Marnie had started off the trip not liking her, but she had to have a different opinion by now. Laverne had saved Marnie's life back at the rest stop, and now she was single-handedly getting her to Las Vegas. What a wild ride!

As the car reached the ramp onto the interstate, Laverne accelerated and merged smoothly into the sparsely populated nighttime traffic. Las Vegas was only two hours and forty-eight minutes away according to the GPS. They'd be there in no time. She turned on the radio looking for some good country music, and when she found a Taylor Swift song, she took it as a good omen. Such a pretty little gal, that Taylor Swift. And so talented too, writing all those songs all by herself. Laverne hummed along to the song and stayed in the right lane, confident that the GPS would get them there.

— — —

When Carson slid over and pulled her into his arms, Jazzy was very glad that the spirit of her grandmother was no longer in the room. When he leaned in and kissed her, she was awestruck at how natural it was to be with this man. She felt a connection to him like she'd never felt to another human being, and she knew that her whole life had led her to this moment. As corny as that sounded.

When he pulled apart and held her face gently between his hands, she was touched by the look of wonder on his face. He gestured between them and said, "Has this ever happened to you before?"

"No, never."

He kissed her again and she wished the night would never end. Given a choice, she'd trade her psychic ability for a lifetime with this man. Hell, she'd trade everything she had, and it would be worth every bit.

— — —

Driving the I-15 toward Las Vegas was smooth sailing all the way, but dark—oh boy, was it dark. Laverne took sips from the Mountain Dew and tried not to look down at the white center line, since it had a hypnotic effect on her. Instead, she concentrated on the road ahead, as much as she could see in the headlights. Other vehicles passed on occasion, but there were long stretches when she felt like she had the road to herself. In the backseat, Marnie occasionally made contented noises. She'd rolled up a jacket to use as a pillow and looked comfortable enough.

After she'd been driving two hours or so, Laverne could see Las Vegas in the distance, so bright that she could imagine the sun coming over the mountains. It wasn't the sun though, she knew, once she got closer, but the lights of the city. What would people in the old days, before electricity, think of such a thing? Would they think it was magic, these lights that shone day and night? And what about those people to come in the future? The ones who weren't born yet? She imagined a time when all the comforts she took for granted—running water, heat, air-conditioning, electricity—were even more precious and rare than they were now. Would future generations get their dander up at all the waste of their ancestors? The way they watered lawns and kept restaurants so cold in the summer heat that customers wore sweaters to be comfortable? She was a little bit glad that she'd be long gone by the time the current generation would be held accountable. No one could point a finger her way.

She followed directions off the freeway and into the city. Glancing back at Marnie's sleeping form, she almost woke her up to let her know they'd arrived, but decided against it. One of them should get some rest. Laverne was too excited to sleep anyway, agog as she was at the palm trees, brightly lit casinos, and hotels. All of it looked exactly as she'd seen on her favorite TV show, *CSI: Las Vegas*. This must be what they called "The Strip." Amazing that all this was built in the desert. People on the sidewalk meandered as if they had no particular destination. Some were dressed in shorts and tank tops, others were dressed to the nines, but all of them somehow gave the impression that they were tourists. This place was Disneyland for grown-ups. Laverne never dreamed she'd see it in person, much less be driving the streets like some kind of hotshot confident person. If only her kids could see her now. They'd never believe it.

Laverne whistled as she drove out of the heart of the city. Good-bye gambling place. They were headed to Kimberly's house.

Chapter Forty-Three

When Marnie finally woke up, they were parked on the side of a street in a nondescript suburban neighborhood and the sun was just beginning to rise. She sat up and rubbed the back of her neck, then noticed that her stitched side hurt something fierce and she remembered everything that had happened in the last twenty-four hours. "Where are we?" she asked Laverne, who was fiddling with the volume on the radio. It seemed to her that her dreams had been invaded by the same country music she was hearing now.

"Kimberly's house."

"What?" Marnie pushed her hair out of her eyes. "You were supposed to wake me up."

Laverne turned around and said apologetically, "I know, but you'd been through so much and you were sleeping so good, I hated to wake you up. I kept thinking I'd go just a little farther, just a little more before I got you up. I even stopped and put gas in the tank just outside the Strip and I thought that would wake you up, but you were *out*. Before I knew it we were here."

"But, but," Marnie sputtered, "it's a gated community. How did you get in?"

"There was a house thing with a window when I drove in, but no one was there and the gate was open, so I kept going. We've been parked here for a long time. I thought we should wait awhile. It's awful early."

The lack of security irritated Marnie, who was sure a stop at the gate would have awakened her. She'd counted on having at least a little time to prepare before meeting up with Kimberly. But Laverne had let her sleep and now they were here.

"That's one big house," Laverne said, pointing.

"Just under eight thousand square feet," Marnie said, rubbing the sleep out of her eyes.

"But the yards around here are kind of small."

"Less than a quarter acre."

Laverne said, "It must have cost like a million dollars."

"Not quite." Marnie knew all about this house. After Kimberly had bought it three years ago, Marnie had found the real estate listing online. The house had a swimming pool, spiral staircase, and skylights. She knew how much property tax Kimberly paid, the name of the school district, and that the house had 4.5 bathrooms, one of which had a spa shower, whatever that was. "I wish I'd gotten my prescription filled at the hospital. Whatever they gave me wore off and it hurts like hell."

"I got something that will fix you right up," Laverne said, and pulled out her Ziploc bag of wonders. "Let's see, you'll need something strong for pain." She held up a bottle and read the label, then discounted it. "Nope, this one will make you sleepy. Can't have that." The next bottle didn't make the cut either. "This one has to be taken with food. You have to be so careful." Her brow furrowed and she dug back into the bag. "Ah, here we go. This'll be good for what ails ya." She uncapped the bottle and shook out two pills, then handed them back to Marnie.

"What is this?" Marnie popped the pills in her mouth and took a swig of water from a plastic bottle she'd gotten off the floor near her feet.

"Sometimes it's better not to know." And then, seeing Marnie's reproachful look, she added, "If it takes away the pain, what difference does it make what it's called?"

"If I overdose it would be nice to be able to tell the paramedics what I ingested."

"Oh posh, you can't overdose. This is medication that was *prescribed*."

Marnie couldn't argue with that logic. In the not too distant past she would have been appalled at the thought of taking someone else's drugs, prescription or not. Somehow, as they'd traveled the miles, she'd become less careful and more open, even to things that were potentially dangerous. Her former self wouldn't have approved, but she didn't care about that. The old Marnie had been kind of a drag. And not all that happy either, if the truth were told.

She got a comb and a compact out of her purse and attempted to fix her hair and face, but no matter how hard she tried, she looked like a woman who'd just slept in a car. The dark circles under her eyes aged her ten years. Her hair was matted to her head like a swimming cap. To make matters worse, the gray T-shirt she wore, which she'd been so grateful to receive only the night before, was now rumpled and shapeless. Midwestern frump was the phrase that came to mind. She glanced up to see Laverne studying her. "I know," Marnie said, running her fingers through her hair, "it's hopeless."

"I was just thinking you looked fine," Laverne said, shrugging. "It's not like Troy will care. He's going to be happy to see you no matter what."

Laverne's comment put everything in perspective. Her appearance didn't matter. She wasn't applying for a job, and she didn't (in theory) care what Kimberly thought of her. Troy was the only reason she was here.

When the lawn care service arrived in a white pickup truck towing a trailer, Laverne and Marnie decided it was late enough to knock on the door. Marnie felt a wave of nervousness rise from the pit of her stomach while they waited on the front mat under the archway. "Maybe we should have called from the car," she said to Laverne. "Given her some notice."

"You gotta be kidding," Laverne said, and knocked again, louder this time. At the curb, the lawn service was in full work mode, unloading equipment off the trailer and giving the two women quizzical looks. Laverne gave them a look and called out, "We are supposed to be here. We are *expected*." The men, all in their twenties, wearing white T-shirts and light-colored shorts, had the decency to look away and get back to their work. One of them waved a hello before turning away. "Yeah, that's right. Back to work," Laverne said, but this time her voice was lower and only Marnie heard.

"God knows what we look like to them. They probably think we're selling something," Marnie muttered, pushing her hair back behind her ear. Now, in broad daylight, she noticed that Carson's Corolla, parked at the curb, looked less than new. In fact, there was a rather large dent by the back bumper and mud splatters around the wheel wells. It sure wasn't helping their image.

"They need to mind their own beeswax." Laverne knocked again, this time like a girl in a horror movie trying to get away from a guy in a mask. "This just beats all," she said, pausing. "I sure didn't drive through the night to get stopped at the door." She turned the knob, and the door opened. "Oh ho ho," she chortled, raising her eyebrows. "Here we go."

"I don't think that's such a good—" Marnie said, but Laverne was already in the house. Marnie sighed. "...Idea." She walked in after Laverne, unsure, but not wanting to be left behind. Once inside she got an idea of the size of the house. No one seemed to be home.

"Woo-eee," Laverne said, standing in the two-story entryway and looking up at a crystal chandelier the size of a Mini Cooper. "Will you look at that?"

"The formal entryway is dramatic and inviting," Marnie said, quoting from the realtor's online description. "The marble flooring was imported from Italy."

"Very nice," Laverne said, toeing the pattern. "Not bad at all." She wandered into the house like it was a public place—a library or museum. "Hello! Anyone here?"

Marnie wasn't convinced that this was the best strategy but felt herself pulled along by Laverne. Maybe it was the effect of the painkiller kicking in, but she seemed to have no choice in the matter. The house was immense. "Can you imagine cleaning a place like this?" Laverne said.

"You'd need help," Marnie said. "A lot of help."

When they heard the voice of a woman speaking, Marnie halted and put a finger to her lips. From the sound of it, this was Kimberly, on the phone. Casting aside her hesitation, Marnie made her way toward the voice. Kimberly was her ticket to Troy. The sooner she spoke to her, the better.

Marnie walked into a large sitting area. Beyond that, an open doorway led to what looked like Kimberly's office. Sitting at a desk, her back to the door, sat Kimberly, a phone clutched to her ear. Marnie knocked gently on the doorframe.

"Back already, Dean?" she said, not turning around. "Just a sec, I'm talking to the administrator at the camp." She was dressed in a pale blue bathrobe and held a pen she jiggled nervously against the desktop.

"It's not Dean." Marnie's voice rose in pitch. "It's me—Marnie."

Kimberly sat up abruptly and turned around. "Just a minute," she said to the person on the phone. "Marnie's here now. She'll be there to get Troy this morning." She gestured to Marnie to sit down, and she wrapped up the conversation, thanking the person on the other end and apologizing for the inconvenience.

She hung up and gave Marnie a relieved grin, then jumped up and hugged her. "Marnie, it's so nice to see you again. I can't tell you how happy I am you're here," she said, and then looked up at Laverne, who stood tentatively in the doorway. "Hello there."

"Who's Dean?" Laverne asked.

"This is Laverne," Marnie said, by way of introduction. "She's with me."

"Oh yes, you're Marnie's stepmom. We spoke on the phone. Good to meet you." Kimberly got up to shake Laverne's hand, then self-consciously rearranged the ties on her robe. "You'll forgive my appearance. You came earlier than I expected. Not that I mind," she said hastily. "My biggest fear was that you wouldn't come at all. That would have been a disaster. The last few days have been so hectic, I can't even tell you. Dean—that's my assistant—got here at the crack of dawn to take the dogs to the sitter, and I've been going nonstop. Every time I cross something off the list I wind up adding something else, so it never gets any shorter." She patted her hair and laughed. "Sorry I'm such a mess." It was not true. Although her hair was mussed and she wore no makeup, no one would deny she was still a stunning woman. She had the fine features and glowing skin that Marnie, for some reason, associated with French women, and she was enviably slender without being too skinny. Her thick blonde hair lay on her shoulders in what looked like natural waves. Doing a mental inventory, Marnie couldn't find anything to criticize. Kimberly's perfectly formed ears lay close to her head, and her teeth were even and pearly white, without looking fake like veneers. The woman was freaking perfect. The only thing that kept Marnie from hating her was that the resemblance to Troy was uncanny. She'd never noticed it in photographs, but in person it was undeniable. There were traces of Troy in Kimberly's posture, her eyes, her smile, even the way she fidgeted with her pen.

"Have you ladies had breakfast yet?" Kimberly asked. "I was just about to grab a bite."

She didn't wait for an answer but got up and led them to the kitchen. Every bit of the house was spacious and filled with light. Marnie wondered where Kimberly kept the clutter. Why were there no shoes by the door, no piles of mail set aside? She and Laverne followed obediently, while Kimberly chatted on about her upcoming trip to London and how the camp called the night before saying Troy had a fever. "Only ninety-nine point eight, which doesn't sound very high, does it? They said they just wanted to keep me apprised, and I'm fine with that, even though I thought it was a little unnecessary. The next thing I know, they're calling saying his temp is a hundred and one, and I have to come pick him up. Their rule, the director said, is anything over one hundred degrees. A despicable woman. Completely without reason. Like talking to a three-year-old. She just kept repeating how this was their policy. Anything over one hundred degrees." Kimberly made finger quotes around the number. "One hundred exactly. How arbitrary is that? And this was at ten o'clock at night, if you can imagine that! I insisted on talking to Troy, and he sounded fine. I explained about my trip, but they didn't care." She sighed heavily and led them into the kitchen of Marnie's dreams: gleaming granite countertops, plenty of cabinet space, and double everything—dual ovens, two stovetops, two dishwashers, and an extra-wide refrigerator. The adjacent breakfast nook held a table for six adorned by a clear vase filled with towering white calla lilies. A doorway on the other side revealed a linen-draped table topped with crimson candles.

"Nice kitchen," Laverne said. The understatement of the year.

"Thanks." Kimberly leaned over the countertop and inspected the coffeemaker. "I didn't know what I was going to do, and then Troy kept asking for you…" She peered intently at the buttons. "The housekeeper has this set on a timer, but there has to be a way to override that."

"Here," Marnie said, leaning around her and pushing a button. A light went on and the unit made a small hissing noise.

Kimberly reared back and regarded her with admiration. "Well played, Marnie." She patted her arm approvingly. "That was brilliant. Just brilliant." She gestured to them to sit, then went to a cabinet and pulled out three coffee mugs. "I called the camp director back. Her name is Helga. The name says it all I think. They won't even give him Tylenol or aspirin. It's against their policy." She wrinkled her nose in disgust. "I told her I wouldn't be able to pick him up, but that his aunt Marnie would be coming in the morning for him. At first she said she wouldn't release him to anyone but me, and she still kept on and on about how I had to come right away, but when I mentioned my attorney she changed her tune and said as long as it was within twenty-four hours and that you were a relative, it would be fine." She rested her elbows on the table and tapped her chin. "That's why I said you were his aunt. On his father's side. We have to make sure we get our stories straight." She looked back at the counter. "I can't believe it takes this long to brew a pot of coffee. Do you think something is wrong with the machine?"

They all glanced back at the coffeemaker where a steady stream of dark fluid filled the glass carafe. "Nah, it looks like it's working to me," Laverne said. "You just got to be patient."

"I'm not good at patient." Kimberly drummed her fingertips on the tabletop. "I'm better at doing than waiting. I suppose you've heard that." She looked questioningly at Marnie, who didn't know what to say. "I'm sure Brian told you how I fell short in the wife and mother department." The air in the room had somehow gotten thicker. Kimberly's fingers stopped their tapping. "You probably heard the story of how I abandoned my son and moved across the country without any warning at all, but that's not completely true. Yes, I did move and I wasn't as involved in Troy's life as I should have been, but you haven't heard my side of the story. I'm not a terrible person."

There was a sharp-edged silence. Marnie finally said, "Brian never said anything bad about you." Which was true. Of course, when they first met, Brian said his wife had abandoned him, but after that he didn't talk about her much at all except in an admiring way. Of course, Marnie had her own opinion of Kimberly. What kind of mother would opt to live so far away from her child? In her opinion, nothing would excuse it.

"Well," Kimberly said, "that's hard to believe. But good, I guess. I'll take it."

"Look, the coffee's done." Laverne gathered their mugs and went to the coffeemaker, which was still dripping but clearly at the end of the brewing cycle, and set to work filling their cups.

"I moved here because of a business opportunity. The plan was that Brian was going to sell the house and join me. I left Troy with him because I travel so much and I wanted to wait until I was settled in. But somewhere along the line Brian changed the plan and forgot to tell me. He didn't sell the house, and he had no intention of moving, I guess." She took a mug of coffee out of Laverne's hand. "Thank you. That smells good." She set it down in front of her. "The next thing I know, the neighbor calls me and says he's dating someone and she's at the house all the time with Troy. I was crushed."

Shocked, Marnie felt her breath freeze in her chest. How could it be that she'd been the other woman?

Kimberly got up to get a container of creamer and three spoons and set them on the table. "Does anyone need sugar? No? Okay."

Marnie didn't know where to begin. "I had no idea," she said apologetically. "He said his wife abandoned them. I didn't have any reason to think otherwise..."

"I know," Kimberly said, sliding back in her chair. "I know. And here's something else. I asked Brian about it and he said you were the babysitter. And after you moved in, he told me he'd hired a live-in housekeeper. The fact that he wanted a divorce around the same time was entirely coincidental," she added dryly.

"The housekeeper?" Marnie felt her ears burning. "That's what he told you?"

"Your husband told you his live-in girlfriend was the house-keeper and you fell for that?" Laverne said, taking a thin sip of coffee.

Marnie shot her a warning look, afraid that Laverne's habit of saying whatever flew into her head might put them at odds with Kimberly. *Just be nice*, she thought. *Quiet and nice.*

"I know, not very perceptive on my part." Kimberly shrugged. "But Brian could be very persuasive. I did wonder at one point, a few years ago, but when I asked Troy about you, he said you and Brian slept in separate bedrooms."

"It didn't start out that way," Marnie said. "The separate bedrooms, I mean. We started out having a relationship, and then…it just sort of unraveled to nothing." She couldn't think of anything that would back up her version of events. Did the fact that she kept track of Brian's checkbook and wrote out the bills give her a higher status? Did her role as Troy's Marnie make her less of a housekeeper? Looking back, she wasn't entirely sure she wasn't the housekeeper. Although if that were the case, she got short-changed in the money department. Instead, she was compensated by the idea she was part of a family. But even that proved to be false. "I didn't know you were married, though. I mean, I knew, but I thought you'd left him."

"I believe you," Kimberly said. "You were like me—you believed what you were told."

Marnie nodded. She and Kimberly had been pitted against each other, never knowing the truth about the other woman. It was Brian's fault, although she wasn't entirely sure it was conscious on his part. He probably felt abandoned, and Marnie filled the void. After that all of them fell into ruts of circumstance. Superficiality was the best he could do. His whole family was like that. She'd met all of his relatives at weddings and funerals over the years. They were all good with the backslapping and joke-telling, but there was never anything resembling in-depth conversation.

"I only bring this up," Kimberly said, picking up her mug, "because I realize that I froze you out of the funeral. Until Troy set me straight last week, I was still thinking you were the housekeeper." She took a sip of coffee. "Also I wanted to thank you for taking care of Troy for me. You were a good substitute mom."

Marnie found herself choking back indignation. "I didn't do it for you," she said, but before she could say any more Laverne jumped in.

"Marnie was a very good mom to Troy," she said with conviction. Someone who didn't know better would have thought she'd witnessed it firsthand. "She's really missed him a lot since he's been here. It's been killing her."

"I had no idea how much work a teenager can be," Kimberly continued, as if she hadn't even heard them. "I figured he's grown. He doesn't need a babysitter. It's summertime so there's no school. He can get his own food. I know I work long hours, but the housekeeper is here. When he said he was bored, I told him I could sign him up for some activities. I even had my assistant look into some different possibilities, but Troy wouldn't have any of it. At his age I would have loved the opportunity to be bored. He has the whole house, the pool, a computer, TV, movies, video games. But none of it makes him happy. He won't go and call on any of the neighborhood kids. I'm about ready to pull my hair out. I don't have time to entertain him."

"Your trip is for six weeks?" Marnie asked.

"Six weeks, yes. I do this every year. I go to a conference for a week and from there I travel and meet with all my suppliers and vendors. It's nonstop and grueling but essential for my business. When I found this camp I thought I'd be covered, at least for the summer, and I signed him up for six weeks. My thinking was that it would keep him out of trouble, and maybe he'd make some friends. But his getting sick threw a wrench in the works. All my careful planning for nothing." She threw up her hands. "I'm telling you, my dogs are less trouble."

"Well, yeah," Laverne piped in, her hands clasped under her chin. "But they're dogs."

"I have an idea," Marnie said. "Why don't you let me take him back to Wisconsin for the six weeks you're gone? I have the summer off, so I can keep an eye on him."

Kimberly tapped on the tabletop with long manicured nails. "Well, I hate to impose on you, but if you wouldn't mind?" She raised one eyebrow.

"It wouldn't be an imposition," Marnie said firmly. "I'd like nothing better."

Kimberly exhaled. "Well, if you don't mind, that would be wonderful. I can compensate you for the expenses he incurs while he's with you."

"Oh no, that's not necessary," Marnie said. "I want to spend time with him. I've really missed him. He can see his relatives on his dad's side and hang out with his friends. It'll all be good."

"Marnie, *you* are a lifesaver." Kimberly glanced up at the clock and pushed the coffee mug aside. "I know this seems abrupt, and I don't want to be rude, but I have a plane to catch later today, and I'm not even halfway ready. I'll give you the paperwork and the directions to the camp. We can work out the other details later on. Will you call me when you get there so I know you have Troy safe and sound?"

Chapter Forty-Four

As they drove through the gates of Camp Future Leaders of America, Marnie muttered, "I can't believe Brian told people I was his housekeeper. It's just unbelievable."

"It's not unbelievable. You can believe it 'cause it happened," Laverne said, in a tone that indicated she was tired of hearing about it. "But it's over and done with. Time to move on."

"I know it's over, but I'm finding it hard to move on," Marnie said, turning to follow a wooden sign marked "Camp Office." "I feel like a fool."

"Why should you feel like a fool? You didn't do anything wrong! Not only that, but you're the one that's still alive. Seems to me you got the last laugh."

Marnie didn't say anything to that, just continued down the gravel drive to their destination. The administration building was a large structure reminiscent of military barracks.

When they got out of the car, Laverne surveyed the landscape and said, "Kind of pretty, in a tumbleweed sort of way." They didn't see any tumbleweeds, though. What they saw was dirt and plenty of it. The sporadic patchy groundcover looked like it was fighting to stay alive in the midday heat. An enormous brown mound on the horizon was their version of a mountain, Marnie guessed. What a contrast to summer camp in lake-covered Wisconsin. If they could export shade from the Midwest to this part of Nevada, they'd make a fortune. Laverne wiped her forehead. "They sure do keep the heat up in this part of the country."

Stepping inside the building, they were relieved to encounter air-conditioning. Oddly, the inside looked much bigger than she'd expected. A long Formica countertop served as a desk for two women, one of whom was on the phone. The other one, a young woman with a curly ponytail, got up to greet them. Her mint-colored polo shirt had the camp name and logo embroidered on one side. She looked as young and chipper as a college cheerleader. When Marnie identified herself, the woman shook her hand hard. "I'm Helga," she said. "We've been waiting for you."

She studied Kimberly's letter and compared Marnie to the photo on her driver's license, then made several copies of each before returning the license to her. "We have to cover ourselves, legally," she said apologetically.

"Can I see Troy?" Marnie said, trying not to sound too impatient. A frantic feeling rose from her abdomen and she felt like she might crawl out of her skin if they didn't produce him soon. She was ready to fight off anyone who would stand in her way. Luckily, that wasn't necessary.

"Of course. He's in the infirmary," Helga said, and led them down a hallway to a windowless room in back. The door was open, and Marnie saw an older woman sitting at a desk opposite two cots, one of which was occupied. A boy lay on his side, a fleece blanket up past his chin. His eyes were closed, but Marnie instantly knew it was Troy. She moved past Helga, who was now talking to the woman about getting Troy's things ready since he'd be leaving soon. Laverne hovered in the doorway uncertainly, but Marnie didn't care. Troy was here. He was right here.

She stooped down next to him. She reached over and brushed his hair away from his face, like she'd done a thousand times before. His skin felt overly warm and his cheeks were flushed. She knew the camp couldn't give him medication, but did anyone even consider a damp washcloth on his forehead? "Troy?" she said quietly.

His eyelids fluttered and then opened. A sleepy grin crossed his face. "Hey, Marnie," he said. The way he said it could have been any school-day morning at home, back before Brian died.

"Hey, Troy," she said, resting her cool hand on his forehead, wishing she could absorb some of the fever for him. "I heard you're not feeling so good."

"I'm sick. I feel terrible."

"I know, honey. I heard."

His eyes closed again. "I knew you'd come."

Marnie stroked his head. "Yes."

"Why did it take so long for you to get here?" he asked.

Marnie glanced up at Laverne, who was wiping her eyes. She said to Troy, "I came as soon as I could."

"I was waiting," he said, his voice sounding as tired as Marnie felt. She was tired but really couldn't complain. It was a good tired. This moment was worth the effort she'd made to get here—all the hours in the car, getting attacked at the rest stop, the hospital visit, and even having to share a room with Laverne. She'd do it all over again if she had to.

She took her hand off his head. "Are you ready to ditch this place and head for home?"

"Yeah." He raised himself up on one arm and regarded her quizzically. "But which home do you mean?"

"I'm taking you back to Wisconsin. Your mom said you can stay with me for six weeks. What do you say to that?"

He grinned. "Yes, please. I would like that very much."

"Someone taught the boy good manners," Laverne said, winking and giving Marnie a nudge. "Wonder who that could be."

Chapter Forty-Five

Rita lingered at breakfast that morning while the rest of the household bustled around starting their day. Jazzy, who assumed she'd be helping at the restaurant again, had set the alarm and gotten up early to take a shower. Very soon Beth, Mike, Carson, and Jazzy would be leaving to set up lunch at Preston Place. Rita alone had opted to stay behind to wait for Glenn to call her back. They'd last talked yesterday evening, and since then, she couldn't reach him. It was unusual for him not pick up his cell phone. She'd left two messages for him. In a little while, she'd try him at work.

While she sat drinking strong coffee, she heard activity in other parts of the house—footsteps along with the sound of the front door opening and closing as different family members loaded the car with the bins they used for transporting stuff to the restaurant. Beth laundered the dishtowels and aprons for the restaurant at home. She wrote up menus and grocery lists and employee schedules from her laptop in the evening, while Mike sat alongside her paying restaurant bills and ordering supplies like fryer grease on his computer. To Rita, the lines between home and work were too blurred. This was a life she'd never want. Mike and Beth were always on the move, either working or playing. They never sat down and read a book or watched television. She longed for her quiet, peaceful home, her husband reading a book on one end of the couch while she did the same on the other end. Just a few days ago she'd wanted to escape her life; now she was desperate to get it back.

She'd picked up her car from the shop yesterday, and it ran perfectly. Such a relief. It was parked outside now where she could see it through the kitchen window. She longed to put her suitcase in the trunk and just drive off by herself. Without stopping, she could make it home in just short of fourteen hours. Think of that—she could be in Wisconsin by bedtime. Would it be so bad to leave the other women on their own? She'd brought them this far—wasn't that enough? Yes, she had agreed to do the driving to Las Vegas and back, but so much had changed along the way. Perhaps they could rent a car for the drive home.

Seeing Davis again was a shock, much more upsetting than she'd let on. The injustice of having him out in the world walking around while her daughter was dead gnawed at her. And the smug bastard didn't seem repentant at all. Dating a police officer's daughter, no less. He acted as if nothing could touch him. And maybe nothing could. She and Jazzy had hung the flyers, and that felt good, like she was putting him on notice and warning the rest of the community, but what did it mean in the long run? If he wasn't welcome here, he'd move on, she was sure of that. Take his charm and manipulative ways elsewhere. Never paying for what he'd done to Melinda. Never getting punished for ruining all their lives.

Jazzy rushed into the kitchen, towing Carson by his shirt. "Hey, Rita," she said. "Guess what?" Rita hadn't a clue and just looked up at her blankly. "Okay, I'll tell you," Jazzy said, exchanging an excited glance with Carson. "I just talked to Laverne. She and Marnie picked Troy up from camp and they're on their way back here! Isn't that wonderful?"

Rita drained her mug of coffee before answering. "Great news." She tried to sound enthused, but her response was flat. "So Kimberly just let her take Troy?"

"Yep. For the next six weeks anyhow, while she's out of town. Marnie's taking him back to Wisconsin to stay with her."

"That'll make the car pretty crowded, don't you think?" Rita asked.

"We'll figure something out."

"When will they get here?"

"Probably not until tomorrow," Jazzy said. "I mean, it's a really long drive. I'm sure they'll have to stop for the night." Seeing the expression on Rita's face, she said, "But we were planning on being gone this long anyway, right? We'll still return right on schedule; you and I just made a stop on the way."

Carson said gently, "You know you're welcome to stay at our house as long as you need to. My folks are fine with it."

"Yes." Rita swallowed back her disappointment. "Your family has been wonderful, and we certainly appreciate it."

Jazzy came up behind her and looped her arms around her neck. She whispered, "I know you're feeling down, but things will get better, you'll see."

Rita patted her arm and said, "Are you saying that as a psychic, or an eternal optimist?"

"A little of both, I think." Jazzy released her hold and then, pulling back, gave her a look of concern. Rita knew that look. Since Melinda's death, she'd seen it many times. People felt so inadequate when a fellow human being was in emotional pain.

She'd gotten good at consoling friends when their well-meaning attempts to bolster her spirits backfired.

Rita summoned up a small smile. Jazzy meant well. There was no point in making everyone miserable. Even so, when they all set off to the restaurant, she was glad to have the house to herself. To keep busy, she organized her suitcase in preparation for leaving the next day, then went outside and tidied the interior of the car, scooping up candy wrappers and plastic bottles. The back was particularly messy, with potato chip crumbs on the seat and something sticky on one of the windows. She wiped the back windows down with a damp paper towel, the best she could do for the time being. When she got back inside, she cleaned up the breakfast dishes and poured herself another cup of coffee and checked the time. Only thirty minutes had passed. Waiting for Laverne and Marnie to return was going to be torturous.

Rita was vacuuming the living room, pushing the cleaner in straight, even rows, when the doorbell rang. The first time it rang she only paused, not sure what she had heard. The second time confirmed it was indeed the doorbell. She shut off the vacuum and listened. There it was again: the loud chime of a doorbell. She considered letting it go and not answering at all. After all, under normal circumstances no one would be home anyway, but something made her lift the curtain and look. The car in the driveway, a boxy blue thing, didn't look familiar. She couldn't see who was at the door from this angle but they were persistent—the bell kept ringing at regular intervals.

"Yes?" she called through the closed door. "Who is it?"

"Rita? Is that you?"

She fumbled with the lock for what seemed to be an interminable amount of time, and yanked the door open to see Glenn, a bouquet of flowers in hand, a smile on his face.

He'd always had an unusual way of smiling, lips closed, almost sheepish, and that was how he smiled at her now. She once asked him to do it differently. "Show some teeth," she'd suggested. When he complied, she burst out laughing. The toothy smile looked forced and uncomfortable. His natural smile was more him somehow.

Rita stared at him in disbelief. "Aren't you going to invite me in?" he asked.

She stepped out and threw her arms around him, crushing the flowers, letting the warm air into the house and the air-conditioned air out into the world and not caring at all about Beth and Mike's electric bill. "I have never been more happy to see you in my entire life," she said.

She kissed his cheek and his ear and his neck, until he said, "All right now, I get the picture. I'm glad to see you too." Such a dear man.

Finally, she let him inside, where he presented her with the flowers, still fragrant and colorful, if not quite as perky as they'd been a few minutes before. She held them across one arm and admired them before setting them on the kitchen table. "Whatever are you doing here?" she asked, leaning against the counter.

"You want me to go?" he teased.

"Heavens no!"

He put his arm around her shoulder, the way he used to do when they were dating. "I heard it in your voice on the phone— you sounded so lost. I knew you needed me. So I called work and told them I had to take a few days off for a family emergency, hopped on a plane, rented a car, and found my way here. I saw the Crown Victoria outside, so I kept ringing that doorbell. My next stop was going to be the restaurant."

"So you came for me?" Rita was touched and relieved. Part of her had feared the worst.

"Of course. Why else?"

"I was afraid you came to kill Davis."

"I'd like to, believe me." He looked down at the floor and took a deep breath before meeting her eyes.

"Did you want to go see him and talk to him yourself?" she asked quietly. "I know where he lives."

He cleared his throat. "It's tempting, but honestly—I don't know what it would accomplish at this point. Not to mention I'm afraid of what I might do to him. I would like to end him." His voice was crisp now. "But we already lost a daughter. I'm not going to prison on his account."

Glenn was serious, she knew. Since Melinda's murder they'd experienced everything from soul-sucking fatigue to uncontrollable rage. Counseling had helped them confront the pain and manage their anger, but it still crept up on occasion. Maybe it always would.

He looked around and broke the silence. "Where are your friends?"

"Marnie and Laverne aren't back from Las Vegas yet, and Jazzy is at the restaurant with Mike and Beth and their son. There's kind of a romance going on between Jazzy and Carson. It's really sweet to see."

"Do you think they'd mind if I stole you away?"

"What did you have in mind?"

He leaned in and whispered in her ear. "The house is lonely without you, Rita. Really lonely. And you sounded like you've had enough. Why don't you just come home with me?" When she started to object, he put a finger to her lips. "Hear me out, first. I know you don't want to leave your friends in the lurch, so my thought was we could leave them the car, and you can fly home with me. When they get back, we can make arrangements to pick it up."

"You'd let them drive the Crown Victoria?" Rita asked in surprised delight. "But that's your pride and joy."

"Ahem," Glenn said. "A little correction—you happen to be my pride and joy. The Crown Victoria is just the best car I've ever had, but it's insured and replaceable. Not that I want to replace it," he added hastily. "I'm just making the distinction."

— — —

Rita led the way into Preston Place, eager to introduce Glenn to Jazzy and the Kent family. The restaurant wasn't open yet, but the front door was unlocked, so they let themselves in. Beth stood on a chair, writing the specials on a whiteboard. Jazzy and Carson were in the process of rearranging tables, pushing and pulling four-tops so that they lined up to make one long banquet table. All three stopped what they were doing when the door slammed shut behind Glenn. Jazzy looked up surprised, and blurted out, "*Glenn is here?*" in such an incredulous way that Rita had to laugh. Beth got down from the chair and wiped her hands on her apron before coming over to say hello.

"This is my husband, Glenn," Rita said. Carson shook his hand and Jazzy gave him a big hug like he was an old friend.

"Have we met?" Glenn asked Jazzy.

"No, but I recognized you from pictures and from how Rita described you." She stepped back and sized them up. "You two match."

"I hope so," Glenn said. "We come as a set."

Mike came out of the kitchen to see what the commotion was, and Glenn greeted him warmly with the kind of backslapping only men could get away with. "Thanks for saving the ladies when the car broke down. You're a good man."

The group chatted for a few minutes, Glenn describing how empty the house was in Rita's absence ("Cripes, the ticking of the clock was driving me crazy.") and how he impulsively booked an early flight and came right away. "I hope you don't mind," he said, "but I'm stealing her back. I need her."

Rita had never heard him speak with such devotion. Apparently absence *did* make the heart grow fonder. He reached over and rested his hand on the small of her back. She wondered at how she could have taken his love for granted in recent years. When you pared away the stuff of life—the obligations, the irritations, the illnesses, and pain—this connection, this love, was all that really mattered. It was trite, a platitude cross-stitched and framed in the gift shop at Cracker Barrel, but that didn't make it any less true. She saw the way Carson looked at Jazzy and thought, *They're so enthralled with each other, they have no idea all that lies ahead.* Maybe it was best that way.

"You're stealing my Rita away?" Jazzy wailed theatrically, putting the back of her hand to her forehead. "All of my friends are abandoning me."

"Poor baby," Rita said.

Glenn explained that they planned to fly home and leave the car so the others could use it to get back to Wisconsin. "We can work out the logistics of getting the car back when you return," he said to Jazzy.

Carson stepped forward. "I don't want to goof up your plan," he said, "but I have another idea." They all waited attentively while he collected his thoughts. "Why don't you just go ahead and take your car? I'll take responsibility for getting the ladies home." He made a sweeping, gallant gesture with one hand.

Jazzy gave him a pointed look. "That's very nice of you, Carson," she said. "But the *ladies* can get themselves home, thank you very much."

His face went slack. "I didn't mean to offend anyone," he said, backpedalling. "Just wanted to help."

"I know," she said, her voice softer. "But we're very capable. We got here on our own, and we can get back the same way."

The group nodded in agreement, nobody pointing out that technically they didn't get there on their own, since the car broke down and they had to be saved. No one mentioned that the ladies would have been completely sunk if not for the motorcyclists coming to the rescue.

"We'd have to take the rental car back," Glenn said, "but that's not a big deal." He nudged Rita. "What do you think? I'm game."

"You really don't mind if I go?" Rita asked Jazzy, getting a sudden surge of guilt. She knew she wouldn't like it if one of the other women changed the plan and left her in a bind. And the timing wasn't the best now that Marnie would have the boy with her. Still, with Glenn here, the thought of getting in the car and just driving home was appealing.

"Of *course* I don't mind," Jazzy said. "I took a look at Marnie's wallet. She's got like four credit cards. We can rent a car as easily as anything. There's no point in you sticking around here." She made a shooing gesture. "Get out of here, lady. Why are you still hanging around?"

Chapter Forty-Six

Marnie still felt under the influence, so she didn't argue when Laverne said she'd take the first shift for the drive back. Before they took off, Laverne rooted through her Ziploc bag and found some over-the-counter medication to bring Troy's fever down, and more pain medication for Marnie. Then she popped something in her own mouth. She called it a "pick-me-up."

Marnie, once disapproving of Laverne's pharmacy, now felt something more like gratitude. Really, who was she to judge? Maybe doctors in the United States were too strict about medication anyway. Whatever worked was her new philosophy. At least for the time being.

Troy took the left side of the backseat, curling up and resting his head on a pillow the camp had sent along with him. Marnie was on the other side—just an arm's reach away, but close enough to check on him. Having both of them in the back was Laverne's idea. They'd be out of the sun for the most part. The GPS told them it was a twelve-hour drive back to Mike and Beth's house. The thought of twelve more hours in the car was almost more than Marnie could bear. But they needed to keep going. In her mind, the interstate was the yellow brick road, and Wisconsin, the Emerald City.

For someone who hadn't driven in a long while before that morning, Laverne drove smoothly. Marnie relaxed once they made it to the freeway. There was something soothing about the hum of a car moving at top speed.

"Marnie?" Troy said, his voice slightly muffled by the pillow.

"Yes, Troy?"

"I miss my dad."

This was not what she expected to hear. He missed Brian? Brian, who kept everyone at arm's length? Brian the workaholic? She drew in a breath before answering. "What do you miss the most, hon?"

"Everything really." Troy sounded like he was holding back tears, which made her want to cry herself. "He always had good advice if I had a problem. He never got mad like some dads. He always said, 'Just do your best.' And when I got good grades he'd say, 'That's the way to do it!'"

True enough, she thought.

"And remember how he always loved your cooking? He'd always eat like three helpings of your roasted vegetables. He said you made the best vegetables in the world."

"Yes, he loved my roasted vegetables."

"We were so happy," Troy said miserably. "No one ever yelled or argued at our house. You and Dad always got along. I could do what I wanted."

"Was there yelling at your mom's house?" Marnie asked.

"There was nothing at my mom's house," he said, getting more upset with every word. "I'm not talking about my mom. I'm saying I miss Dad and how things were at *our* house." He turned his head toward her for just a second and she saw him blink away tears.

"Okay, I'm sorry I interrupted," she said. "I should have let you talk."

"I just miss my dad is all," he said, and settled back into the pillow sniffing.

Memories came flooding back to Marnie. Brian in the kitchen, lifting lids from pans on the stovetop in anticipation of a good meal. Brian writing checks for charities at Christmastime. Brian reorganizing the garage. None of it benefitted her, but she saw now that even with all his faults, Brian had good qualities. He was a decent man, a reliable guy, and apparently a good-enough dad to Troy. She'd been too busy feeling shortchanged to acknowledge the loss. "I know you miss your dad," she said. "I'm sorry that you're having such a hard time, Troy."

"I missed you and all my friends too. My mom said I shouldn't bother you. She said you probably had another job with another family." His voice quavered. "She thought you were a house-keeper."

"I know. There was a misunderstanding."

"When you called I was really mad at you."

"I could tell."

"You didn't even try to stop my mom from taking me to Las Vegas," he said. "I kept waiting for you to say something, but you never did. And you could have, if you wanted to."

"It wasn't really up to me," Marnie said. "But you're right. I should have tried harder."

He drew in a big breath. "I'm not mad at you anymore."

"That's good," Marnie said. "When we get back, you'll have to give Matt a call so you guys can get together. What do you think?"

"Okay." He shifted and stretched so that his legs pushed against her, but she didn't object.

"Get some sleep, Troy. It's going to be a long drive."

— — —

On the expressway a few states away, the Crown Vic headed eastward with Glenn at the wheel and Rita next to him, enjoying the view. "It's so nice to have someone else do the driving," she said.

"Does that mean you're not going to take a turn?" he asked.

"Oh no, I'll definitely do my part. It's just nice not to have to do all of it."

"So, are you sorry you went?" Glenn faced forward. The road ahead had his full visual attention, but his hearing, Rita knew, was tuned in for her response.

"No, I'm not sorry I went, but I'm not sure it accomplished anything."

"Was it supposed to? Accomplish something, I mean?"

"I thought it might." Rita fiddled with the sun visor, putting it up, then thinking better of it and lowering it again. "At first it was an adventure. I thought I'd help Marnie out in visiting with her stepson. And then it was exciting when the deer surrounded Jazzy at the rest stop. I was so happy to know she got a message from Melinda." She stole a look in his direction to get his reaction, but his face was still. "I know you're skeptical, but I could *feel* her. I was so hopeful that something miraculous would happen. But then the car broke down and it was stressful. And then seeing Davis dredged up all kinds of terrible feelings." She thought of herself as a peaceful person, but the sight of Davis caused something deep and dark to come to the surface. If she'd had a gun in her hands, she'd have pulled the trigger and killed him right in the parking lot. "All kinds of terrible feelings. I almost think it would have been better if I'd never seen him at all. To know for certain that he's out there…" She shuddered. "Officer Dietz said she'd have him questioned, but that if he denied knowing anything, there wasn't much else they could do. Since I haven't heard anything, I'm assuming that's what happened." Just talking about it brought back feelings of sadness. She turned on the radio, looking for a good song, but after a minute of trying and not finding one, she lost interest and shut it off.

In the silence that followed, Glenn spoke up. "I know you wanted more out of this trip than you got, but from my perspective, I think it's good you went," he said matter-of-factly.

"You do?"

"Sure," he said. "It took you out of your comfort zone. You made some new friends and had some new experiences."

"Did I ever," she said, a bit glumly.

"And it gave you the opportunity to miss me."

Rita gave him a smile.

"And just look how it ended up," he said, drumming his fingertips against the steering wheel. "Here I am on a weekday afternoon driving with my sweetheart instead of sitting at a desk. Tonight we'll stop somewhere for a nice dinner, and then we'll stay at a nice hotel." He smirked. "And you know I always get lucky at hotels."

She laughed. "Well, we'll see about that." But there really wasn't any question about it. He always did get lucky at hotels.

Chapter Forty-Seven

Jazzy decided to take charge of the last leg of the trip. She knew Marnie and Laverne would be rolling into Colorado in the wee hours of the morning, way too late to show up at Mike and Beth's house. She came up with an alternate plan, but since she knew Marnie would never go for it, all the scheming had to be done through Laverne.

While the trio was at a rest stop in Utah—Marnie busy in the bathroom, and Troy getting Doritos from a vending machine, Laverne and Jazzy plotted over the phone.

"Here's the deal," Jazzy said. "Rita's husband flew in earlier today, and the two of them took the car and drove back to Wisconsin. She didn't abandon us. I told her she should go," she added, just to clarify. "She really wanted to go home, so I said we'd manage on our own."

"So how're we going to do that?"

Jazzy could picture the way Laverne's face scrunched up when she was puzzled. The thought made her smile. "I'm making an executive decision," Jazzy said. "This is what we'll do. You meet me at the Marriott hotel near the Denver airport. You can find it using the GPS. We'll all stay there tonight and fly out tomorrow. I checked and there are flights available. Hopefully they'll still be available when we're ready to book them."

"So we're not driving back?"

Her voice was so incredulous that Jazzy almost laughed out loud. "Nope, we're flying home. My brother said he can pick us up from the airport."

Laverne said, "Well, isn't that something! I've never been on a plane before, you know."

"I figured as much."

"I don't know if Marnie is going to go for it though. You know she's got that thing—that fear of flying."

"I know," Jazzy said. "But it's going to be fine. Trust me."

— — —

Several hours later, Jazzy and Carson sat on a couch in the lobby of the Marriott, waiting for the other three to arrive. Jazzy had already booked two rooms and left her suitcase in one of them. Beth and Mike had dropped them off at the hotel; the plan was that Carson would pick up his car from the ladies and say his good-bye from there, but he didn't seem too eager for that to happen.

"I can't believe you're going back tomorrow," he said forlornly, resting his arm on the back of the couch behind her shoulders. He was respectful, almost shy, surprising since they'd had a pretty intense make-out session at his parents' house. But this was the lobby of a Marriott hotel, within earshot and eyesight of the two employees at the front desk and anyone who walked through the front door. So he held back. "I just found you and now you're leaving."

Jazzy felt it too, a kind of magnetic pull that would make it hard for them to be apart. Strange that they'd known each other for such a short period of time and she'd already memorized the angles of his face, the shape of his beautiful ears, the way he could speak volumes with his hands, his lopsided grin. They'd talked for hours, and he'd shared so much about himself, but she wanted to know more. There were stories from childhood right up through college left unsaid. Maybe she'd never know it all, but she'd know more as time went by. She was looking forward to that. "I *am* going back tomorrow," she said. "So believe it. I have to get back to work, and I have a few other details to arrange. But don't worry, we'll be in touch."

Truthfully, Jazzy wanted nothing more than to stay in Colorado for the rest of the summer, but she sensed that she needed to pull back. There would be time for this relationship to unfold. Plenty of time.

"What kind of details are we talking about?" Carson asked, moving in his lips close to her ear. "Anything involving me?"

"It might involve you eventually," Jazzy said, suppressing a smile. "But for now I have to talk to a woman about a job."

Chapter Forty-Eight

At the rest stop, Marnie decided to let Troy stretch and sleep in the backseat, so she moved to the front passenger seat for the duration of the trip. She was dozing when the car finally stopped; the sound of the GPS saying "Arriving at destination" jarred her awake. She'd been under the impression that they were going to return to Beth and Mike's, so she was startled to see they were in the parking lot of a hotel.

"Are we there?" Troy asked from his nest in the back.

"We're here," Laverne said brightly, reaching over Marnie's lap to put the GPS unit in the glove compartment.

"Where are we?" Marnie said, looking around. "Why are you stopping here?" She twisted her head from side to side while rubbing at a spot on the back of her neck.

"Change of plan," Laverne said. "We're staying in a hotel. Jazzy is meeting us here."

Despite Marnie's questions, Laverne wouldn't say any more on the subject, instead telling her Jazzy would explain it all. "She's in the lobby waiting for us," she said.

Even though Laverne had done most of the driving, Marnie was exhausted. Walking felt like moving through a whirlpool, and she was sure she looked like hell. A hot shower and a hotel bed might be just the thing.

Troy perked up considerably, especially since less than twenty-four hours before he'd been languishing on a camp cot. He ran to the hotel entryway to get a luggage cart and helped Laverne empty the trunk. Marnie, meanwhile, stood idly by, wanting to help but feeling like the walking dead.

The feeling stayed with her even when they met Jazzy and Carson in the lobby and as they made their way up to their adjoining rooms. Jazzy said, "I thought Laverne and I would share one room, and you and Troy would have the other one."

When the elevator stopped on their floor, Marnie came out of her mental fog long enough to realize someone was missing. "Where's Rita?" she asked Jazzy as they pulled their suitcases down the hall with Troy following happily behind. With his large backpack slung over one shoulder and a duffel bag dangling off one arm, he looked like an escapee from a Boy Scout overnight.

"Yeah, about Rita," Jazzy said, hedging for just a moment. "She went home."

"She went home!" Marnie said. "What do you mean, she went home? With her car?"

"No need to panic," Jazzy said, handing her a key card. They'd arrived at their rooms. "Her husband flew here and they did drive the Crown Vic home, but I told them to. I said that we'd figure out another way home."

Marnie held the card but made no effort to open the door. "Well, isn't that wonderful. I can't believe she left us without a way to get home."

"Oh, we'll get home all right," Laverne piped up. "Jazzy has a plan, and it's a doozy." She spoke to Troy. "I know this isn't a big deal for you kids today, but this old lady has never been on a plane before and I'm pretty excited about it."

"Oh no." Marnie's heart was racing just thinking about it. "I don't fly. I hate flying. I did it one time and it was terrible."

Down the hall, a doorway opened and a man stuck his head out. "Could you people keep it down? Some of us are trying to sleep."

"Sorry." Jazzy gave an apologetic wave, then said to Marnie, "Let's continue this conversation inside."

Marnie knew she wasn't going to feel any less panicky inside the room, but once she was on the other side of the door, she realized there was something comforting about being in a hotel room. After so many hours in the car, the beds and bathroom looked inviting. Laverne made a beeline for the bathroom on her side, while Troy grabbed the remote, claimed a bed, and immediately began flipping through channels. Jazzy took this opportunity to give Marnie the lowdown. Rita was gone, she said, and so was her car. They now had two options: they could rent a car or fly home. "I know you're afraid," she said, "but it's a very short flight and we're all tired of driving."

"I'm tired of driving too. I say we fly," Troy chimed in, although no one had asked him.

Jazzy said, "I just checked and there are still openings on flights tomorrow morning. We can be home in no time."

"It's not that I'm afraid," Marnie said, trying to think of how to explain the enormity of the problem. "If it was just that, I could do it, no problem. It's that my body goes crazy. Even thinking about it makes me nuts. I know if I get on a flight, I won't be able to breathe, my heart will start beating out of control, and I'll get sick to my stomach." She remembered the one and only time she'd flown. She was a teenager, excited to go on a class trip to Orlando. On the flight there she was fine, but on the way back they'd encountered horrible turbulence, the plane lurching so severely that several of the girls screamed. The pilot came on the speaker to reassure them that everything was fine, and the class chaperone, Mrs. Garneau, had shouted out that this was just like a bus ride going over bumps. The difference being, Marnie had thought at the time, that buses don't fall out of the sky. The turbulence had gone on for at least half an hour. Despite her best efforts, she'd thrown up into the little bag the airplane provided for that purpose. She was glad to have made it into the bag (and actually proud of herself for having remembered it was in the pocket in the seat in front of her), but it was still horrifying. Worst of all, she had to sit with her bag of vomit until the flight attendant came by fifteen minutes later and took it from her, holding it away from her body like it was a dead rodent. Her classmates talked about the incident for years. As recently as six months ago, a former friend had mentioned it when they bumped into each other at the mall. (*Hey, remember when you got sick on the plane ride home from Orlando? That turbulence was killer!*) She had vowed she'd never fly again.

"None of those things will happen this time around," Jazzy said. "I promise you with complete certainty that you'll be fine."

Marnie said, "I know you're psychic and you know things, but I also know myself. There's no way I'm going to be fine." She cast a longing glance at the empty bed. All she wanted to do was sleep. "Look, I don't want to debate this with you, Jazzy. If you and Laverne want to fly home, feel free. I'll figure something out."

But Jazzy wasn't about to let it drop. "Just hear me out, Marnie, just for one more minute, and then I'll leave you be. We don't have to decide anything until tomorrow, but would you at least consider it?" Before Marnie could answer she plowed ahead. "You're making a decision based on how you used to be, but that's not you anymore!" She was becoming impassioned. "Two weeks ago your index card was blank. You didn't want to share a day brightener with a bunch of women at the rec center. And now, you've driven across the country with three complete strangers, confronted Kimberly, and taken charge of Troy. You're not the woman I met not that long ago."

Marnie sighed. "Your point being?"

"Look," Jazzy said. "No one can force you to do something you don't want to do, but would you at least think about the *possibility* of flying home?"

She'd promise anything to finish this conversation so she could wash up, brush her teeth, and crawl between the sheets. "Okay, I'll think about it," she said. Jazzy looked triumphant, but Marnie knew they were only words.

Chapter Forty-Nine

The next morning after a stay in a hotel and a nice breakfast, Glenn and Rita were driving through Iowa when her purse blasted with the sound of Beethoven's Fifth Symphony. She pulled the phone out and put it up to her ear. "Hello?"

It was Judy Dietz on the line. She said, "Rita, I'm afraid I've got bad news."

Rita listened intently, then answered, "Oh my." Glenn glanced over as he changed lanes, and she held up one finger to indicate he'd know soon enough.

When Judy was done giving her the news, Rita thanked her for calling and added, "Please let us know if you hear anything else." After saying good-bye, she rested the phone on her lap for a moment and stared out the window, processing the news. The sight of the Iowa cornfields was soothing in their predictability and sameness.

"What was that all about?" Glenn finally asked.

Rita sighed and put the phone back in her purse before answering. "That was Judy Dietz. You remember me telling you about Officer Dietz, the one who's daughter, Sophie, was living with Davis?"

"What happened?"

Rita couldn't get the words out to tell him the whole story—how Davis had been smooth and confident in his denial of having anything to do with Melinda's death. How Sophie Dietz had confronted Davis with a copy of the poster once he'd returned to their apartment, and how things had escalated into a big screaming match. And the aftermath—how he had fled, like the coward he was, leaving Sophie heartbroken. Rita would tell Glenn the details later, but for now she simply said, "Davis never admitted to anything, but he took off and they're not sure where he is right now. He's just gone."

"Really." Glenn's voice was even.

"I guess it's good that Judy's daughter is out of danger," she said, trying to look on the bright side.

"That's something, anyway." But they both knew it wasn't enough.

"I'm glad I'm with you," she said, her eyes filling with tears. "Because no one else could understand what I'm feeling right now."

"I love you, Rita. We'll get through this," he said, which was exactly what she wanted to hear.

Chapter Fifty

Marnie was at the airport, her boarding pass in hand, still not entirely sure how it happened that she'd been talked into going on this flight. The night before she'd slept soundly enough, waking in the morning to see Troy in front of the window, one hand holding the curtain aside, the other pressed against the glass. She fumbled for her glasses on the nightstand and put them on, blinking from the light. When her eyes adjusted, she saw he was staring at something down below. "What are you looking at?" she asked, half wondering if he was admiring the mountains.

Troy answered, "There's a guy down there with a dog on a leash and he's letting the dog crap right in the parking lot. Geez."

She smiled, so glad to have him back. It put her in a good mood. Between that and the solid night's sleep she found it easy to swing into action, getting herself and her suitcase ready to go in record time. Troy watched TV while she bustled around. Laverne and Jazzy were doing the same in the adjoining room, and they planned to go downstairs to eat breakfast and have a talk. At that point, Marnie was entirely sure that there was nothing that could convince her to board a plane. She'd have bet every dollar she had in savings, which was a considerable amount, since she'd banked most of her paycheck for a decade.

All through breakfast, she was firm in her decision, even to the point of thinking she and Troy would take the airport shuttle with Jazzy and Laverne, to rent a car there. Somehow, though, before she even finished her coffee, they tag-teamed her. Jazzy started up again about how Marnie had evolved as a person. "It's like you were here," she said, pointing to one edge of the table, "and now you're over here." She slid her finger all the way to the other side.

While Marnie was trying to figure out what that meant, Laverne started yammering about how she'd never flown before and how she couldn't wait. "I can't believe we'll get there in only two hours. Imagine that. Two hours!"

Both of them asked her to reconsider, and she felt herself getting angrier and angrier that they wouldn't drop it. She was just about to snap when Troy said, "Marnie, couldn't you just give it a try? It's really not such a big deal."

Poor boy did not realize that there was no such thing as giving it a try. Once the plane was in the air, she'd be stuck. "It's not that I don't want to, Troy," she said, starting to explain, but then stopped when she saw the sweet, serious expression on his face.

Troy looked at her intently. "I'll be right next to you the whole time." And then he said the thing that made her falter. "You can hug me if you get scared. I'm going to be there. You know I won't let you down."

She was losing her resolve and everyone at the table knew it. When Laverne pulled the Ziploc out of her purse and said, "I got just the thing to help you relax. You take one of these and you won't even care where you are," Marnie knew it was all over.

Against her will, she'd been swept along in a current of persuasion.

Now she sat in a plastic molded seat in the airport, nervously fanning herself with her boarding pass. Oh why had she agreed to do this? And why had Jazzy been so insistent she fly? Laverne and Jazzy could have flown without her. It wasn't like her presence was necessary. She felt her nervousness ratcheting up a notch; she swallowed a lump of worry. Just when she was afraid of launching into a full-blown panic attack, Troy appeared at her side, back from buying a Snickers bar at the newsstand. "I checked the board and our flight is right on time," he said joyfully, oblivious to her pain. And just when she'd been thinking how self-absorbed teenagers were, he ripped open the wrapper and offered her some. When she shook her head, he proceeded to polish it off in four bites.

They'd checked all their luggage, including her cooler, another reason she couldn't back out of the flight. In retrospect, she wondered if Jazzy had encouraged that decision on purpose. "Let's just check it all," she'd said. "Then we don't have to fuss with getting it into the overhead bins." Everyone sitting around Marnie seemed to have carry-on suitcases, duffel bags, and laptops. Her purse somehow seemed like not enough.

Across the aisle, Laverne and Jazzy sat side by side, leafing through entertainment magazines. If Marnie didn't know better, she'd have thought Laverne was Jazzy's grandmother. They sat apart because they hadn't been able to find four seats together, a problem that would follow them on the plane where they would all be separated. Troy and Marnie would sit closest. They were at least in the same three-person row. Unfortunately, there was someone else in the middle. "I'm sure that person will let you switch," Jazzy said. "No one wants to sit in the middle anyhow."

Marnie hoped so. She'd just taken the anti-anxiety medication Laverne had foisted on her, and was hoping it would help. She was counting on Troy to bring her comfort in the event she had a meltdown. She knew it was a lot to expect from a teenage boy, but she thought he was up to the job. Besides, he'd offered.

When they announced that the plane was boarding, Marnie quelled her doubts by concentrating on Troy. She shifted into stepmom mode, shepherding him into line and telling him to get out his boarding pass. "Can I see Matt as soon as we get home?" he asked while they were still in line.

She couldn't see past the next ten minutes, but to make him happy, she answered, "Yes, of course."

Down the ramp and into the plane, she repeated a sentence in her mind: *It's just for two hours. It's just for two hours. It's just for two hours.* To distract herself even further she did mental arithmetic, calculating what percentage two hours was in the course of a day, a week, a month, a lifetime (assuming her lifetime was seventy-five years). Ahead of her, Jazzy and Laverne made their way into seats in the back of the plane. Jazzy's laughter floated forward in the cabin. Marnie found their assigned spots in a row of three seats, midway in the plane. Troy scooted into place next to the window; she was supposed to be on the aisle, but she took the middle one instead, telling Troy, "When that person comes I'll explain that we're together."

As the other passengers settled into their seats, Marnie felt a wave of mellowness wash over her, dulling the edges of her anxiety. Laverne's drug was kicking in. She imagined it working its way from her stomach into her bloodstream and traveling through her body, relaxing every muscle and soothing her ragged nerves. It made her feel a little numb, but that was preferable to raw, bone-grinding fear. She looked at the ceiling of the plane and said a prayer of thanks for the invention of whatever it was making her feel better. She closed her eyes and muttered, "Thank you, God."

A male flight attendant walked through, closing the flaps of the overhead bins, checking to see that seat belts were fastened. Troy kept his eye on the window, watching the luggage handlers as they unloaded another plane. He'd flown many times with his dad, but the novelty hadn't worn off.

Just when Marnie thought her adjacent seat would remain empty, a young man wearing a tan baseball cap came down the aisle and stopped in front of her row. He reached up and shoved a carry-on bag into the overhead bin; all the while Marnie only had a view of his trim midsection. She looked discreetly away. Now she heard the solid sound of the passenger door shutting in the front of the plane. Without Laverne's medication she'd be in complete panic mode right about now. Thank God for modern chemistry.

The young man slammed the bin shut and slid into the aisle seat. Marnie turned to explain about the seat change. "I'm in your seat," she started, and then, recognizing him, stopped talking, shocked.

"It's okay," he said. "I like the aisle." He stretched his legs forward and put his head back, lowering his baseball cap over his eyes. His arm rested on what should have been her armrest. She pulled away, not wanting to touch him.

In disbelief Marnie stared, and blinked, and stared some more. There could be no mistake, it was Davis Diamontopoulos. And he hadn't recognized her from the encounter in the restaurant parking lot. Her fear of takeoff was momentarily forgotten, replaced by the knowledge and horror that she was sitting next to a murderer. She looked around, unsure what to do with this information. Over the loudspeaker, a woman's voice asked them to read along with the pamphlet in the pocket in the seat in front of them. Troy nudged her, and she glanced over to see him holding an instruction sheet. He said, "Dad always made me pay attention to this, just in case."

Marnie nodded. The words *just in case* applied to emergency landings, but no one had ever prepared her for what to do if she was stuck sitting next to a killer on a plane. She had only a vague awareness of what was going on in the rest of the plane in the next fifteen minutes: the announcements, the takeoff, Troy putting in his earbuds when given the okay to start up electronic devices. She felt the skin on her left arm crawl, even though she wasn't actually touching Davis. The rest of the passengers proceeded with their business, unaware there was a killer in their midst. *What to do? What to do?* It wasn't like she could inform the authorities. He wasn't wanted by the law. But she couldn't stop looking at his hands resting loosely on the armrests. Those same hands had strangled Rita's daughter. *Someone should cut those hands off*, she thought, and was immediately horrified that something so vile had even entered her head.

She had to tell someone he was here. When the light for the seat belts went off, signifying passengers could move around the cabin, she got Troy's attention and told him she was going to the bathroom. "Excuse me," she said, bending her body in an awkward way to get past Davis. He didn't even try to get up to let her pass, but brought his legs in.

Marnie made her way down the aisle toward the back of the plane and stopped when she saw Jazzy, in the middle of a row on the left. "Jazzy," she hissed. "I need to talk to you."

Jazzy looked up from her magazine. "Now?"

"Now." Marnie motioned to the back and then kept walking until she reached the line for the bathroom.

"How are you doing?" Jazzy asked, coming up behind her.

Marnie spoke through gritted teeth. "I am sitting next to Davis Diamontopoulos." She waited a moment for it to sink in, but Jazzy didn't look shocked. "The man who killed Rita's daughter," she said. Oddly enough, Jazzy only nodded in response. Somehow Marnie had expected a bigger reaction. "I think we need to tell someone."

"Well, okay, sure, if you think so." Jazzy looked around. "Who did you want to tell?"

"I don't know," Marnie said, exasperated. "You're the one who knows things. I'm asking you what we should do."

"I can call Rita or Judy as soon as we land," Jazzy said calmly. "There's not too much we can do when the plane is in the air."

True enough, but that wasn't what Marnie wanted to hear. The line inched forward and an elderly gray-haired woman came out of the bathroom and pushed past them, the scent of floral perfume trailing in her wake. Marnie said, "I'm just creeped out sitting next to him." An involuntary shudder came over her.

Jazzy gave her arm a reassuring squeeze. "Do you want me to switch seats with you?" she asked. "Because I will."

"No, that's not the answer," Marnie said, and then remembering she'd left Troy alone with Davis, she turned around and headed back without even wrapping up the conversation. She maneuvered past a young woman carrying a toddler and waited to let a heavy-set man with a cane get by. The plane had been in the air for only a short time, yet everyone, it seemed, needed to visit the restroom. When she got back to her seat, she was alarmed to see Davis had moved. He was now sitting in her seat talking to Troy.

"Ahem," she said. When the two looked up, she saw that Davis was showing Troy something on some electrical device.

"Hey, Marnie," Troy said, gesturing enthusiastically. "He's got the thing I was telling you about. The—"

"Could you move, please," Marnie said, pointing. "I'd like to sit down next to my son." She knew she sounded rude, but she didn't care. Laverne's medication made her fearless.

"Hey!" Troy said, protesting Marnie's bad manners, but Davis didn't flinch, just got up and moved out of the row, allowing Marnie to get back to the center seat.

"You didn't have to be that way," Troy said, when she'd settled back in, clicking her seat belt and reclining her seat.

"I'll explain later," she said.

Troy gave her a grumpy look and then put his earbuds back in and turned his gaze toward the window. Someday he'd understand that she was only trying to protect him. Right now he wasn't seeing the big picture.

Marnie managed to keep her face tilted away from Davis for the next half hour, but when the drink cart came through, she had to turn in that direction to place their orders: a Coke for Troy, and a diet Sprite for herself. She looked past Davis as the attendant poured the soft drinks out of cans into wide-mouthed plastic cups. Marnie took Troy's drink and set it on his tray; when she turned back, Davis had her drink in hand and was offering it to her. "Special delivery," he said. She took it without saying a word.

After they'd finished their drinks and the flight attendant collected their empty cups, Davis turned to her and said, "You have a problem with me, don't you?"

She didn't respond.

"I wasn't doing anything to the boy," he said. "Honest, I'm a good guy."

Marnie couldn't help herself. "That's not the way I hear it." She said it between clenched teeth, but she knew he heard.

"What did you say?" He tilted his head toward her, getting way too close for comfort.

"Nothing."

"No, you said something. What was it?"

His mouth was so close she got a whiff of breath mint. "Never mind," she said.

Davis sat back in satisfaction. "If you've got something to say to me, best to say it to my face. Or not at all."

Marnie was going to let it go until she saw the smug look on his face. She sat up straight and spoke loudly. "You said you were a good guy, and I said, 'That's not the way I hear it.'"

"Oh yeah, what do you hear?"

"I hear that you're a murderer." The words came out as rapidly as machine-gun fire.

"What?"

"A murderer. That's what you are."

He tipped his baseball cap back and gave her a wide-eyed look. "Lady, I don't know what you've been smoking, but I think you've got me confused with someone else."

"You killed Rita's daughter, Melinda." She struggled to keep her voice steady. "You strangled her with her own scarf and then left her in the car like a coward."

"Not true," he said, but she could tell a nerve had been struck. Both of his hands curled up in fists, like he was trying to hold back.

She should have let it go, but she didn't. "Murderer."

"Stop it. That's enough!" he yelled, startling Troy, who took out his earbuds and clutched at her arm. Around them, people stopped talking. "Who put you up to this?" Davis's face flushed red. "Who's saying these things?"

"Marnie, what is it?" Troy asked, clearly afraid.

"It's okay, hon, don't worry about it," she said, shielding him with her body.

"You have a lot of nerve," Davis said loudly. "You don't even know what you're talking about."

Troy wouldn't let go of Marnie's shirt. "What's going on?" he said.

Marnie turned away from Davis and said, "There's nothing to worry about. This man killed a friend's daughter, and I—"

"Bitch!" Davis screamed, jumping out of his seat. He stood over her, slapping her across her head and shoulders, blows raining down from above.

She ducked down, crying out in pain and trying to get away but trapped by the narrowness of the row and her seat belt. He landed a blow against her head that was so hard, she felt her brain snap against her skull; entire constellations glistened behind her eyes. Before she could recover, his hands went around her neck and she felt the unbearable pain of her windpipe being compressed. Marnie couldn't breathe.

Troy got to his feet and yelled, "Stop it! Leave her alone!" while frantically trying to wrest Davis's hands off Marnie's neck.

The young male flight attendant came running and two young guys dressed in Wisconsin Badger T-shirts bolted from the back of the plane to help. It took, Marnie found out later, three men to pull Davis off her.

Chapter Fifty-One

They were at the hospital in Milwaukee for a few hours getting Marnie checked out and answering questions for the police. Davis had been arrested as soon as the plane landed, and several of the passengers gave their account of what had happened. Marnie felt a bit foolish to have so many people—Troy, Jazzy, Laverne—hover around her bedside in the ER, while Jazzy's brother, Dylan, their ride home, sat in the waiting room. She offered to let them go, but like true friends, they'd have none of it. They stayed.

When the ER doctor, a young guy with a narrow face and wire-rimmed glasses, asked about the stitches in Marnie's side, for a moment she couldn't remember how she'd gotten them. The rest stop encounter with Max, once so traumatic, seemed like a lifetime ago. Luckily, Laverne was there to fill in the gaps. "I was there and saw the whole thing," she said, and launched into a colorful version of the story, with her role as hero the most important part of the tale.

Dark-colored finger marks were now evident on Marnie's neck and would, according to Laverne, get even worse because, she declared, "That's how bruises work. You wait and see. Tomorrow your neck will be a lot of different colors."

It was easier to let other people talk, so Marnie didn't say much. *This is what it must feel like to be in shock*, she thought. She put her hands up to her throat and probed the tender areas, the place where Davis's thumbs had pressed into her windpipe. The attack had happened very quickly and was over just as fast, but that didn't lessen the emotional trauma. She was completely shaken and jittery.

But looking over at Troy sitting on the edge of the bed, Marnie knew she had to pull it together and soon. She wouldn't be able to go home and crawl into bed for a week. When you were responsible for someone else, you couldn't be completely self-absorbed. Besides, she'd discovered there was more to her than she'd previously thought. It would take time, but Marnie knew she'd get through this.

As the doctor entered information into a laptop, he asked if she'd taken any medication in the last twenty-four hours. Marnie looked guiltily at Laverne and decided to confess. "I did take something. I have this fear of flying, and I took a pill for anxiety," she told him.

The doctor looked up from his laptop. "I need to know the name of the drug and the dosage. Do you have the bottle with you?"

Laverne dug into her purse and pulled out the Ziploc, and Marnie cringed, imagining what the doctor would have to say about Laverne's unauthorized plastic-bag pharmacy. "I gave her some of this," she said, handing him a bottle.

He looked at the label and then handed it back to her. "We don't put melatonin in the same category, but I'll note it."

"Wait a minute!" Marnie said. "That's not right. Tell him what you really gave me."

Laverne said, "That's what I gave you. Melatonin. It helps me relax at bedtime, so I figured it would take the edge off."

"No," Marnie insisted. "I've taken melatonin before. You gave me something much stronger. I could feel it coursing through my blood. It took the fear right out of me."

The doctor said, "It's important that I know exactly what you took." He peered at Laverne over the top of his glasses.

Laverne said, "That's what she took."

Jazzy spoke up. "It was melatonin, Doctor. I saw Laverne take it out of the bottle." Seeing Marnie's look of dismay, she added, "I swear on my grandmother's grave, it was melatonin."

"But that can't be. I felt it…" Marnie said, stunned.

"The placebo effect is incredibly strong," the doctor said. "You'd be amazed at the power of the human mind."

— — —

In the car on the way home, Marnie, who was sandwiched in the backseat between Troy and Laverne, cried out, "Oh! We never called Rita to tell her what happened."

"She knows. I called her when you were in the ambulance," Jazzy said, turning around to reassure her. Dylan, serving as chauffeur, had sensed the seriousness of the situation and hadn't said a word since they left the medical complex.

"What did she say?" Marnie asked.

"I think she was a little stunned, to tell you the truth. She felt terrible that you were attacked, but she was relieved to hear Davis is in jail. She said she'd call you tomorrow." Jazzy pulled her hair over one shoulder. "She didn't want to overwhelm you. She sends her love."

She sends her love. Such a heartwarming expression. The instant Jazzy said it, Marnie felt it. Love surrounding her from all sides. This, despite the pain, the stitches, the sore neck. Overcome with emotion, she sniffed. Troy gave her a concerned look. "Are you okay?" he asked.

"Never better," she said.

When they pulled up to the curb in front of the duplex, Marnie stared dully at the house. They'd been gone only a few days, but living there felt as distant from her current life as a childhood home. And yet, it was exactly the same—red brick with white shutters, colonial-style pillars flanking the front stoop. Dylan unloaded the trunk and helped the women carry their luggage into the house. When Laverne unlocked her door and said good-bye, Marnie reflected on how much had changed in such a short time. Before, her neighbor had been the mystery woman downstairs. Now they were friends.

When it was time to part, Jazzy gave Marnie a hug and said, "Give me a call if you need anything. I can run to the store or whatever."

"Okay, thanks."

When she and Troy were finally home alone, she said, "So do you want a tour of the place? I promise you it won't take long."

He sat impassively on a kitchen chair, his backpack and duffel at his feet. Slouching, he looked much younger than his fourteen years.

"Troy? Is something wrong?"

His eyes glittered with tears. "When you said we were going home, I thought we were going back home."

His meaning dawned on her instantly. She pulled up a chair and sat down facing him. "Oh, honey. I don't live in our old house anymore. It doesn't belong to me. Remember? Your mom hired a realtor and is selling it?"

"I knew that, I…" He wiped his eyes with the back of his hand, embarrassed. "I just forgot. In my head I pictured us going in the door and me going up to my old room. I was thinking one thing and it turned out to be different."

Marnie sighed. "I know how that is. A lot of life seems that way."

Chapter Fifty-Two

That night, after the sun had gone down, Rita found herself leaning against the window frame in her darkened dining room. Just a few minutes earlier, she and Glenn had been viewing the news on TV when the anchorman, Spencer Spellman, announced, "A local woman was attacked by a fellow passenger on a flight from Denver to Milwaukee this afternoon." Rita had been knitting, not really been paying attention, but at that point, she set down her needles and yarn and gave the TV her full attention. Just as she thought, the story was about Davis's attack on Marnie. Rita and Glenn held perfectly still while watching the footage of Davis being escorted off the plane in handcuffs; another clip showed Marnie being transported by gurney into an ambulance. A reporter at the airport interviewed two other passengers, a middle-aged woman and her teenage daughter, both of whom said that Davis looked crazed. "It took three men to pull him off that poor lady," said the mother. "He was like totally possessed," the daughter said.

When the segment was over, Glenn muted the TV and gave her a sad smile. "How're you holding up, hon?'

"I'm just glad Jazzy called and told us about this," she said. "It would have been worse to find out on the news." Before she could say any more, the phone rang. Rita would have let it go, but Glenn didn't have the same instincts. He got up to answer it, and she called out after him, "I'm not talking to anyone." She heard him in the kitchen speaking to her sister, Carolyn, who'd apparently seen the news and wanted to let them know. Rita didn't know how to feel. She had so many contradictory thoughts and emotions swirling through her mind. Guilt was one of them. If only she and Glenn had been on that flight, maybe they would have been the ones confronting Davis, and Marnie would have been spared. How horrible it must have been for Troy to be right there and unable to stop it. That poor kid. She was truly sorry that Marnie had been attacked. But she was relieved too. Davis was in jail now and would go to prison, where he belonged. Best of all, the fact that he choked Marnie made him look guilty of Melinda's death. *The same MO*, she thought. She hoped this would shine some new light on the case.

As Glenn continued his phone conversation, she wandered into the dining room, not switching on the chandelier above the table, but standing in the dark and looking out the window. The room was just big enough for the table and the china cabinet. A large picture window looked out over the backyard. It was one of her favorite rooms because nothing was ever out of order. The clutter on the kitchen counter—the not-yet-sorted mail, the rubber bands, and other odds and ends—never made their way into the dining room. The dining room table always looked impeccable, draped in linen and topped with a floral centerpiece.

The contents of the china cabinet too stayed precisely the same, except for spring cleaning, when she pulled everything out for hand washing. The wood in the room smelled faintly of lemon polish, a clean, comforting smell.

Standing in front of the window now, she had a clear view of the backyard. A full moon hung overhead, the orb so small that she could cover it with her thumb. Funny that such a tiny dot could cast so much light. Once her eyes adjusted she could see beyond the patio to the vegetable garden along the back of the property. Earlier in the season, Glenn had helped surround the garden with chicken wire to keep the rabbits at bay, and so far it had worked.

The moon, she noticed, was surrounded by a slightly foggy halo, making her think of a saying Glenn had taught Melinda when she was a little girl: *Circle around the moon, rain or snow soon.* Maybe there would be rain; it was humid enough. She was glad Glenn had turned on the central air as soon as they'd returned home. The house was comfortable now.

When Glenn was done on the phone, he came looking for her and found her still at the window, enveloped in darkness. Hearing him fumble for the light switch, she said, "No, don't turn it on. I like it this way."

He came up behind her and put his hands on her shoulders. "You like being in the dark?"

"It helps me think."

"Think about what?"

"I'm sorting out my feelings."

"You feel bad for your friend," he said.

"I do," she admitted. "I feel terrible for what Marnie went through, and it makes me think about what Melinda went through…"

"Don't think about that," he said.

"I can't help it. And I feel guilty that I'm happy Davis choked Marnie because it proves that he's that kind of person, and it got him arrested. What kind of horrible person am I that I'm happy about something like that?"

"Don't be too hard on yourself. It's complicated." He rested his chin on the top of her head.

Rita closed her eyes and rested against him, happy to have his support. Without Glenn she would have caved in from grief long ago. He wrapped his arms around her. She said, "I know it's complicated. You always say I overthink everything."

"Me? I say that?" he teased. "You must be thinking of someone else."

"No, I'm not thinking of anyone else. It's you." She nudged him with her elbow. "But I know you're right. I do have a tendency to overthink things."

They stood together, not saying anything at all, their breathing harmonizing. Such an obliging man. She was lost in thought when Glenn whistled and said, "Would you look at that." Opening her eyes, it took a moment to follow the line of his arm and see what he was pointing at, but when she did, Rita let out a gasp. It was a deer. A doe delicately walking over from an adjacent yard, as casually as a neighbor coming by to borrow a hose. She leaned closer to the glass. Glenn became alarmed and said, "If that thing goes near the garden—"

He jerked toward the door, but Rita stopped him saying, "Wait." She felt a little notch of hope build from the pit of her stomach. The deer continued with dainty steps, bypassing the chicken-wire-enclosed garden and heading straight toward them. Rita had heard of deer seeing their own reflection and thinking it was another deer, crashing through picture windows, but this deer moved slowly and deliberately.

Glenn tensed up next to her. He was one inch away from bolting outside to shoo it away. He didn't understand. Rita said, "It's okay, Glenn. Just watch." The deer leisurely walked onto the patio, facing them. Stopping a few feet short of the window, the doe stared straight at them, nodded, and twitched her ears forward, as if waving. Glenn whispered, "Well, I'll be damned. I've never seen anything like this."

Rita didn't take her eyes off the doe. When the deer turned to go, it paused for only a second before bounding across the yard. In a moment it was gone.

Glenn shook his head, bewildered. "What was that all about?"

Rita said, "This is like what happened at the rest stop. Remember me telling you about the deer and Jazzy? That it was a message from Melinda?"

It was hard to gauge his expression in the dim light, but Rita was fairly certain he was skeptical. Given time and some thought, he might come around. In the meantime, it didn't much matter if he didn't believe the deer had special significance. The sign was meant for her. Things had happened as they were supposed to and she didn't need to worry anymore.

Chapter Fifty-Three

When Marnie had moved into the upper duplex in the spring, she never dreamed she'd be moving out before the summer ended. She hired a different moving company, Hernia Movers, this time around, mostly because their slogan, "The Potentate of Totin' Freight," amused her to no end. Even with hiring professionals, there was still plenty to do beforehand, the wrapping and boxing and packing that was so tedious and necessary. She and Troy ate breakfast at Laverne's that morning because all of their food was packed away. "I can't believe you're leaving me," Laverne said, hovering over her kitchen table. She pushed a plate of toast at Troy, who took another piece even though he already had one in front of him.

"We aren't leaving *you*," Marnie said. "You'll still see us. Remember, I'm going to see you on Friday when I drive you to the clinic." Laverne had finally set up an appointment at the sleep apnea clinic at Marnie's urging, but only after getting the assurance of a ride both ways. She'd talked about renewing her driver's license for the last several weeks, but didn't seem to be in any hurry to actually do it.

"I still don't see why you have to go," Laverne said. She gave Troy's shoulder a poke. "Wouldn't you rather stay here with me and Oscar?" Upon hearing his name, the cat mewed from under the kitchen table.

She was clearly teasing, but Troy answered in all seriousness. "No, I want to go home." And he meant that literally, because Marnie had bought their old house back from Kimberly. In retrospect, it was fate. She and Troy had driven past the old house one Sunday, and noticing there was an open house, stopped to tour the place. One last time for old times' sake. Walking through the house, she was surprised to see that much of the furniture was still there. A flood of memories washed over her. The spot to the right of the fireplace was where they always put the Christmas tree, the pull-out spice rack Brian had custom built for her (in their early years) was still tucked into one of the cabinets, the window seat where she curled up and read on rainy days was still there, paisley cushion and all. Every room called up something special. It hadn't been just Brian's house, she realized with a start—it had been her house too. Maybe even more so.

After they walked in the door and she signed in on the clipboard, Marnie had explained to the realtor, a lady wearing a pantsuit and dark red lipstick, that she and Troy used to live in the house. Good thing she came clean right away, because Troy couldn't hide his reaction. "It looks the same," he exclaimed. "Can I go up and see my room?" She'd given him the okay and smiled when she heard his footsteps clattering on the hardwood floor above her head. While a young couple with a baby made small talk with the realtor, Marnie picked up the information sheet and read the specs. All things she already knew. It was a two-story colonial with three bedrooms, two bathrooms, central air, a two-and-a-half-car garage, and a wooded lot. The price, she saw, was in line with other homes in the area; in fact, it was a little on the low side. She was surprised Kimberly hadn't gotten an offer yet. It wasn't that much money, considering the neighborhood and the home's amenities. In fact, Marnie had more than that amount in her savings account. She could afford it.

By the time Troy came downstairs, she had put in an offer on the house. It was crazy and impulsive, which was unlike her, but it felt right. When the realtor explained there could be a delay in hearing back from the owner because she was in Europe, Marnie said that was fine. She could wait.

When Troy got wind of what she'd done, he was beside himself with joy. In the car after they'd left he asked, "Do you think my mom will let me live here with you?"

"I don't know, Troy. That's a lot to ask." Kimberly had already agreed to let Troy stay until the end of summer and agreed to future visits to Wisconsin. Marnie was afraid to push her luck.

"But she has to." He clicked his seat belt on. "*Everything* is here."

Teenagers were all about the absolutes. Everything was here. Nothing was there. As if Las Vegas had nothing to offer, but suburban Wisconsin was a hotbed of activity. "It's not that simple," Marnie said. "She's your mother. I'm not related to you."

His face fell. "That bites," he said angrily. "What's it to her, anyway, if I stay here? It's not like she has time for me."

"To be fair, she has a very demanding career. Give your mom some credit. She runs a multimillion-dollar company."

He didn't care about her multimillion-dollar company. "She can't make me stay. I'll run away. I'll come back on my own."

Marnie started the engine. "Troy, don't be that way. I'll call and ask her, if you want, but don't count on it," she said, not wanting to get his hopes up.

Marnie waited until after the closing on the house to make the call. Once the papers were signed by Kimberly's attorney and the deal was finalized at the end of July, she felt she had a stronger case. She picked up the phone and took a deep breath, ready to launch into a speech about the advantages of having Troy live with her. But when Kimberly answered, Marnie got a surprise. Before she even had a chance to give her argument, Kimberly said, "Well, maybe if you could hold onto him for the time being that would be best. I've got a big project coming up and I can't even see straight right now." She laughed. "It's been crazy, Marnie. And you know Troy doesn't really roll with my schedule." She spoke with the familiarity of an old friend, like Marnie would sympathize.

Marnie's heart filled with joy. Still, she needed to clarify, just to be sure. "So he can move with me to the old house, and I can enroll him in school for his freshman year?" Next to her, Troy held his hands together like he was praying. When Marnie nodded yes in his direction, echoing Kimberly's response, his fist pumped the air, and he got out his phone to text his friends. When she finished the call, Marnie said to Troy, "You understand that this is just for now? She left it pretty open. I got the impression this is not long term."

Troy blew off her concerns. "That's how Mom is about everything. She's not like you, Marnie. She always makes it sound like she's going to do things later on, but she never does. If it's not about her company, it doesn't happen."

"Well, I'm sure she means well," Marnie said, feeling suddenly charitable toward Kimberly. "And you probably need to plan on visiting her during school holidays." But she might as well have been talking to herself, because his attention was completely on his phone. Just like old times.

And today, they were finally moving back to the house that both she and Troy thought of as home. The movers were scheduled to come at ten that morning. "Moving back to a place where you used to live—does it seem like you're going backward in life?" Laverne asked, pouring more coffee into Marnie's mug.

"Backward? No," Marnie said. "I might be moving to our old house, but I'm not going backward. I'm definitely moving forward."

Chapter Fifty-Four

Jazzy was going to be late, but this time around she would be late on purpose. Her road trip friends were throwing a surprise going-away party at Marnie's, although Jazzy wasn't supposed to know it was a party. The invitation was for dinner with Laverne and Rita. "So you can all see my house and we can say good-bye before you move to New York," Marnie had said over the phone.

"Sounds good," Jazzy said, jotting down the date and time. "Can't wait to see you guys!" She knew, of course, that there was more to it than Marnie let on. Jazzy's grandmother had given her a preview, the most detailed vision she'd had to date. In her mind's eye she saw that Marnie's house would be festooned with crepe paper and balloons. Above the fireplace would hang a long white banner with gold letters that spelled out, "BON VOYAGE, JAZZY!" The kitchen table would be filled with trays of appetizers and petite desserts, while the countertops would hold warming trays full of meatballs and other hot dishes. A case of champagne would be stored under the table, along with an ice bucket and a box of champagne flutes. This would be saved for the toast at the end of the evening. Jazzy could see the house crowded with people she knew from all the compartments of her life: Mrs. Griswold, the neighbor lady from her childhood home; assorted coworkers from the store, one still wearing his blue vest; the other women from the grief group at the rec center; and various high school friends and their dates. In her preview, she mixed graciously among the guests, wearing a summer dress and strappy sandals, her hair pulled back in a ponytail. Troy would be there too, along with Matt Haverman, his best friend since grade school. The boys would mill around, trying to figure out if it was possible to snitch a bottle of champagne without anyone noticing.

Jazzy also knew that arriving on time would ruin everything. Several of the attendees were going to be a few minutes late, and Marnie would meet guests at the door and ask them to move their cars around the corner. Knowing this, Jazzy had Dylan drop her off a few blocks away, and as she walked to Marnie's house, she used the extra time to practice looking astonished.

When she walked up the path to Marnie's house, she was impressed. The front blinds were drawn, and Rita's car was in the driveway, but otherwise, nothing gave it away. She rang the doorbell and thought she heard the hushed sounds of a large group of people trying to be quiet. Marnie opened the door breathlessly. "Jazzy!" she said, and embraced her before she was barely across the threshold. "I'm so glad you could make it." She pulled back and gave her an appraising look. "Don't you look pretty! You'll make the rest of us look bad." Marnie ushered her into the house, chattering nervously about what she was serving for dinner, all of the talk bogus, Jazzy knew, but she played along. "Rita and Laverne are in the kitchen," Marnie said. "Come along."

Jazzy followed obediently, ready to do her surprised look: eyes wide, hand covering her mouth. She'd even practiced saying, "You guys!" while tipping her head modestly to one side.

Like a compressed slinky, she was ready to let go, but when she got in the kitchen, there was no party. It was only Laverne and Rita, standing at the counter, each holding a glass of wine.

"You're late, gal," Laverne said. "But I'm glad to see you anyway."

They greeted her with hugs and compliments, and Jazzy was so confused she didn't say a word. Finally, she couldn't help it. "Where is everyone?" she blurted out.

The other three women looked confused. "We're all here," Rita said.

"Who else were you expecting?" Marnie asked.

"Well," Jazzy said, suddenly sheepish, "I thought Troy would be here, and maybe Glenn."

"Girls' night means no boys allowed," Marnie said firmly, pouring another glass of wine and handing it to Jazzy. "Troy is spending the night at a friend's house."

"And Glenn is enjoying the solitude," Rita said, an amused smile crossing her face.

Marnie gave them a tour of the house, and they ate dinner shortly thereafter: pork tenderloin, broccoli casserole, and fresh beet slices. Marnie was a nervous host, jumping up from the table every few minutes to get a pitcher of ice water or "check on things in the kitchen." At every turn, Jazzy expected a large group of people to jump out and surprise her. By the time the dessert was served she realized it wasn't going to happen. What had gone wrong?

"So tell us about your new job," Rita said to Jazzy.

Jazzy stopped eating her chocolate cake. Where to begin? She had been reluctant to take this offer when she'd first met Scarlett Turner on their trip, but she'd done a complete reversal since then. Knowing Carson was going to be nearby was a big part of her change of heart. They'd been in constant touch every day since she'd been home and planned to meet up in New York in three days. The wait was killing her. If she had a time machine, she'd jump in and program it to take her three days in the future.

"Ha, look at her blush!" Laverne said. "She's thinking about more than just the job."

"I am very much looking forward to starting my new job," Jazzy said primly. "I believe it will provide me with opportunities for personal, professional, and financial growth."

The ladies whooped, and Laverne said, "Gal, you are so full of hooey."

When the laughter died down, Marnie asked, "So where are you going to be living, then?"

"With my boss, Scarlett Turner, at first," Jazzy said. "She's got a big apartment on Central Park West."

"Fancy," Rita said approvingly.

What Jazzy didn't say was that she doubted she'd be living there for long. She needed a place to stay, rent was high in New York, and Scarlett had offered. For now this was the easiest solution. Carson, on the other hand, had a rental arranged for him by his new employer. She had a very strong feeling that eventually they'd be together, but she didn't want to start out that way. All in good time.

After dinner, they carried their wine glasses into the living room and exchanged stories about what was new in their lives. Laverne had recently been diagnosed with sleep apnea. "Turns out my sleep was constantly being interrupted all night long, even though I didn't know it. No wonder I was so darn tired all the time." The solution, she was told, was to wear a CPAP mask at night while she slept. "As if it wasn't hard enough trying to sleep with this thing strapped to my face," she said. "My cat, Oscar, likes to sit on my chest and he bats at the air hose, like this." She illustrated with her cupped hands. "Darn annoying. I finally had to lock him out of my room, and now he cries like a baby."

"Oh, don't be so mean," Jazzy cried. "Let Oscar play with the medical device."

"Maybe you could get him his own CPAP," Rita suggested.

"Yeah, that would be one expensive cat toy," Laverne said.

The doorbell interrupted the conversation, and Marnie said, "That's probably a salesperson. I'll get rid of them."

She left the room and Rita said, "It seems like the cable people stop by every week lately, wanting to talk to me about upgrading my plan."

When Marnie returned, she wasn't alone. Trailing shyly behind her was Carson, carrying an enormous bouquet of roses. "Look who showed up," Marnie said, gleefully extending her arm. The other women jumped up and shouted, "Surprise!"

"Carson?" Jazzy stood up, stunned but happy. She crossed the room and threw her arms around him. "What are you doing here?"

"Are you surprised?" Laverne said. "We've been planning this for weeks."

Speechless, Jazzy put her palm on his cheek and shook her head in wonder.

"She's surprised," Rita said. "No one could fake that reaction."

"I came early to pick you up," Carson said. "So we can drive to New York together."

"But my brother already booked a plane ticket for me," she said.

"No, he didn't," all the women said in unison, laughing.

"He didn't?" Jazzy looked around the room at her friends. "So all of you were in on this? Even Dylan? I can't believe you pulled one over on me." Her grandmother's energy drifted into the room and Jazzy picked up on how pleased Grandma was with herself. Clearly, her grandmother's surprise-party preview had been a ruse to throw her off her game.

Good one, Grandma, she thought. *You had me completely fooled.*

Chapter Fifty-Five

Carson drove the Corolla, while Jazzy was in charge of the GPS, music, and snacks. She thought it was a good arrangement, and he didn't seem to mind a bit. "Fifteen and a half hours from my house to Manhattan," she told him.

"That's driving time," he said.

"Yeah. If you had a bunch of middle-aged women in the car you'd have to add ten more hours for bathroom breaks."

"That's a lot of bathroom breaks."

"Tell me about it."

Carson apparently appreciated Jazzy's taste in song choices, because he grinned and nodded his head in time to the music as he drove. He wasn't one of those people who felt the constant need to talk. She could be quiet with him and just enjoy the ride. She needed that.

The view going east was different from the trip westward she'd taken with the ladies, but the sense of anticipation and new beginnings was the same. At Marnie's house the other night, she'd planned on telling Rita that Davis would eventually confess to killing Melinda, and that he would get the sentence he deserved. She knew because she'd woken one night from a sound sleep and seen it all in a vision: the courtroom scene with the slamming of the judge's gavel, and Davis being led off, his head down. She knew other things too—that Troy would live with Marnie all through high school and that Laverne would finally be able to sleep with the CPAP mask on all night. After a few weeks she would be amazed at how much energy she had. "I feel twenty years younger," she would crow to anyone who would listen.

Jazzy knew all these things and wanted to share them with her friends, but when she opened her mouth to talk, her grandmother's spirit advised her to keep it to herself. *Let them find out on their own.*

"So, psychic girl," Carson said, interrupting her thoughts. "Any new predictions? I'd be interested in knowing what you see for the two of us."

"For the two of us?"

"That's what I said. For the two of us," he said cheerfully.

"Hmmm, give me a minute," Jazzy said, closing her eyes. Almost immediately she saw their lives stretched forward in front of her, a series of road trips. Like a movie in fast-forward she saw it clearly: the two of them driving to the church to get married and then, three years later, a trip to the hospital—Carson driving, Jazzy nine months pregnant and urging him to hurry. Family vacations with one, now two, now three children strapped into car seats in the back of a silver minivan. Visits to friends and family. A collage of driving expeditions to graduations and weddings and births and funerals. "As a matter of fact, I do have a prediction," Jazzy said, opening her eyes and giving him a smile. "I see us going on a road trip."

Ahead of them, a ribbon of concrete stretched endlessly forward. Anything could happen.

Acknowledgments

Once again, my eternal gratitude goes to Terry Goodman. He's a good man and terrific publishing partner, and I really like him too. Maybe someday I'll drive a convertible and be as cool as Terry. Probably not, though.

When I think of Amazon Publishing, it's the people who come to mind. The team has always gone the extra mile for my books, and what author wouldn't love that? Kudos to the always efficient and personable Jessica Poore. She assures me I'm never a bother, which can't possibly be true, but I appreciate her saying so. A big thank you to publisher Victoria Griffith, who once said I'm *one* of her favorite authors. Now my goal in life is to become her absolute favorite. Thanks also to Jeff Belle, whose signature I treasure. I'd like to acknowledge other members of the team including Jacque Ben-Zekry, Sarah Tomashek, Katy Ball, Katie Finch, Brooke Gilbert, Rory Connell, and Nikki Sprinkle. My apologies to anyone I inadvertently excluded. My gratitude is enormous even if my memory is faulty.

When it comes to this novel, Jeannée Sacken started it all by using the phrase "women on a road trip" in the context of a different conversation. Thanks, Jeannée. I always cherish our talks, but this one was particularly helpful.

Early readers Geri Erickson, Gail Grenier Sweet, Alice L. Kent, Neve Maslakovic, and Jon Olson gave me valuable feedback and needed reassurance, and I owe them all, big time. Thanks, guys! Your collective wisdom made this a better novel. (And Jon—I really do know the difference between the hood and the trunk of a car. I have no idea how *that* particular snafu happened. Someone must have snuck in during the night and changed it on me.)

Charlotte Herscher read every word of the manuscript multiple times, suggested improvements, and caught numerous errors, thus saving me from certain humiliation. She's an editing wizard, and I'm happy this novel received the benefit of her skill and care. Any remaining mistakes, however, are really and truly mine.

To Jennifer Williams and Jessica R. Fogleman, copyeditors extraordinaire—thank you for lending your expertise to this book! Your dedication to the written word did not go unnoticed.

Publicist Kathleen Carter Zrelak is an absolute wonder. She got me past security and in front of a camera at ABC Studios, something I still can't get over. There's no one I'd rather have lunch with at the restaurant in the Trump Tower, even if we did have to sit at the bar because we didn't have reservations.

I raise a glass to Kimberly Einiger who thinks I'm funny and who also allowed me to use her name for one of my characters. Kim-ber-ly. Three syllables of awesomeness.

My husband, Greg, always supportive, was particularly so with this book when he did the majority of the driving from Wisconsin to Colorado and back again, in just four days, so I could fact-check some of the more pertinent details. My driving makes him a little nervous, so I suspect he wasn't being completely altruistic, but that doesn't diminish the joy of getting to be a passenger for thirty hours. Thanks, Greg!

I love my kids beyond measure, and I'm lucky they keep me up to date on so many things. Credit goes to Jack, Maria, and Charlie, just for existing, and also for making Mother's Day the best holiday of all.

Book bloggers are the unsung heroes of the publishing industry. I've been the recipient of many thoughtful reviews, and I don't take any of them for granted. My thanks to book bloggers everywhere, now and forever.

And finally, if you're one of those people who respond to my books, connect with my characters, and enjoy my stories, you have my heart. Because of you, I get to write for a living. I am sending infinite thanks your way. I hope you can feel the love.

About the Author

Photo by Greg McQuestion, 2011

Karen McQuestion writes books for adults as well as for kids and teens. She is a best-selling author on Kindle. Two of her novels placed in the top 100 Customer Kindle books for 2010, based on sales and reader reviews. Originally self-published, she now writes for Amazon Publishing and Houghton Mifflin Harcourt. McQuestion lives in Wisconsin with her family.

READING GROUP GUIDE
The Long Way Home by Karen McQuestion

1) The four women in the book become friends based more on circumstances than commonalities. How likely is this to happen in the real world?

2) Laverne's son thought she didn't leave the house because she was afraid, something she didn't agree with. Why do you think she became homebound after her husband died?

3) Is the ending of the novel satisfying? If not, what would you have changed?

4) Of the four women, which one could you most identify with, and why?

5) Jazzy's motto, "Do the thing you long to do and become the person you're destined to be," spurs the women in the grief group to share their hopes and dreams. What hopes and dreams have gone unrealized in your life, and why?

6) If this novel is made into a movie, how would you cast it?

7) Have you ever gone on a road trip with a group of friends? If so, did the experience bring you closer?

8) At the beginning of the novel, Marnie suffers from a lack of confidence. By the end of the novel, with help from the group, she's grown as a person and has taken charge of her life. Where do you see her going from there?

9) Kimberly seems to lack a maternal instinct. How realistic is this? Do you know any women who fall into this category?

10) Rita is convinced that the deer are the conduit through which her daughter, Melinda, communicates with her. Do you believe deceased loved ones can send messages to friends and family? Do you have any stories you'd like to share?

16107652R00194

Made in the USA
Lexington, KY
05 July 2012